NO COMFORT ON A CHILLY NIGHT

NOEL BRAUN

Published in Australia by Sid Harta Publishers Pty Ltd,
ABN: 46 119 415 842
23 Stirling Crescent, Glen Waverley, Victoria 3150 Australia
Telephone: +61 3 9560 9920, Facsimile: +61 3 9545 1742
E-mail: author@sidharta.com.au

First published in Australia 2023
This edition published 2023
Copyright © Noel Braun 2023
Cover design, typesetting: WorkingType Studio

Braun, Noel
No Comfort on a Chilly Night
ISBN: 978-1-922958-30-3
pp336

ABOUT THE AUTHOR

Noel Braun commenced his working life as a country school-teacher then moved into a corporate career, which took him from Melbourne to Perth and Sydney. He has had a lifelong passion for writing and wrote the first words of his novels fifty years ago. After a busy career and raising a family of four, he has found the time in retirement to fulfill his long-held ambition to see his work in print.

Noel has published two previous novels: *Friend and Philosopher* and *Whistler Street*. He has published a memoir, *No Way to Behave at a Funeral*, which describes his grief journey following the death by suicide of his wife Maris, and three explorations of the Camino de Santiago de Compostela: *The Day was Made for Walking*, *I Guess I'll Just Keep on Walking* and *Keep Pressing On, Brother*.

Noel has taken his time with his third novel, *No Comfort on a Chilly Night*. He commenced the first draft twenty years ago and wrote four other books in the meantime. He is working on other manuscripts. He lives in the Snowy Mountains where he is involved with the community. He is a keen walker and enjoys getting out in the national parks surrounding his home.

PART ONE

DAYS OF PROMISE

Chapter 1

The Camino passed through an arid stony land interspersed with olive groves and vineyards. A rough pebbly track climbed around the hills, descended the valleys and followed a dry rocky riverbed. No breeze offered respite in the heavy atmosphere. The songs of the cicadas, sharp and strong, could have been the voice of departed spirits who had walked this track before they succumbed to the deadly heat, which hung over the land like a dense, suffocating fog. The sun shone down fiercely, intense heat radiated from the earth and the light reflected off the chalky ground was just as lethal. The occasional tree struggling for existence along the track provided scant shade in this oven-like world.

He had begun walking early, two hours before dawn, to take advantage of the cool morning, but the heat, like a beast of prey, was waiting for the sun to rise and make its fiery assault. In the bar where he stopped for breakfast, the weather forecast on the television predicted a string of forty-degree-plus days across Spain. Apart from the weary bartender and a faded customer sipping coffee, he saw no one that morning except for an old lady with a sharp beak for a nose dressed in black. Just as he passed her house, she shuffled out with a pan of water to pour on potted geraniums on either side of her door, their red flowers a contrasting touch of beauty against stark whitewashed walls. She greeted him with a *Buenos Dias*, but then scurried back like a frightened rodent into the cool, darkened interior, wondering why this red-haired sunburned youth was out in such heat.

He was following the shell symbols of the ancient pilgrimage, Camino, which wound its way through France and Spain and converged on the city of Santiago in the northwest of Spain. Not that he regarded himself as a pilgrim. No way. He just knew that this was a cheap way for a backpacker to get around, see the country and meet the people. Following graduation, he travelled to France to bum around before he committed himself to the serious business of finding a career. Big cities like Paris were no place for an Aussie with next to no money, so he abandoned the din and unaffordable prices and took to the country. He walked along the network of trails called *Grandes Randonnées*, which crisscrossed the country. The French countryside was beautiful. He walked along mountain tracks with views over a patchwork of farmlands and forest, where the air was clear and the only sounds were the rustling of the breeze in the trees, the songs of the birds or the tinkling of cow bells or distant church bells. He walked by canals built in the days of Louis XIV along paths shaded by mature plane trees. Those waterways were designed to transport grain but were now the domain of tourist boats from which passengers sipping their cool drinks stared at this lone walker.

He came upon lovely, restored villages and groups of houses clustered around the church where life continued servicing the tourists from Germany and Britain. Yet, he passed by abandoned hamlets where the old had died out and the young had deserted for the attractions of the town.

He enjoyed the freedom (*la liberté*) and feeling of going nowhere in particular, with no special destination and just taking each day as it came. By day he preferred to walk on his own, allowing his mind to drift, occasionally getting it into gear to admire a wayside flower or greet a cud-chewing cow in an adjoining paddock. At night he enjoyed company. He passed most evenings with other walkers, sometimes with one or two, sometimes with a crowd. He relished the opportunity to speak French over a meal and copious glasses of wine in conversation with ordinary people. He asked his fellow walkers questions – how long they were walking and where they were heading, where they had come from, where did they live and what sort of place that was. They were curious that he spoke the lingo and came from Australia, so far away. Most of the walkers were French but many were from Germany, Holland and Norway.

The conversation turned to French politics of which he knew little. The topic was fresh because France had just emerged from an election campaign that produced the first left wing president of the Fifth Republic, François Mitterrand, to the dismay of supporters of his predecessor. Valéry Giscard d'Estaing believed he lost only because of disunity among the right-wing parties.

'I cannot believe the passion and ferocity with which the French discuss their politics,' Felix wrote in a letter to his sister. 'Although I've witnessed no fisticuffs, I can appreciate the place of violence and revolution in French history.'

One night, he shared a decanter of scruffy red wine with Marcel, a skinny Frenchman with one arm. His extreme thinness made him appear nearly two-dimensional, like a character out of a comic book. He looked as if he had been walking all his life and, along the way, had shed his baggage.

'Where are you heading?' he asked the young Aussie with red hair.

'Nowhere in particular.'

'You should have a destination.' He spoke with passion like a zealot. 'You should cross the Pyrenees into Spain and follow the route to Santiago. Accommodation is plentiful, much cheaper than France and a bar every few kilometres. The Camino is a sacred way which pilgrims have been following since medieval times. Walkers make their pilgrimage to the shrine of Saint James at Santiago.'

'Good idea,' Felix replied, as he took a mouthful of wine. 'Why not?'

'It will do your soul good.' Marcel was pleased to be giving a young man a life direction. 'You might discover something about yourself.'

The young man looked down at his plate of duck confit, moved a leg in an anticlockwise direction and helped himself to more wine from the stone decanter. He lifted his glass to his companion.

'I'll give it a go.'

A week later, he found himself south of the border in the Spanish heat. He knew more about Spanish politics through his reading on the Spanish Civil War. The reign of General Francisco Franco was replaced by King Juan Carlo. Earlier in the year, Felix read a newspaper account of an attempted bizarre coup when a contingent of the civil guard occupied parliament. It sounded like a page from a comic opera libretto.

That blistering day, he was on his own. Even the walkers who had stayed the previous night in the same *albergue* had vanished. No surprise, no one was dill or imprudent enough to be walking in this stinker, the cicadas his company on his blighted road. Long distance walkers tell you it is an addiction. Once you commit yourself, you must keep going whatever the conditions. He was carrying two litres of water and had already drunk over a litre.

Usually tolerant of heat, used to the Australian summer, Felix found this day intense and oppressive and wondered how long he could last. The only thing he needed to add to the day's unpleasantness was the sirocco, the Mediterranean wind from the Sahara that blows across Southern Europe, sometimes up to hurricane speeds. His sweat evaporated and left him with dry salty skin. He should have given himself a day off. He was desperate for decent shade where he could take a breather, remove his boots and backpack and rest. As he came around a hill, the path descended into a deeper valley, and at the bottom, trees provided much-needed shelter from the scorching heat. In the cooler rainy seasons, the water rushed down these tracks and gullies and collected in these valleys, providing the moisture that enabled the trees to thrive. There might even be grass, unlikely to be perfectly cut, moist or lush, like in the middle of a manicured garden, but just enough to stretch out on. He quickened his pace to reach an oasis.

He found the shade and, sure enough, the green grass invited him to remove his pack and boots and stretch out. He drank from his water bottle. One was already empty. This was one of those days when the veterans' advice was to drink four litres, so he was hoping there might even be a small refreshing stream. He lay down on his back, feeling like a grease spot, with his pack as a pillow and looked up through the leaves to the cloudless sky, thankful for the brief relief from the torture of the road.

'I will go looking for water as soon as I rest,' he muttered to himself. He was about to close his eyes when he heard a small sigh.

He looked around. Someone was sharing his oasis. A girl was stretched out on the grass about ten metres away. Her eyes were closed. She was slim and dressed in shorts. She had removed her T-shirt and used it as a pillow. Her hair was bouncy black and, in another world, could have been licked into shape to model for hair conditioners. Her skin was pale. She seemed vulnerable and needing help. Beside her lay her backpack. A water bottle was lying about a metre away, discarded as if empty. His first thought: *There is no waterpoint here.* His second: *That girl has run out of water and succumbed to the heat. She is in trouble.* He got up and walked across. He recognised her as one of the walkers who had stayed at the same *albergue* the previous night but had not had a chance to speak to her. A slight tingle like electricity ran through his body and he could feel internal organs he hadn't given much thought to as he admired her beautiful slim body and bare breasts. In her nakedness, she seemed so weak and fragile.

'*Hola! Bonjour!* Hello!' He usually greeted people in several languages and then continued in the language they responded in. She opened her eyes – they were dark and soft – and looked at him as if she wasn't seeing, then whispered,

'*Bonjour!*'

'*Voulez-vous de l'eau?*' (Would you like some water?)

'*Merci.*'

By now, she was focussed enough to recognise her angel.

He stayed in the same *albergue*, but they did not speak to one another as he was in the midst of a rowdy group. Walkers around him had plenty to say, curious to know why he, an Australian, was walking in Spain. Weren't there places in Australia to walk? they joked. She was curious and would have enjoyed talking to him. She would have her chance. He walked back to his backpack and grabbed his water bottle. By the time he returned she had sat up, placed her T-shirt across her breasts and propped herself on her left elbow. He leaned over her and offered the bottle. The smell of his sweat was pungent but not unpleasant. Such unselfconscious masculinity so close to her; she could have grabbed him and held his vibrant body close. She accepted the bottle and took a long drink.

'J'ai manqué d'eau. C'est une journée si chaude.' (I ran out of water. It's such a hot day.)

She sat up and returned the bottle. Her face was drawn, and she felt exhausted, but the water restored some life, and she could feel a vibrancy, subdued at the moment, ready to bubble forth at the right time. As he accepted the bottle and screwed on its top, he felt a strong connection with her. She had trusted him and accepted his help. He felt a yearning for her, more tender than carnal although he held the bottle in front of his body to hide his arousal. He wanted to protect her, to see her recover from dehydration and regain her strength.

'Comment ça va?' (How are you feeling?)

She lay back and placed her hand on her forehead. She was lovely and beautiful in her weakness.

'J'ai mal à la tête.' (I have a bad headache.)

'C'est parce que tu es déshydratée. Laisse-moi te trouver

quelque chose.' (That's because you're dehydrated. Let me find you something.)

He returned to his pack and from the top removed a small first-aid kit. He took out an aspirin and returned.

'Ici! Prends ça. Tu te sentiras mieux.' (Here, take this. It'll make you feel better.)

One of the unwritten laws of long-distance walking is to offer help to someone in distress and for the other to accept aid when offered. They were doing no more than what any would do, but he felt her acceptance was different. She trusted him. In this remote and isolated place, he could have allowed the flesh to take control. No doubt about it. She was desirable, but to take advantage of her would be an immense breach of her trust. He wanted to protect her.

She needed to lie down and close her eyes. She was content when he sat down beside her and leaned against a tree. She needed someone to be nearby. The air was warm and stifling and, although ridiculously hot in the shade, the heat would have been unbearable on the unprotected path. Even the cicadas found the heat too much for they had taken a rest from their song. Both closed their eyes too and mused, thinking about nothing in particular, just content to be with each other. He took a deep breath and allowed his mind to meander through the field of possible outcomes of their encounter. The only thing she knew about him was that he was Australian, spoke French and was gallant. He seemed different to other boys, French and Spanish boys, who only thought of what stirred below. Australian boys were probably no different but this one was courteous and respectful. She had heard that redheads (*les rousses*) can be very passionate, but she felt she could trust him. In turn, he knew little about her. She spoke French and was lovely. At university he had slept with girls who had offered themselves. He was happy to oblige but such relationships never lasted, if they could be called relationships; they were so ephemeral. He had met girls in France. They were interested in him because he was different, an Australian who spoke French. A German girl whose name was Sybille he would have willingly slept with, but such liaisons were difficult to organise in dormitory-style accommodation. This girl beside him was unlike any he had met. She connected with something deep inside him. He wanted to get to know her.

He was not sure how long he sat there when he heard her stirring beside him. He opened his eyes, and she was looking at him.

'*Comment ça va?*' he asked.

'*Mieux. Je me sentais terrible. Je pensais que j'allais mourir. Je me suis embrouillée. Et je ne pouvais pas savoir où je me trouve. J'aurais dû transporter plus d'eau. J'avais une autre bouteille mais je l'ai perdue hier.*' (Better. I was feeling terrible. I thought I might die. I got confused and couldn't work out where I was. I should have carried more water. I had another bottle but I mislaid it somewhere yesterday.)

As she spoke, she was gazing nowhere in particular. Then she turned and looked at him with eyes that stirred his heart.

'*Tu m'as sauvé la vie. Merci.*' (You have saved my life. Thank you.)

She was being dramatic, but he did not mind her gratitude one little bit. She turned her eyes, looked at the ground and spoke quietly.

'*Tu ne veux pas continuer à marcher?*' (Don't you want to continue walking?)

Despite the distraction of a palpitating heart, he managed to reply.

'*Je resterai avec toi pour m'assurer que tout va bien.*' (I'll stay with you to make sure you are okay.)

He tried to sound nonchalant, as if it were the normal action. One should help a fellow human being in distress and make sure they are okay before continuing on their way. Underneath, his heart and stomach were stirring. The last thing he wanted was to depart. The last thing he wanted was to let her go. If he were to leave her now, he would never see her again.

'*Merci. Ce serait bien.*' (Thank you. That would be good.)

The first thing she wanted was to see him stay. She needed someone to protect her until she was confident enough to walk on her own. She liked the way he paid attention to her, how he looked at her. She wished she could explain his eyes and how the sound of his voice gave her butterflies and how his smile made her heart skip a beat. Together, they rested in silence. The afternoon passed. The sun made its descent, the shadows lengthened, the crickets resumed their song, birds returned to the trees and on the ground squirrels scampered looking for food. Nothing was out of the ordinary, yet everything had changed. Eventually, she spoke.

'*Je m'appelle Pascaline. Comme t'appelle-tu?*'

'Felix.'

Chapter 2

They stayed in the shade until late afternoon when it was cool enough to continue. A passing pilgrim stopped for a rest and told them in halting English a village not far ahead had three refuges.

'*Es-tu assez forte pour marcher?*' *(Are you strong enough to walk?)* Felix asked Pascaline.

'*Oui, je pense que oui,*' (Yes, I think so) she replied.

He helped her with her backpack and they walked in silence the few kilometres. She conserved her energy for the physical movement while he was happy to be her silent companion. Thankful for the long twilight, they did not arrive until about 9 pm. The houses were ancient, built of solid stone with overhanging wooden verandahs and external steps almost black with age. The first refuge displayed the full sign (*completo*) and so did the second. Around a corner, the third had two bunks available on opposite ends of the dormitory. They sought the showers and, in adjacent cubicles, cleansed themselves under the tepid water. They surfaced. Pascaline wrapped her towel around herself while Felix held his in front. They turned their backs to each other but not before Pascaline noted that Felix looked good without too many clothes on. They ran their towels over their refreshed bodies.

'*Comment ça va?*' (How are you feeling?) he asked.

'*Mieux, merci.*' (Better, thank you.)

'*Tu dois manger.*' (You should have something to eat.)

'*Oui.*'

They returned to their bunks, dressed, emerged back outside and just down the street saw the lights of a bar/restaurant. Inside, pilgrims were drinking, recovering from the extremes of a hot day. Although approaching 10 pm, a young girl welcomed them and showed them a table outside under the overhanging verandah. They saw the pilgrim's menu on the blackboard (*Menú del Peregrino*) – three courses with a choice of salad or soup, burgers or chicken, ice-cream or fruit, and two jugs: one of water, the other of red wine (*vino tinto*).

They did not have much to say during the day, but, relaxing over a glass of red wine, they found the energy for conversation.

'Thank you for staying with me today. I'm not sure where I would be without you. Now, tell me something about yourself, my gallant rescuer.'

'You're speaking English,' Felix replied.

She nodded.

'You speak English as well as I speak French.'

She lifted her glass and smiled.

'Thank you. Now tell me about yourself.'

'Okay. I'm Australian and I live in Melbourne.'

'You're far away from home.'

The girl returned with their salad and a candle, which she placed on the table. Its light shone in their eyes and lit up their souls.

'I finished my studies and I'm travelling before finding a job and starting a career.'

'And what did you study?'

A burst of laughter from inside almost drowned her voice. He sipped his wine and waited until the noise subsided.

'Psychology was my major focus, but I also studied French.

That's why I'm here, speaking to you in your maternal language.'

'You must like learning languages?'

'Yes. While I'm in Spain, I'm learning Spanish. I'd like to be at least bilingual and possibly multilingual. I admire the way Europeans slip from one language to another.'

People were leaving the restaurant and as they passed, the candlelight stirred and danced over their faces.

'You must also like walking. Have you always been a hiker in your own country?'

'Not particularly. I enjoy walking because it's a cheap way of getting around and seeing the country. I was walking in France first and decided on the Camino for no reason other than I was told there was always good company and cheap places to stay.'

'You should walk the Camino for a reason,' Pascaline replied.

'I'm always asking people about their walking. Why are you walking?'

'I'm walking the Camino because I want to find myself, to see if I can handle the challenge.'

The girl appeared with their chicken.

'How come you speak English so well? I love your accent.'

'My mother is a language teacher. She teaches both French and English and through her I learned English because we spoke both French and English at home. It was just as important for my mother as for us children, my brother and me.'

'My father was a teacher, too. He's retired now. He taught in primary schools, and we moved around the country. He had various appointments. He was the principal. We moved from place to place. Just as I was getting used to a town, we moved, and we had to make new friends, me and my sister. In the last place, I made good friends. We went to university together. We shared a house, but we studied different courses. The others got jobs, but I wanted to travel first.'

'What about your sister?'

'She stayed at home. She had a boyfriend and I'm sure they'll marry soon.'

'I've always lived in the place where I was born.'

'Where's that?'

'I live with my mother in Chambéry.'

'Where's that?'

'In the Auvergne Rhône-Alpes region. It's near the frontier with Italy and Switzerland.'

They finished their ice-cream and were the last to leave. He did not want to let Pascaline slip away and, as they strolled back to the refuge, he suggested:

'We should walk together tomorrow.'

She looked at him, and, in lighthearted fashion, replied, 'Okay,' as if it could be an adventure. He sighed. He should take the next step.

'Perhaps we could walk together the day after that and after that.'

She looked at him again and, as she returned her gaze to the path, replied, 'That would be good,' but this time with a faint smile. They returned to the refuge just in time before curfew. The dormitory was in darkness. Pilgrims were asleep and snoring, and they stumbled around finding their beds, trying to make as little noise as possible. Felix took his torch and helped Pascaline find her bunk and belongings, made sure she was settled and that she had found her own torch before he crept back to his own bunk and settled in for the night. He was tired, too, but he dozed off with images of Pascaline. What lively company she would make and how he looked forward to their days together.

The refuge stirred about 5 am. The forecast was for another sweltering day. The early birds were on the move, trying to make little noise but managing to make a racket, dropping boots, rustling plastic, zipping bags and whispering loudly. He rose at about 7.30 just as the light was showing through the window. Pascaline was still asleep, and he woke her gently. She opened her eyes and smiled at him as he leaned over her, the light shining off his red hair. He was tempted to kiss her.

'We should have breakfast at the same place.'

They were the last to leave, passing the sign requesting everyone should depart by 8 am. Cleaners were already on the job in the showers.

The day was already hot. They walked together mostly in silence, content with their own thoughts. They passed through vineyards, the vines heavy with fruit, and in places the machines were busy harvesting. By early afternoon, they arrived at a small village with a beautiful, restored refuge by a stream. According to the notice, the refuge was used in medieval times and was a favourite because the stream gave the grimy pilgrims an opportunity to wash. It was a favourite, too, with the modern pilgrims as they were already splashing about or lounging in the shade on the grass. The refuge was not yet full, and they were able to take the same bunk. Pascaline chose the top bed, and he was more than happy to sleep under her.

They joined the others by the stream, Pascaline in her

bikini and Felix in his briefs. They delighted in splashing around after the heat and exertion of the morning. Pascaline scooped down into the water and splashed him. He leaped after her and she made a halfhearted attempt to escape. He picked her up, waded to a deeper part in the middle of the stream and demanded,

'*Dis que tu es désolée.*' (Say you're sorry.)

She shrieked, and he dumped her in the water. They played a game, clowning around, chasing each other, laughing like little children – a game of seduction. The spectators lying on the grass laughed, too, and urged him to give her a good dunking. The young men were admiring Pascaline, and one of the cheekier ones stated that she would be good in bed tonight. (*Elle sera bien au lit ce soir.*) He sounded good-hearted, just playful and jealous he had in tow such a beautiful girl, but Felix told him in his best gutter French to get lost. (*Va te faire foutre!*)

They joined them on the banks and relaxed on the grass. Pascaline was ready to sunbake, but he encouraged her to join him in the shade. 'This hot Spanish sun will cook you.'

They remained there for the afternoon, thankful they were not walking. He wanted to put his arm around her beautiful bikini-clad body, but he lay beside her, content that he had made timely progress. He did not want to rush. They both snoozed until Pascaline sat up and gave him a gentle playful slap.

'*J'ai soif, j'ai faim.*' (I'm thirsty. I'm hungry.)

He gave her a playful slap back .They returned to the building for a shower, dressed and went out into the village looking for a bar-restaurant. They were not as late as the previous night returning to the dormitory. She had no problem undressing in his presence. Nudity didn't seem to be a problem for the French, he thought. Felix gave her a gentle kiss on both cheeks before she climbed into her bunk. His thoughts were on this beautiful girl just above him, and in the dark, he listened for changes in her breathing; she may already be asleep. Remembering the young man's comments, he would have happily climbed into her bunk, but a dormitory was no place for lovemaking. It was difficult to have sex silently. He imagined waking up the other pilgrims. Some would be grumpy because their slumber had been disturbed, but the young blokes would be happy to be woken, to watch and encourage him.

The next morning, over a breakfast of coffee and rolls, Felix commented, 'We should walk together until we reach Santiago.'

'You are such a courteous, gallant fellow, my dear Felix, always seeking my approval instead of just saying we'll do this or that.' She stabbed the air with her finger as if giving directions.

'I'm not sure what you want, Pascaline, but I was taught to show respect, to open a door, to say hello when I enter a room, to say please and thank you.'

'Oh Felix, you are such a silly boy. Of course, I would love to walk with you to Santiago.'

'Do you want me to order you about and tell you what to do?'

'Of course not. That was my father's way. No. I like you just the way you are – gentle and soft.'

He was tempted to ask about her father but was content to wait.

Each day followed the same pattern. They left their place of refuge before the sun rose. They were travelling west and the sun behind cast long shadows on the track ahead. The shadows shortened as the morning advanced.

'They are our guardian angels,' Pascaline commented. 'Their job is to show us the way.'

'They don't do a decent job,' Felix bantered. 'By midday, they've vanished.'

'They have all but done their job for the day. They are resting now but will always be back next morning.'

'They're slack sometimes, particularly on a cloudy day. Where are they then?'

They stopped walking early afternoon and searched for a place to sleep. After a shower, change of clothes and some washing, they rested and then explored the village or town. There was always something to see – ramparts, castle ruins, fountains, beautifully restored houses, or craft shops selling local products. Pascaline loved to visit and inspect the range, sometimes pottery or tableware, sometimes clothes. Then they would find somewhere to eat, chat with other pilgrims and eventually find their way back to their refuge. They slept in dormitories in bunks because they were cheap. Sometimes, he thought it would be great to go upmarket and find a double bed in a private room.

Once, as they were about to enter a village, Felix ventured to suggest, 'It would be nice to sleep together tonight.'

She looked at him with a frown and gave his hand a gentle slap.

'Not yet, my silly boy. Wait until the end of our pilgrimage. Be patient.'

Not until they reached their destination, Santiago, were they to become one. They arrived early on a Saturday morning.

'I would like to attend the midday Pilgrims' Mass in the cathedral,' Pascaline said.

'I'm not a churchgoer,' he confessed. 'My parents were bush Baptists.'

'What does that mean?'

'It's Aussie slang for having no religion.'

'Everyone goes to the Pilgrims' Mass whether they are religious or not. Come with me. That will be a happy end to our pilgrimage.'

The Santiago de Compostela Cathedral has been a pilgrimage destination since the Early Middle Ages and marks the traditional end of the pilgrimage route. An imposing building in the Romanesque style with Gothic and baroque additions, it faces a large square known as the Praza do Obradoiro. After walking through the modern town, they arrived at this open space and paused to admire the façade, like millions before them, before climbing the stairs into the building. They arrived in good time and found a seat in the second row before the incredibly ornate altar with its gold leaf and semi-naked angels, compelling in its decoration. In the meantime, tour groups arrived, each with their flag-waving leader trying to explain in a variety of languages the features of the cathedral, all the while a priest on the microphone calling for silence. Organised groups of pilgrims followed, singing as they passed through the doors, wearing the same T-shirt, their leader carrying a banner. Individual pilgrims arrived wearing their backpacks, breathless, as if they had rushed to get to the cathedral in time. The building was full. Some had walked hundreds of kilometres, some the last hundred, others were walking for the weekend and the tourists had arrived by coach. The priest on the microphone managed to quieten the chaos. The noisy crowd settled down for mass. In the second row, they had an unobstructed view. Around them, tourists, well dressed, their designer handbags tucked under their arms, were taking up the seats while tired pilgrims, Felix noted, had to stand. A group of these tourists arrived late and tried to stand in front, between the altar and the pews, but the priest on the microphone chased them away.

The ceremony began. The priests, twelve of them, dressed in their finest vestments, were accompanied by an army of altar boys. First, as a symbol of welcome, a list was read of the pilgrims who had arrived within the last twenty-four hours plus their nationality and the place where each had begun their pilgrimage. They were invited to give thanks to God for the experience of their adventure and for having reached the goal. The language was Spanish but Felix understood what was going on. He heard Australia mentioned.

The liturgy was dramatic, in a variety of languages, such as Spanish, Latin, English and French. The singing, by a solo soprano, was beautiful, and towards the end, the baroque organ broke in with an anthem to Saint James, in such a blast that it shook the building. It didn't matter that they didn't understand much of what was said. Witnessing such an amazing event that swept along both the faithful and the non-believers was enough. The ceremony concluded with the botafumeiro, handled by six strong men, swinging twenty metres high above the congregation, reaching a speed of sixty-eight kilometres per hour and spewing incense smoke. Every head was craning for an unobstructed view of a relic from medieval days when the incense smoke was needed to suppress the stink of unwashed pilgrims.

Felix found the ceremony exhilarating, and Pascaline was reduced to tears.

'What's wrong?' he asked. She leaned into him, placed her head on his shoulder and wept. He wrapped his arms around her. Her emotions had reached a deep primaeval place. She felt the presence of millions of pilgrims who had pressed into the building down the centuries. After battling with the elements, fatigue, pain and their own demons, they had arrived at this sacred place, overwhelmed by their feelings and the joy of arriving. She was a mess – disoriented, vulnerable and uncertain, grateful for his calm, reassuring presence. They remained in the seats in the second row while the crowd swirled around taking copious photos and the organ, after a thunderous surge at the end of mass, played gently in the background. She found it difficult to articulate her emotions to Felix, but he was gentle and patient and asked no more questions.

They entered a bar near the cathedral where they sat at a window table and watched the crowd crossing the road back up to the cathedral. Pascaline recovered over *tortilla de patatas*, an egg and potato dish, and they ate in silence.

After lunch, they found accommodation for two nights in a luxury hotel that was once a seminary, this time in a private room with a double bed. He felt as excited as a small child and could not wait for the night. They spent the afternoon exploring the medieval town, descended the steps below the altar to view the shrine to Saint James, visited a museum next to the cathedral (*Museo de la Catedral de Santiago de Compostella*) and wandered along arcades of shops where Pascaline bought souvenirs for her mother – a brooch shaped like a pilgrim shell and silver rosary beads. They went upmarket and had a romantic dinner, a classic Spanish paella of chicken and mussels, with candlelight in a small intimate restaurant that could have been standing for hundreds of years. Then they strolled back to the hotel, arms around each other like lovers. The night was calm, and the floodlit ancient buildings stood out in beautiful silhouettes against the darkened sky. The Spanish red wine left Felix content, but his body tingled in anticipation.

As soon as they entered the room, he kicked his shoes off into a corner and unbuckled his belt.

'Attends,' (Hold on) she whispered.

'Je suis fatigué d'attendre.' (I'm tired of waiting.) He had held on for a month. He had been holding his breath and was on the point of letting it go.

'Nous devrions nous réjouir de chaque instant.' (We should delight in every moment.)

They faced each other and she stepped forward to give him a long passionate embrace. She stepped back as if to draw breath and said, *'Déshabille-moi.'* (Undress me.)

His hands were shaking as he tried to undo the buttons down the front of her blouse.

She teased him as if she were dealing with an impatient child. *'Pas si maladroit, mon petit. Lentement.'* (Not so clumsy, my silly boy. Slowly.)

He was successful on his second attempt. She helped him remove her blouse and bra, then he knelt and removed her shorts and panties. His heart was beating out of control. Soon he would lose all restraint. She was more adroit as she undressed him, removing his shirt and belt and allowing his trousers to fall to his feet. His underpants followed. He stepped out of them, and she took his hands, his socks the only item of clothing between them. They gazed at each other's bodies and ran their fingers over each other's shoulders. She looked down at his endowment, which was showing its impatience, and fell back on the bed. She was ready for him. He removed his socks, threw them after his shoes and followed. The night was warm, and they lay on top of the smooth sheets. He pulled her towards him, feeling the warmth of her body. His hand travelled down her back and thigh; her warm hand explored his back and buttocks. He was on fire. The passion that had been pent up for so long released and he abandoned himself to entering her and they became one. At first, he could find no words to describe his feelings, just a series of grunts, but then his tongue found his heart and out poured the love. She set his heart on fire; she was the best thing that had ever happened; she completed him and made him feel a whole man; she made his world a better place; he lived for her love; she was everything to him; he wanted a lifetime with her. Over and over, he repeated the words of that most popular of French songs: '*Que je t'aime, que je t'aime, que je t'aime, que je t'aime*'. He uttered those words 'I love you' with every gram of his being. He may have sounded like a ham actor in a soppy movie, but he meant every phrase and she heard them.

She heard his commitment. She heard his body. She gave herself immense pleasure as she stimulated herself with his engorged penis. She shrieked as his thrusts and movement inside extended her excitement. She needed him to stay and when he removed himself, she pleaded him back into her, with a solid push of his buttocks. She loved the way he lost all inhibitions and gave his whole self to her. His movement gave her intense pleasure and, from the noise he made as he ejaculated, they shared each other's orgasm. His sexual attraction was exquisite. She admired his body. His nipples and penis stood erect, and she ran her hands over his back and buttock. She loved the way he gazed at her with gentle smiling eyes. They settled down. He fell asleep in an instant, nestling into her while she lay on her back and stared at the ceiling. She leaned over him, watched his chest breathing and ran her hands over his softened penis. He had the look of innocence but in bed he was adult. He was great for a casual night of sex, but she wanted more. She wanted a man who was excited to see her and would miss her terribly should she happen to be absent. She wanted a relationship with a man who was not only good in bed but whom she could trust, with whom she felt safe, who could talk himself out of a sticky situation at, say, 3 am on a darkened street.

They made love again during the night and slept late. When he woke, it took him a moment to clear his head, but when he saw a sleeping Pascaline beside him, he felt a deep sense of gratitude as he realised what a precious gift he had been given. He placed his hand on her thigh and, in that action, recognised that the most beautiful moments in life do not reside in the grand, but in the simple. He could die that day knowing that he had spent a night of breathless moments with her.

During the day, they wandered hand in hand around the town, looked at the sights but didn't see much, listened to the sounds but failed to hear except for the street performers, *troubadours*, with songs of love. They were in a daze, drunk with love, absorbed in each other and longing for the night when they could press their naked bodies together.

During the afternoon they found the Parque de la Alameda and admired its graceful stairs, fountains and manicured lawns, and later, they sat down for a drink at an outside table of a bar, feeling the wind kiss their cheeks, seeing the sun set and watching the pilgrims with backpacks crossing the street on the way to the cathedral, just as they did the previous day.

Their pilgrimage complete, they spent a moment thinking about the future.

'Et maintenant?' (What now?) he asked Pascaline.

'Tu dois rencontrer ma mère.' (You should meet my mother.)

Another joyous moment of simplicity. She reassured him that their relationship was more than a holiday romance with sex thrown in, to be relished while it lasted and then forgotten. She wanted him to stay around. She was like the beach, and he was the ocean that flowed over her. They were different but inseparable, irrelevant to say where he ended, and she began.

When night arrived and laid its mantle over them, they resumed their lovemaking with the same passion and vigour and with the knowledge of what each one wanted. This was the best thing that had ever happened. She had made him a whole man. She was everything and he could look forward to a life at her side. She, too, was hopeful of a life of promise, of a flowering into womanhood. Falling in love was like hearing a beautiful song that got better every time it was heard.

Chapter 3

The next day, they took a plane to Barcelona and then Paris. They were tired and slept most of the way. At Barcelona airport they did not bother with the shops but found a bench and dozed. At Orly Paris airport they did the same. He was running short of cash and an expensive night in a Paris hotel was out of the question. In the morning, Pascaline rang her mother to let her know when they would arrive.

'Etes-vous des amoureux?' (Are you lovers?) She asked her daughter.

'Oui.'

'Bon. Je vais faire un lit.' (Good. I'll make up one bed.)

'Oui.'

'J'ai pris un jour de congé. Je vous rencontrerai à la gare. J'aimerai rencontrer Felix.' (I've taken the day off. I'll meet you at the station. I will enjoy meeting Felix.)

They caught an early train through the suburbs of Paris, first to Gare de Lyon.

'Comment s'appelle ta mère?' (What's your mother's name?) he asked Pascaline.

'Ghislaine.'

'Comment est-elle ?' (What's she like ?)

'Tu le sauras bien assez tôt.' (You'll find out soon enough.)

On to Chambéry in the TGV, the high-speed train. This time, they did not doze but spent the time admiring the French countryside flashing by at incredible velocity. Felix was apprehensive about the impending meeting with Ghislaine. How would she receive him? Well, he hoped. How should he present himself? His personality confused people; at times it confused him. He enjoyed being alone, but he liked people and could be outgoing and sociable. Sometimes he was loud; sometimes he was quiet. He read the energy of his environment and adjusted. There were times when he wanted to turn up and there were moments when he needed to process thoughts alone or read a good book. Perhaps she would be a formidable and critical old French biddy, not to be messed with, with a strong and intense interest in the bloke with whom her daughter was sleeping. He should be nonchalant and appear laid-back. He dismissed those thoughts. Ghislaine would be a perceptive, intelligent woman and quickly see through pretence. He should be himself, a young man with an eye on her daughter and nervous at the prospect of meeting her mother.

At Chambéry Challes-les-eaux, they were among the first to leave the train. They moved with ease, their backpacks no encumbrance. The other passengers alighted, their baggage a clumsy burden, and joined them walking along the platform. He saw her standing at the entrance. Ghislaine was well groomed, elegant. Nothing sloppy about her; she showed none of the ravages of middle age and could have been glamourous in her youth. As soon as she saw them, Ghislaine waved. She rushed forward and embraced Pascaline, gushing all the way and held on to her with a mother's love. He was sure she would have been elated to see her daughter looking so well and healthy and (he hoped) in good company. A breathless Pascaline managed to disengage and introduce him.

'Maman, voici Felix!'

Ghislaine stepped towards him and embraced him just as tightly.

'Enchantée! Bienvenue!'

Her welcome was warm and unreserved. He had nothing to fear. She was positive and lively, an older version of Pascaline – same slim build, similar hair aided by some colouring. If Ghislaine were what Pascaline would be like at her age, he would be content. Around them, the scene was replicated. Other groups, family groups, were greeting their travellers just as warmly, shouting, laughing, embracing, kissing, full of joy at seeing them home.

'Allons-y. Let's get out of this chaos.' Ghislaine spoke in English and waved her car keys in the direction of the car park. In no time, the packs were in the boot, and they were seated in the vehicle, making their way through the Chambéry traffic. Pascaline sat next to her mother, and Felix sat in the back. Ghislaine talked the whole time. She was relating the news. He heard little above the traffic, car horns and all the sounds of a city. Every now and then, Ghislaine turned, shouted at him, and pointed out features, the university, the châteaux of the dukes of Savoy.

'Chambéry was once the capital of Savoy,' Ghislaine explained above the road noise, 'and joined France late in the nineteenth century.'

'I see there are three flags displayed on the buildings,' he shouted back.

'Yes, that's the European Union, the French tricolour and the flag of Savoy. That's the white cross on a red background. Even today, many residents regard themselves as Savoyards first, and French second.'

Ghislaine was just like any mother, excited to have her only daughter home. He was pleased that she tried to include him, speaking in English in case he didn't get the drift.

They left the city and drove through the countryside, a lush green valley surrounded by towering mountains. Vineyards crept up the hillside, sheep and cattle were grazing in the fields in between.

'*Vous habitez un beau pays, Ghislaine.*' (You live in beautiful country, Ghislaine.)

'*Tu dois tutoyer.*'

He had used formal language, addressing her as '*vous*'. The young French use '*tu*' in addressing each other; parents use '*tu*' in the family setting. Younger persons use '*vous*' in speaking to an adult. He was correct in using formal terms. No way was he going to be familiar with an older person. His immaculate politeness would have made his French teachers give him a standing ovation. She told him to '*tutoyer*', that is, use '*tu*' rather than '*vous*'. Her invitation was another signal he was welcomed into the family and would be treated as such. He felt good.

'Felix, your parents gave you a nice name,' Ghislaine shouted.

'Yes, I like it.'

'I'm pleased you are attached to your name. It's come from the Latin and means happy and prosperous. That's what your parents wanted you to be.'

'I haven't thought about it

'Names are important. Every name has a meaning. They give you identity. They play a key role in the destiny and life of the owner. They are a gift from God.'

'Names run in families. My grandfather's name was Felix.'

'I named Pascaline after her father. His name was Pascal.'

'Pascaline has a lovely name. It sounds melodious, like a song.'

'Names are far more than a group of letters put together to make a pleasant sound. They are the most important word for a person. Did you ever carve your name on a school desk?'

'Can't say I did.' He shrugged his shoulders. 'I was the schoolteacher's son.'

He felt the weight of the penny dropping that Ghislaine was an astute lady.

'What is your work?'

'I teach French to foreign students at the Institut Français de Chambéry.'

After ten minutes, Ghislaine turned off the road along a short drive to a rambling farmhouse. A courtyard was surrounded on three sides by buildings that could have been there for centuries. Large blocks formed thick fortress-like walls, but the timber door and windows were modern. At one time, he imagined, it was a ruin, like so many deserted houses in rural France, but the whole had been restored. Over the courtyard was a lattice of vines and in the middle was a large table and benches, an ideal spot for summer dining. Inside were all the modern conveniences. There seemed to be many rooms and he wondered about sleeping arrangements, whether Ghislaine would put him in a separate bedroom, but she ushered him into Pascaline's, which had a double bed.

Ghislaine knew, by the way they looked at each other, that her daughter and this young man were lovers. She liked the way he looked at Pascaline, how he stopped everything just to look at her; there was no need to be coy. Before dis-illusionment, she was in love with Pascal, and, from that experience, knew that whether in the light of day or the dark of night, a moment did not pass when lovers did not think of each other. Lovers believe that they've always been linked in the silence of their souls until they find their time and place together in the world.

The young man didn't know why he felt awkward, but he did, so he blushed. A string of '*merci beaucoup*' followed. He overdid the thanking and she laughed at him.

'You should get some rest now.'

They rested for the afternoon. Felix slept and awoke to find that Pascaline was already up. He lay on the bed, listening to the chatter coming from the kitchen. Mother and daughter were preparing the meal and catching up with each other. Now and then, they spoke quietly. Felix assumed they were talking about him. Ghislaine would want to know as much as possible about this bloke who turned up with her daughter. He got up and joined them in what he imagined a rural French kitchen would be. Shelves on the walls were adorned with pots and pans; bunches of garlic, onions and grapes hung from hooks, and in the middle of the room was a large solid wooden table where the women were preparing the meal. They looked up and smiled when he came in.

'Could I help?' he asked Ghislaine.

'No! No! No! Pascaline and I have everything under control.'

'I can tell that this meal is going to be delicious. I wish I could contribute something. Like some wine.'

'Don't worry. Anton is coming to dinner. He wants to

welcome home his sister. And you, too. He will bring wine. He works in a vineyard. He will bring their best.'

Ghislaine and Pascaline resumed their chopping and stirring. They worked together well, now and then commenting on their work. They seemed happy together. Ghislaine wasn't bossy, ordering Pascaline about. The daughter wasn't objecting, saying she'd do it her way. Their meal preparation was a collaboration of equals, each consulting the other – a joint effort. He sensed a strong bond between mother and daughter and an absence of tension.

'Go and sit outside. It's nice there.'

He left them and sat outside in the courtyard. The afternoon was warm and balmy, perfect to dine outside under the vines. He felt content, at peace with himself and this household. He fell in a reverie and reflected on his good fortune in finding Pascaline. If they'd never met, his life would not have been complete. He would have continued to wander around Europe with no idea of who he was searching for.

He wasn't on his own for long. His meditation was interrupted by the arrival of Anton, along with his partner Mireille and three bottles of wine. Out came the ladies in exuberant welcome. It was easy to tell that Pascaline and Anton were sister and brother. He was almost two metres tall. He bent down to embrace and kiss her on both cheeks. He embraced and kissed Felix and so did Mireille. Felix felt welcome. The ladies returned to the kitchen and Mireille joined them.

'*Ouvrons une de ces bouteilles,*' (Let's open one of these bottles.) said Anton. The table was already set, and Anton filled two glasses, went inside to fill the ladies', returned and sat opposite.

'*A la Vôtre! Bonne Santé!*' He raised his glass and together they drank, as if they were performing a ceremony of male bonding. Anton looked at Felix and got to the point with a double-barrel.

'*Qu'as-tu fait en France? Comment as-tu rencontré ma sœur?*' (What have you been doing in France? How did you meet my sister?)

Felix was pleased that he used the familiar '*tu*'.

'*Je suis venue en France après mes études et j'ai fait de la randonnée en France et en Espagne. J'ai rencontré Pascaline lors d'une canicule. Elle était déshydratée par la chaleur et je suis resté avec elle. Nous sommes amoureux.*' (I came to France after graduation and have been hiking in France and Spain. I met Pascaline in Spain in the middle of a heatwave. She was dehydrated from the heat, and I stayed with her. We fell in love.)

'*Très galant! Ma sœur est une fille adorable. Tu as fait un excellent choix pour rester avec elle.*' (My sister is a lovely girl. You made an excellent choice to stay with her.)

By the time the ladies came out with dinner, Anton and Felix felt like old mates. They had a delightful meal of four courses, with salad as starters, a main course of chicken, cheese platter and a dessert of strawberries and ice-cream. The conversation flowed. Anton and Mireille talked about their vineyard, Pascaline told stories about the Camino and the people she met. Felix told them about Marcel, the skinny Frenchman who directed him to the Camino. Ghislaine spoke about her pupils and the quaint ways of her colleagues. They finished Anton's wine and Ghislaine found a bottle of cognac. There they were, in regional France, a French family, mother,

her children and their partners, dining under the stars. Even the foreigner (*un étranger*) was accepted.

Anton was exuberant as they left and insisted Felix visit his vineyard.

'Tu dois visiter mon vignoble demain.'

In the absence of a father, Anton was the head of the family. Felix thanked him and his family for welcoming him so warmly. He laughed the same as Ghislaine at his string of thank yous.

'A demain!' (See you tomorrow!) he said upon leaving.

'I will leave my car home for you to show Felix around. I will ask one of my colleagues to pick me up,' Ghislaine mentioned as she prepared to leave them.

'Thank you, Ghislaine.'

On their own that night, Felix asked Pascaline two questions.

'Where's Pascal, your father?

She sat on the bed and began to undress, pausing before she replied.

'He lives in Lyon. I don't see him very often. He's lost interest in us. He didn't stay with Mum for long.'

He removed his shirt and trousers.

'Long enough to conceive the two of you.'

Pascaline sighed, as she slipped into bed.

'After me, my mother had a miscarriage. She was sick, and they had to operate. She could not have any more children.'

He slipped into bed after her.

'That was sad.'

'My father wanted more children. He has another family, now.'

'It must have been tough on Ghislaine, bringing up two children.'

'Grandma helped her.'

'Where's your grandma now?'

'Gone to God.'

He cuddled into her and asked his second question.

'Does your mother have a man in her life? She is very attractive.'

'No, nothing serious.'

She turned towards him and kissed him as if to say that's enough talk. Time to make love. He was happy to comply. As he settled down to sleep, his thoughts ranged over this family. He was happy with what he had seen. They got on well, different to many families who wage war with each other. He dreamed that Pascaline and he visited the forest near her home. They made a fire, lay down beside it and counted the stars that shimmered above the trees.

In the morning, they had a late breakfast of croissants, which Ghislaine had left them. It was early enough to spend the morning at Anton's vineyard. Perched on the side of a steep hill, it required hand picking. Harvesting had just been completed and the grapes were being pressed. Anton who was manager and winemaker, delighted in showing them around. He took pleasure in telling Felix that the vineyard had been in operation for centuries and included a small museum of ancient equipment. He paused to explain a collection of wine presses and tools to cultivate around the vines as well as baskets to gather the grapes. Felix was fascinated to learn that vines had been cultivated in this valley since Roman times. They had lunch with Anton and Mireille then drove up into the picturesque mountains and found walking trails. From the valley below, he saw a large cross and was interested to visit. They had a magnificent view over the valley, over the town and a large lake. Pascaline pointed out the railway yards, of strategic importance during the war, a constant target for American bombs with the odd one straying off course to hit the ancient town, by now faithfully restored. They visited Chambéry's monuments.

'I must show you the *Fontaine des Eléphants*,' Pascaline exclaimed. 'It's an extravaganza left to the town by a grateful citizen who made his fortune in India. It's a favourite place where townspeople arrange to meet each other. We call it *les quatre sans cul* because none of the four elephants have backsides.'

Those days he shared with Pascaline's family were some of his treasured memories. Gathering with loved ones around the table was full of promise and anticipation. Felix sighed as he realised the time for him to depart was approaching far too quickly.

Pascaline liked his old-style protective chivalry, like a medieval knight, except that his awkwardness made her smile. He was giving her an opportunity to travel with someone who would look after her.

'I would like to go to Australia, Felix. Would you like me to come with you?'

Pascaline posed the question.

His heart leapt with joy and threatened to burst out of his chest. He could barely believe that his decision to stay with Pascaline, made on impulse, had worked out so well. He wanted to ask her the same question, but was scared witless she would say no. To leave her family and travel to the other side of the world with a man whom she had known a few weeks would be too presumptuous to ask and expect.

'Pascaline! I couldn't think of anything nicer.'

He loved her name. Pascaline! He pronounced every syllable, allowing the sound to roll around. Too nice a name to shorten or rush. He loved the way she spoke French. She was slower and more measured than most, melodious in the flow of her sentences like water running over pebbles. The way she spoke English in an accent was a delight to hear. He loved to see her naked. Her smell in bed and the way she allowed him to enter her, guiding him in his clumsiness, were rapture. He loved her climax with her little shrieks, imploring him to press on. He loved her lying against him, relaxing in his arms as if she trusted him completely.

He loved everything about her.

Now she was ready to commit herself by following him to the other side of the world. He could not believe his good fortune. He felt unworthy of her affection and an immense sense of responsibility that he would not measure up and live up to her expectations – a thorn in their bed of roses.

Felix's visa was due to expire. He hadn't yet booked a flight. He wanted to delay as long as possible in case that meant separation and the prospect of never seeing her again.

'You must visit the travel agent tomorrow,' she whispered as they settled down to sleep.

He felt guilty of wanting to take Pascaline so far away from the close bonds of a loving family.

The next day, he sought out Ghislaine for a quiet chat.

'I'm taking your daughter away. Different if we were going another place in France or another country in Europe.'

Ghislaine sighed.

'I have trained my children to be independent,' she said. 'I am happy that they are so thankful and loving to me. We will always have that bond, no matter where we are. I am happy to see my daughter happy and I believe she will be happy with you. But I am sad for myself to see my daughter depart for the other side of the world.' She laughed. 'I don't mind that you are a foreigner, but why aren't you Spanish, or Swiss, or German, or Italian?'

He was no longer the carefree backpacker. He had responsibility.

'I promise I will take care of your daughter.'

Ghislaine embraced and kissed him and hugged him for some seconds.

'I'm sure you will.'

Chapter 4

Rob Champion liked the young man on the phone. He fitted in with his plans for company expansion. But from the delay, uncharacteristic of the rhythm of his conversation when they met, Rob sensed that he was ambivalent. He needed more persuasion.

'We've got our Christmas barbeque Saturday night. You should join us. You'll meet the blokes. They're a great bunch. They're a great team to work with. You'll know you've made the right decision.'

On the other end of the phone, Felix Schmidt looked out of the window, inhaled, and held his breath before letting it go.

'Thank you very much, Rob. It sounds very exciting but let me think about it.'

'That's okay. It's a big decision. But we'd very much like to have you on board.'

From his office in St Kilda Road Melbourne, Rob rang his brother Sid who was running a training programme at an oil refinery in Geelong.

'How did you go?' asked Sid.

'I've got a good feel about him. He mightn't rush into decisions, but if he commits himself to us, he'll give us a hundred per cent plus.'

'Good! That's the sort of bloke we want.'

*　　*　　*

Rob Champion wasn't meaning to fan the flames of Felix's anxiety but that's what he did. Felix was excited and hesitant about both the job offer and the party invitation. He already had a job and an invitation that Saturday night. He worked in family welfare, his job after returning to Australia, and felt obliged to attend the work Christmas party, held at the home of the director. How different to his student days! If he didn't like the party giver, he didn't bother. He disliked the director – Jonathon Grant, a tall, bulky man. Old Jonah, his staff called him. What irritated Felix most was Old Jonah's habit of peering over his glasses at his staff as if he were dealing with pieces of low life. Once he had made up his mind, attempting to change his view was like trying to shift a beached whale.

Felix had nightmares about his colleagues. He shared an office with one phone with Dave. They were both supposed to answer the phone, but Dave never did. He'd just let it ring even if he was right next to it. Dave's preoccupation was his superannuation. He always seemed to be working on a page of calculations – his contributions, his likely pension as a percentage of his final salary and determination of his take-home pay should he decide to increase his contributions through salary sacrifice. If Dave was in his fifties or sixties, Felix could understand his concern, but he was Felix's age. He was a timid old man in his twenties, and he sounded as if he had settled to spend his working life in the department even though he saw nothing enjoyable. Despite his irritation at having to share an office, Felix felt sorry for him. Dave needed structure and certainty. He was in a job he didn't like but was afraid of losing it. Having a go or taking a risk scared him witless.

Felix worked on projects with Margaret. At their first meeting, he opened the door for her.

'I can open the fucking door myself,' was her response with an expression that was a cross between astonishment and contempt.

Her disposition didn't improve. She'd abuse him if he displayed normal courtesy. She scared the wits out of him. He did not enjoy working with this loud, uptight, angry lady, operating on the edge, who was always alert to any insult, real and imaginary. He was amazed at her paranoia, at the manner in which she could misconstrue simple remarks or actions, accusing him and others of all manner of devious motives.

'What do you mean?'

He concluded Margaret was a secret hoarder. She had a bag full of bad memories and had never parted with one. She had never faced the mess in her bag, tipped its contents on the floor and figured out what to take with her and what to sweep away. While the job of sorting herself out remained undone, she was a powder keg ready to explode and a danger to herself and everyone else.

His immediate boss was Travis McCully, a hyperactive self-absorbed attention seeker who should have been wearing a cowboy hat and unbuttoned shirt rather than a faded business suit that had left Lowes decades ago. He was probably married in it. A frustrated person in a job entirely unsuited to his vanity. He was also thick and usually missed the crux of an issue. Felix felt he sucked him dry and gave nothing in return. McCully valued people only for as long as he needed them. He'd usually treat Felix as the invisible man but then, he'd say: 'I want to pick your brains, Felix!' Dutiful Felix ventured worthy ideas, pleased to be noticed, only to find McCully later spouting them as his own. Once, he asked Felix to present a paper at a conference, which he was supposed to deliver but could not, out of illness, cold feet or fear of exposure of his own incompetence. Felix spent several nights undertaking the necessary research and wrote the entire paper. He showed it to McCully. He made no contribution. At the conference, Felix's jaw dropped slack in disbelief when the chairman of the session introduced him as reading a paper that an indisposed Travis McCully had prepared from his sick bed. He felt out of place, an outsider, a mere conveyer of the message stick. At least, he was invited to the luncheon. A lady at his table commented on what a good paper he had read. He was busting to tell her the truth. It was his paper, not McCully's, but some twisted misguided sense of loyalty to his boss resisted the temptation and kept him silent. Felix was not sure how long Old Jonah would take to work out that McCully was an idiot. Blind Freddie could have seen his incompetence.

Felix realised from day one that he had made a mistake and had been looking for other jobs. He'd not had much luck. His confidence was waning. He would never get out of this toxic wasteland, in a perpetual state of descending from bad to worse. He had images of endless trudging through the contaminated mire and suffering the same negativity as his colleagues. For the poet, April was the cruellest month, but for him every month with the department was equally savage and detrimental to his psyche. He applied for other jobs in the public service, but he always had to nominate referees and had none other than McCully and Old Jonah. Late one Sunday evening, he was glancing through Saturday's *Age*, listless at the thought of having to continue the battle Monday, feeling as if he would have to muddle through another day. He read a job advertisement from a management consultant firm calling for qualifications in psychology. He'd not given much thought to moving out of the public service into private enterprise. He could do a lot worse. Come Monday he posted an application, not mentioning referees because the advertisement didn't ask for them.

What kept him off the insane list was going home each night to his Edwardian house in East Melbourne, not unlike his old student digs but with a French ring door knocker, very appropriate, for inside, his beautiful Pascaline was waiting. She walked with him like she had always been there, like his heart was a home built for her. In her erotic presence, he could forget the torture of the day and give himself over to excitement, to desire and to reconnecting to parts of himself that he thought he had lost. He succumbed to the exhilaration of entering her nest and listening to her expressions of joy in her native tongue *('Encore! Encore!')*. In her language and culture, he found a freedom from the imprisonment of his daily routine.

His other refuge was his books. He was always an avid reader, a gift from his bibliophilic parents. His sister, Nell, and he were both excellent readers. They grew up in a house full of books and had read from their earliest memories. Felix returned to the authors and poets of his school days, such as TS Eliot, who were a puzzle then, but in his adulthood were making sense. Pascaline's influence led him to French literature. He had studied the classics at university (Victor Hugo,

Alphonse Daudet, Guy de Maupassant, Honoré de Balzac) but he consulted her on contemporary authors. She introduced him to Anna Gavalda, Jacques Prévert, Marcel Pagnol and Christine Arnothy. Jacques Prévert (*Paroles*) appealed to him as a poet and screenwriter (*Les Enfants du Paradise*), always photographed with a cigarette hanging from his mouth. She borrowed the books from Alliance Française, and they both read them. At work he buried himself in a book at lunch breaks to minimise interaction with his colleagues.

On Wednesday he was reading a French translation of Stephen Crane's *The Red Badge of Courage (La Conquête du Courage)*, always a favourite, when he received a phone call.

'Would you come in for an interview Thursday at 5.30?'

He was impressed. He posted the application on Monday. He arrived at an office in St Kilda Road late afternoon. The buildings along this boulevard were mostly modern but this one reminded him of a once elegant old lady seeing out her last days. Now an office suite, it was waiting to be knocked down and replaced by a building as bland as its neighbours. A shiny plaque announced the name of the firm 'The Champions'.

'Sounds corny! They must think themselves good,' he mused as he entered the office. He was greeted by a tall, slim, earnest young man about his age, with large freckles and red hair, by the name of Owen, who told him he was one of the consultants.

'You were quick off the mark.'

'When we see someone good, we don't muck around.'

Owen's enthusiasm boosted his confidence. He'd been ground down of late, coming from an organisation where the norm was to criticise rather than praise. The interview proceeded. He told Owen about his studies and work, and Owen told him about the company. The firm was in staff recruitment and used psychological testing to assess job applicants.

'That's why we're looking for psychology qualifications.'

'But I don't know much about psychology tests, I've never used them,' he said. *You fool*, he said to himself. *That's no way to sell yourself.*

'That's not a problem. We can teach you.'

'I'm intrigued by the firm's name, The Champions.'

'The firm was founded five years ago by two brothers, Sid and Rob Champion.'

'Are they still in the business?'

'Very much so,' Owen laughed. 'Rob calls himself Managing Director and Sid calls himself Chairman.'

'You haven't asked for referees.' Felix was worried because neither McCully nor Old Jonah boss would speak well of him. In fact, he was sure of it, for the only time that he had nominated Old Jonah as a referee for a job in another department, he had heard through a grapevine source with connections someone in his department didn't like him.

'We don't place much reliance on them,' replied Owen.

'Why is that?'

'Because no two organisations are the same. A person will behave in one organisation quite differently in another because the organisations are different.'

'That makes sense.' He could imagine that he would be open and ready to engage in a supportive organisation where he didn't have to watch his back.

Owen looked over his notes. *This bloke looks promising. He should go to the next step.*

'We'd like you to do a battery of tests.'

'What kind of tests?' Felix didn't know much detail about testing. The subject was treated in his university course, but the lecturers focussed on the controversy about their effectiveness. To some they were God's gift to assessment, but to others they were a con job with little scientific validity.

'They cover abilities, interests and temperament. They tell us more about a person than you could work out from an interview. They tell us whether a person would be effective in the job or not.'

Owen sounded like a prophet. Before he could stop himself, Felix reacted.

'I must admit I'm sceptical,' he said to Owen, but instantly to himself: *Idiot! You'll talk your way out of the job. If testing is the next step, so be it.*

'That's okay,' Owen replied. 'Many people are, but once they see the results ...'

The following Saturday morning saw Felix undergoing a four-hour test session with three other hopefuls – applicants for jobs the company was handling. Another consultant was administering the tests. As young as Owen, he introduced himself as Tim. He took an interest in Felix as a potential colleague. On one of the tests, verbal reasoning, he had reached the last item when Tim said, 'Time's up,' but he allowed Felix to write down the answer. They stopped for a break and Tim served morning tea. Tim stayed in the room and invited people to ask questions. Felix liked that touch, a good PR effort, to calm anxieties and take the mystery out of the process. Questions were about the next step and whether people would see the results. Felix asked if Tim administered the tests every day.

No! During the week a girl did the job, and on Saturdays, the consultants took it in turns. He liked Tim. He liked Owen, too. They could be good colleagues.

Saturday afternoon, Pascaline and he walked in the park close to their home. People were strolling while children ran and rolled on the grass. He talked about the morning.

'They seem nice people. I've met two now, Owen and Tim. They look like good blokes to work with.' He sighed. 'Not like my present colleagues.'

He tried to relax but he was in a state of tension, suspended between two worlds, one in which the work itself was okay but the organisation was chaotic, and the people were toxic, the other full of the promise of the unknown where the people seemed fine. Over the weekend he could not get those tests out of his mind. The Champions relied heavily on them. He would have to manage his scepticism should they offer him a job? His heart was full of hope and his head the delicious prospects of escape.

He didn't have to wait long. On Monday, he received a call from Owen.

'Could you come tomorrow afternoon to meet Sid and Rob?'

'Sure. How did I go on the tests?'

'Rob will give you feedback when you come in.'

He couldn't get home quickly enough to tell his beautiful Pascaline.

'I must have done all right if they're keen to see me so quickly. Or, the results are bad, and they just want to put me out of my misery.'

'Silly boy! I'm sure you did amazingly well. They want you badly.'

'This mob doesn't stuff around.'

Pascaline had confidence in him and over dinner he came round to thinking that they could offer him a job.

Nerves tingling in anticipation, he was back at St Kilda Road for the third time within a week. The tablet with 'The Champions' written on it invited him to enter. Owen greeted him warmly, called him 'Mate' and led him into an office where he introduced him to Sid and Rob Champion. They were seated behind a large desk and rose to greet him. They didn't look like brothers. Chairman Sid was big and filled the room. He shook hands with a fierce energy, more in keeping with a man wearing an open leather jacket over a bare chest and tattoos rather than a business suit. Managing Director Rob was smaller and less imposing in his presence, younger looking, almost boyish, but possessed a determination underneath, like a wolf masquerading as a puppy. Both had a cigarette in their hands. The air was thick with smoke and expectation. Both lit a Camel from another. If he joined these people, he thought, he'd be joining the rat race. Rob offered him a cigarette. He was tempted to take one, but he was in the process of giving them up, having bought his first packet on his seventeenth birthday. If he took one, he'd be back on the fags and in no time be like these blokes, lighting one Camel from another, smoking sixty a day.

Rob didn't beat around the bush. He came straight to the point.

'We'd very much like to have you on board, Felix.'

To say he was surprised was an understatement. Rob had never met him before, so what did he know that he could offer him a job so promptly? Felix dropped his jaw. Rob sensed his puzzle. He glanced down at the pile of papers on the desk.

'We have your test results here.'

'How did I go?'

'You got top score on verbal reasoning. We need people with excellent verbal skills for report writing. The temperament scale indicated that you'd fit in very well.'

Sid had his turn:

'This is not the public service, you know. We don't stop at five o'clock. We work 'til the job gets done.'

'You're not talking about the public service I know. I'm so busy seeing people all day that I have to take files home and write them up at night.' No need for Sid to know that he stopped, no matter how urgent the report, when an impatient Pascaline asked in a seductive way he could not resist, 'Whenever are you coming to bed?' or more often than not, '*Tu veux te coucher avec moi?*' He dropped everything and replied, '*J'arrive!*'

'Okay.' Sid was happy. Felix passed this test just like he had passed the written tests, and Rob made him a job offer paying a lot more than his current salary.

He was taken aback! A job offer after one interview. He was used to job applications taking months over multiple interviews. It hit him. What the hell was he doing? He was stepping out of the solid, safe, secure environment of the public service, where it was difficult to get the sack, where receiving a pay packet every fortnight was guaranteed, whether times were good or bad, into an unknown environment where employment was tenuous and where firms could go down the gurgler the instant the climate turned sour. The work in the public service was varied, but the job had turned him into a bureaucrat, more concerned with policy than with the welfare of clients. Tired of the battleground, he should have been outgoing and contributing his ideas with zest in a creative and receptive environment. Instead, he felt drained and experienced a dreary malaise in which the struggle was against withdrawing into himself, like a bunny backing into its burrow.

That evening Felix went for a long walk in the cool night air of the park near their flat, hoping the gentle breeze caressing his face might allow an inner space to open where he could think.

'What do you reckon?' he asked Pascaline back home.

She was annoyed with his procrastination.

'I am sick of you moaning about your job. Here is your chance.' She thumped the table and tossed her head. Then she was sorry because he was crestfallen at her anger. He reminded her of her brother Anton when he was a little boy, who burst into tears whenever chastised. She softened and chided him in French, *'Petit idiot. Arrête tes bêtises! Couche-toi avec moi!'* (Silly boy. Stop your foolishness. Come to bed.)

She clinched his decision. He felt a relief. Their sex had an extra delicious edge that night. The agonising indecision was gone. As they lay back, he felt a peace and a joy that new pathways had opened. She ruffled his hair and he snuggled into her for warmth, comfort and affection. He needed her approval. She felt tranquil as he could now give her all his attention. Whether or not he had made the right choice, their journey of love would continue forever.

He rang Rob the next day.

'I'd be lying if I said I wasn't scared.' He paused for a few seconds trying to push down his nervous stomach. 'But I think I'll accept.'

'That's tremendous,' said Rob. He had hoped for a definite yes, but he had to accept that Felix Schmidt was slow to commit.

Felix battled with his anxiety but was thrilled with Rob's enthusiasm. He was acknowledged. He was accepted. He was important. He was relieved. The chains that had tied him down to the department had been cast off and the key to the padlock thrown away as well as the padlock itself.

'Why don't you join us for our barbeque next Saturday night?' Rob continued. 'You'll meet the blokes. They're a great team. That'll help you know you've made the right decision.'

The work Christmas party was also scheduled for Saturday. Sensible Pascaline decided they would go to the work party, stay a respectable time, and then complete the evening at the second. Apart from the number of cars parked in the street outside, there was no indication that a party was on hand. It was a sober affair, as sombre as Old Jonah's house, built in Victorian times – no loud music, balloons or loud laughter. Old Jonah liked quiet, sedate affairs where the people sat or stood around and talked. People were usually guarded because they were alert to each other to see who was going to make a fool of themselves. As usual, McCully did. He thought he was a ladies' man. Felix resented the way he perved on his beautiful Pascaline.

'Thank God I'm leaving this mob of wankers,' he said to Pascaline as they walked out to the VW Beetle. He read the boredom in her lovely eyes.

'I do not like the way Mr McCully looks me up and down

as if he is undressing me. Only men who love me and whom I love can do that.'

He gave her a hug and a long kiss before starting the engine. He would have been happy to drive straight home. They drove for fifteen minutes to the address in the outer suburbs that Rob had given him. As he parked the car, they heard loud music and laughter.

'The party's under way,' he said.

'Je pense que ce sont des gens qui s'amusent,' (I think they are people who enjoy themselves) said Pascaline.

Chapter 5

Sid's house in outer suburbia was modest, a triple-front brick veneer. His mind's eye viewed a far more imposing edifice. The night was mild and moonless, but the poet in Felix felt the crispness of an early morning where the sunlight kissed the flowers and bid them open to a new day, a new society, a new world order, a new career.

The party noise floating from the rear was an invitation to join. As soon as they walked in, they felt the warmth of welcome. Rob stepped forward, shook Felix's hand and introduced himself to Pascaline. Sid's backyard was no different from a million others, but it looked like fairyland, decorated with lights and balloons. A fire was blazing in a pit, grill on top for the meat. The air was buzzing, lots of laughter, in contrast to the party they had just left. Music was playing from within the house and people were shouting to be heard. Then Rob began a giddy round of introductions – wives, family, girlfriends, even neighbours. Felix hoped he would remember names.

It did not take long for the party to split into two. The blokes gathered around the barbecue with beer cans and the women drank wine around a large table on the patio. Pauline, Sid's wife, insisted that Pascaline sit next to her. The ladies took a strong interest in her. The fact she was French and spoke English with a delightful accent made her different. She was nervous, sometimes struggled to find the right word and the ladies fell over each other to help. The men took an interest in her, too.

'She's a stunner,' was Sid's comment. 'Where did you meet her?'

'In Spain,' Felix replied.

Sid was busting to ask how, but the banter swung around to serious topics like, 'What about another beer?' Every now and then, Felix cast an eye at the ladies to see how Pascaline was faring. She was listening then talking, joining in, and looking as if she was enjoying herself and her company.

Throughout the evening in snatches of conversation, he learned something about the other consultants. Tim had been with the company for twelve months. He came from South Australia. The company brought him and wife Amily over from Adelaide. Aaron who was joining with Felix had just returned to Australia from England and had been looking for a job. He saw the same advertisement. He had a girlfriend in London but, unlike Pascaline, she was not interested in leaving her family for the other side of the world.

'You're taking on two more consultants at the one time,' Felix said to Rob. 'That's a significant increase in staff, going from four to six. That's a third of the company.'

'Yes, Sid and I decided it was time to add one more, but both you and Aaron looked good, so we thought why not take on two. The work's there. The business is growing.'

When the barbeque was finished, the fire died down and the neighbours went home. Sid said they were good people but he invited them so they wouldn't complain about the noise. The men joined the ladies on the patio. Felix was happy to settle down for a quiet chat.

'I appreciate the way you old hands have welcomed me and Aaron as if we were old mates,' he said to Sid.

'We want everyone to feel they are part of the company. That includes their families as well. One tight-knit family.'

'Camaraderie is important,' Rob added. 'With their families on side, our consultants are prepared to work their guts out for the company. Sid and I are hoping for you new blokes to be infected by their enthusiasm and be as zealous.'

'I haven't formally resigned from the public service, but I'll give them the heave-ho on Monday.'

'That's the stuff,' added Rob, finding another beer for them both.

'You have drunk a lot of beer. I will drive,' Pascaline said.

Felix did not mind. He was tired.

'They are nice people,' Pascaline added on the way home. 'They ask a lot of questions.'

'Like what?' He was dozing off.

'How we met, why I came to Australia and what my family back in France thought.'

They slept late Sunday and went for brunch at a local restaurant.

'I'm going to join them.' He reaffirmed his intention over a hearty meal of eggs Benedict.

'When will you join them?

'It's coming up to the holiday break. After that, in January.'

'We should have a holiday. There might be time to go back home and see *Maman*.'

'That would be good. I'll have to talk to Sid and Rob.'

'I want you to come, too.'

Pascaline hadn't been back to France although she rang Ghislaine weekly – Sunday evening in Melbourne, Sunday morning in Chambéry. Felix was grateful that she didn't want to take a trip on her own.

He could not imagine life without her. The world went dark when she wasn't around. He just wanted to hold her hand, not just in public for the world to see, but in their private darkness where the feel of each other was all they had.

Felix didn't mention he was bursting to start work, and, although he was happy to fly to France with Pascaline, he was enthusiastic to get cracking with The Champions.

On Monday he sought an interview with Old Jonah and formally resigned. He had little to say, just grunted. He did not mention that staff turnover was disastrous, and Felix was just another resignation.

Back on the phone with Rob.

'I've handed in my resignation.'

'Great! When can you start?'

'I was hoping I could start middle-to-late January. We would like to take a short trip back to France to see Pascaline's family.'

The silence on Rob's end buzzed around his ears. He waited for his answer.

'Have you booked flights?'

'No, not yet. We were only discussing the idea yesterday.'

'Sid and I were hoping to start you and Aaron together. We've got a whole induction programme worked out to take you through. There's a lot to learn. If you started later, we'd have Aaron twiddling his thumbs waiting for you.'

Felix ran his hand through his hair in a dilemma. Whom to please, Pascaline or Rob? He didn't want to appear hesitant. Not a good look for his new employer. The Champions won the day.

'Okay, I'll start straight after the New Year.'

'Great. That's the stuff. Looking forward to it.'

He rang Pascaline.

'I'm sorry, Pascaline! They want me to start as soon as New Year is over.'

'I was looking forward to seeing *Maman*. I told her last night on the phone. She is very excited, and I'm sure she's already told Anton and Mireille.'

He felt lousy that he hadn't talked to her first.

'*D'accord*. That's okay,' she said, but she cast her eyes down and her guts flooded with pangs of resentment. Her silence told him she was disappointed and felt let down. She was learning that not every day with Felix would be a good day, and not every day would be a step forward.

Felix leaned back, raised his arm, and stretched, looking for inspiration to save the situation.

'We have about ten days. We can take a break and get out of the city.'

'*D'accord*,' she agreed but was still disappointed, not that she would miss seeing her family, but that he didn't notice she was hurting, as if he were so self-absorbed that even when he was looking directly at her wound, he wasn't aware that she was bleeding.

Instead of her family, they visited his. They spent Christmas with his parents, sister Nell and family in the Victorian highlands. His parents lived in a small cottage in the town, a delightful place to gather, full of antiques and nostalgia. Whereas he left the bush for university and travel, Nell stayed home and married her school sweetheart, Charlie, who wasn't one of his friends but a likable bloke. Charlie was a carpenter while Nell was the homemaker. They lived out of town in a half-built house that Charlie had hoped to finish earlier but he was flat out with his trade. Nell and Pascaline got on well and enjoyed their chats. Pascaline was delighted in their two small twin girls who were about to have their first birthday.

'Felix never told me much about the girls. They are so sweet.'

'Sometimes he forgets what really matters.'

'She a lovely girl, Felix,' Nell said to her brother. 'Don't let her go.'

'I don't intend to.'

Between Christmas and the New Year, they crossed the border into New South Wales and travelled north to the Snowy Mountains, and, despite it being the summer holiday season, they found seclusion. They camped in the bush by a river, and passed joyful days on a tiny beach, skinny dipping, sunbathing, hiking in the hinterland and making love in their tent at night while listening to the sound of nocturnal animals and witnessing evidence of their presence in the morning. Pascaline enjoyed this time together. She was not a good actor, but she concealed her disappointment, and her performance was good enough to convince him that nothing was wrong.

*   *   *

Brand new day!

Back in Melbourne, Felix was excited as he drove along St Kilda Road. The building was set back from the road and boasted a small garden, not well maintained but it provided a space from the busy roadway. Just as dandelion seeds were waiting for the breeze to convey them to new beginnings, a sense of elation carried him like the wind to his new day.

Rob was waiting.

'Welcome to The Champions!' He greeted Felix with a vigorous handshake and broad grin, as if he were sealing the bond of camaraderie. Felix felt he was being admitted into a secret society. If not secretive, certainly exclusive. Sid followed, then Owen and Tim, all equally exuberant in their greeting and handshake. He was feeling at home, hyped up and ready to leap into the game. Aaron arrived. Rob took the two of them around the office to meet the office staff – Camille, the receptionist, Rebecca who ran the test room and two girls in the typing pool, Angela and Mary. Then, The Champions, the six of them, Sid, Rob, Owen, Tim, Aaron, and Felix, gathered for the induction programme in the test room, its only natural light coming through double-glazed doors that led to an enclosed verandah, probably a bedroom in its residential days. After five minutes of small talk, which focussed on what everyone did during the Christmas break, they spread themselves among the small tables and chairs.

Sid stood at the front before a whiteboard, the room's only decoration, and launched into a long-winded speech.

'Welcome everyone. Welcome especially to our new consultants, Aaron, and Felix.' The rest clapped and echoed the welcome. 'You know, this is a significant day in the company's history. Rob and I started the business six years ago with just ourselves and a girl. For three years we worked hard to get the company off the ground. I focussed on getting out and finding the business and Rob worked on developing the systems. We were pioneers in the application of psychology to the business world and we wanted to offer a distinct and unique range of products. It was touch and go. At first, we took no drawings but made sure the staff were paid. Our gamble paid off and business flowed. Owen joined us two years ago and Tim last year. You, Aaron, and Felix are the fifth and sixth. This year, we are planning to open a Sydney office and employ two consultants. The company had grown, and I see no reason it couldn't expand further.'

All the while, Rob was nodding his head in agreement. Both were already onto their second cigarette.

Felix was impressed. No doubt about it, Sid was persuasive; he had charisma. His enthusiasm was infectious. He sat down, pulled another cigarette out of its packet although he still had one in his mouth. He handed over to Rob.

'Business will be quiet this week as many firms are yet to return to work. A suitable time to focus on staff training – the reason our old hands, Owen and Tim, are included. I hope the flow won't be one way and that everyone will contribute their ideas.'

Rob described the ranges of services. The company provided management training and selection as well as psychology services. Psychological services consisted of testing candidates as part of a recruitment assignment. Clients also forwarded candidates whom they had sourced. If the testing found the candidate wanting, they were advised that the company could always recruit for them. Aaron asked about the fees. There were strong incentives to sell full recruitment assignments because the fee was based on a percentage of the starting salary. The higher the salary of the position, the higher the fee. The fee for testing was a flat fee, regardless of the level of the position. Individuals also referred themselves for career guidance and parents referred their school children for vocational guidance.

Rob explained the testing framework. Candidates underwent a series of tests covering abilities, interests, and temperament. The abilities and interests tests were available from local publishers, but the company had gained exclusive Australian rights for a temperament scale developed in the UK. This was the company's USP (unique selling point), which set them apart from other consulting and recruitment firms. The theoretical basis of the test was complex, but Rob had developed a framework that was simple enough for clients to understand and to believe there was substance in the services they were being offered.

'I reckon that the strengths of my brother and me complement each other. I develop the ideas and Sid sells them. However, we don't regard ourselves as specialists. Both of us sell and develop ideas. That's our intention, too, for all consultants. Of course, everyone has their special strengths, but consultants should be allrounders capable of offering all the services the company offers. They must sell them, too.'

'Look at it this way,' Sid chipped in. 'There are two classes – people who are relegated to the roadside market to sell their crafts – called consultants – and the people passing by who have the option of not buying those crafts. If they buy, the stallholders flourish. If they don't, they fade away.'

Felix took a moment to fix the squint he used to convey scepticism. He was apprehensive about that word *salesman*. When he thought of salesmen he had an image – a caricature selling used cars, possessing the gift of the gab, smooth on the surface but manipulative to the core, ready to conceal the blemishes from any potential client. There was something immoral or unethical in sales, forcing services and products on prospects, which they did not need or want. His expression returned to normal as he realised that his image was stereotypic and false. Whereas he could have nurtured this thinking in the public service, he was now in an environment that demanded that good sales and selling techniques were vital to the success of any enterprise.

Sid returned to the front again, cigarette trailing behind, this time to talk about mission. Their mission was to introduce the insights gained from the development of psychology to commerce and industry.

'We're pioneers in this field. Instead of flying by the seat of our pants, we base our work on solid scientific principles. This gives us a distinct marketing advantage over competitors. Marketing means getting out and letting the world know how good we were. Nothing will happen if we just sit on our bums and wait.'

Sid spoke about motivation. Money was a good motivator, but so too, was the desire to do an excellent job.

'Motivation is a fire from within. If someone tries to light that fire under you, chances are that it will burn very briefly. Every job is a self-portrait of the person who does it. You should aim to autograph your work with excellence. You can always do better than you think you can.'

'Sometimes success can be a matter of luck,' Tim commented, 'happening to be in the right place at the right time.'

'Luck's a matter of preparation meeting opportunity,' Sid replied. 'I'm a great believer in luck myself. The harder I work the more I have of it.'

Sid was the patriarch, passing on his wisdom to the 'young blokes'.

At the end of the day, Sid and Rob invited everyone to stay back for drinks. The beer was kept in an old fridge, a hand-down from one of the families, in the small kitchen. The spirits were kept in one of the cupboards. The drinks, supposed to be for the entertainment of clients, were very much a staff amenity and the alcoholic vapours that seeped from their systems bonded one with the other.

'It's good to linger over a beer. It's a chance to unwind and to catch up with what was happening,' was Sid's justification.

The rest of the week was devoted to Rob as he went through the theory underlying the temperament scale. He had a class of four. Aaron and Felix were the new chums, but Owen and Tim were included because they had never undergone a formal training programme. They had learned on the job in a haphazard, informal fashion, snatching moments here and there, and often over an after-hours beer. This was an opportunity to consolidate their learning. Felix could see why Sid and Rob were so keen for him not to delay his starting date. The first week of January was a golden opportunity to conduct formal intensive training before the clients returned to work from their holidays. As it turned out, Sid departed to Queensland to undertake training with one of his clients. His client, too, had organised staff training in a quieter period.

'Sid's often away on training assignments,' explained Rob. 'He likes to get away to a mining site in some remote locality. He spends the day training, but he's in his element in the evening in a bar where they are all hard drinkers, and he entertains them with his many stories. When he's in Melbourne, he spent most of his time calling on clients. I'm happy to stay inside and run the show. We complement one another.'

Their week together was a fun time to get to know each other. Each one told their story. Tim, an engaging character, was recruited from South Australia. Coming from a well-known pastoral family, part of the establishment, his uncle was a member of the South Australian Legislative Council. He grew up on the family's property and was expected to join his father, but he was an excellent student at his Adelaide boarding school and decided to study psychology at university. Felix admired his natural easy self-assurance that enabled him to mix at all levels and to get on well, a positive person who everyone liked. Felix admired his intellect and his ability to grasp the core of an issue. Not possessing the same confidence, he was envious of his talents. Tim demanded respect if not outright admiration. Small in stature, he did not fit the image of a burley farmer, used to tossing sheep and bales of hay around, so it was not surprising that he left the farm behind, at least for the time being.

Owen joined a large international manufacturing company as an executive cadet after leaving university and was employed in the Personnel Department. At first, he had ambitions of transferring to the parent company in the US but felt stifled by the systems of a large organisation. He met Sid on one of his marketing calls. When he mentioned his dissatisfaction, Sid invited him to meet Rob. Nothing happened for a few months and Owen thought they had forgotten him, but one day he received a phone call. He was tall and skinny, quieter than Tim, but he had a nice quirky sense of humour, which made one smile rather than guffaw.

The Falklands War, Britain under Margaret Thatcher and two winters in the clammy English climate were more than enough for Aaron but long enough to have picked up traces of the 'toffy' English accent. In London, he worked for one of the large banks, and Aaron's colleagues, he said, spoke with public school accents and a little of their mannerisms, he claimed, rubbed off on him. That made him appear entitled. That was not his intention, for underneath he was a dinkum Aussie. He was big and strong. At school and university, he was a footballer in winter and a surfer in summer. He missed both his Australian rules and his beaches and was pleased to escape the cold and return to the warm Australian climate. What kept him sane was his music. He played a guitar and followed closely the British rock scene.

The four of them were the 'young blokes,' to use Sid's term, the hope for the company's future. They enjoyed each other's company and over the week's training, developed a camaraderie that Felix never experienced in the public service. It was as if they were a small army unit where, if they were to survive, they would need to rely on and trust each other. At the end of the week, Rob invited the four of them to dinner, along with wives and girlfriends. They went to a classy restaurant in the city, expensive but Rob saw it as a sound investment. Not only did he want the consultants on board, but their families as well.

*   *   *

So began the pattern of his early time with The Champions. They were heady, euphoric, intoxicating days. The public service was never more than a job. He never got to work before nine, left right on five and Pascaline was used to seeing him home shortly after, even though he often had to write up his reports at home. Pascaline did not mind. His presence kept her happy. The Champions was another life. He looked forward to work each morning and stayed late, finishing the day with a few drinks. Pascaline was not keen on his new vision.

'The company is competing for your love,' she said one evening in bed. 'At least, it's not another woman that I must worry about.'

'There is no other woman, Pascaline. But I'm gaining great satisfaction from mastering the job, learning something new every day.' He thought she was joking, yet he detected a distraction in their lovemaking, as if some thought was troubling her.

'*Qu'est ce qui ne va pas?*' (What's wrong?) he asked.

'*Rien!*' (Nothing!)

His main work was drafting reports based on test results. Mastering the interpretation of the temperament scale was the main challenge, and gradually he appreciated more of its subtleties. The next challenge was writing the interpretation as succinctly as possible in a way that clients could understand. As he became more confident, he gave a verbal report over the phone if the client was anxious to get the results or visited the client's premises to deliver and explain the report. The marketing objective was to develop client loyalty and repeat the business.

One afternoon while they were having drinks, Aaron mentioned that the British rock group Queen had released a song entitled *We Are the Champions*. He brought out his guitar. The tune was catchy, and in no time, they were singing together.

The song became the company's unofficial theme song. Whenever a successful sale was made, someone would burst into song, like a victory anthem after a long, hard struggle against the odds.

At that time, Sid was away every other week on training assignments. Often, he paired with an independent consultant. Charlie lived in Sydney. Together they would travel together and deliver the programme.

'Charlie has skills relevant to the mining industry,' Sid explained. 'Although he's independent, I regard him as part of the company.'

A request came from Mt Hedley Mines in Far North Queensland. Sid had visited the company in its remote outback location many times.

'It's time I introduced you young blokes to training in the mines,' he announced one afternoon over their beers. 'I'm feeling tired and need a break. This will be a valuable opportunity for one of you to gain the experience.'

'I would love to go.' Felix spoke out. Visiting a mining company in North Queensland sounded exotic.

'No. You don't have enough experience, Felix. I'll get Tim to take my place. I reckon he's about ready. He'll have Charlie to hold his hand if he's in trouble.'

Tim was delighted. Felix was envious, but he knew he wasn't ready. He mentioned the trip to Pascaline.

'Tim's got more experience than me. I'd love to go.'

Je suis content que tu n'y allies pas, (I'm pleased you're not going),' she replied with emotion. 'How long would you be away?'

'About ten days!'

'Diable! Tu passes assez de temps avec l'entreprise telle qu'elle est.' (You spend enough time with the company as it is.)

Tim spent time closeted with Sid who took him through the paces and sent him home with training manuals for further study. The night before he departed, they farewelled him with a rendition of *We Are the Champions* over their drinks.

'Tim will fly to Sydney, pick up Charlie, they'll fly together to Townsville, and from there, in a small plane to Mt Hedley.'

Like an umbrella parent, Sid was on the phone every day, either to Charlie or to the Personnel Manager Mount Hedley Mines. The reports from both indicated that Tim had been readily accepted. He fitted in well and was doing an excellent job.

'Not as good as me, of course,' Sid told them. They could see from his smile that he was pleased that his protégé was doing so well. He was no different from a father, proud of his son's success. Charlie and Tim were due to finish on the Wednesday, fly early Thursday morning to Townsville and back to Melbourne via Sydney. Sid told Tim to take Friday off to spend a long weekend with his wife, Amily. They were looking forward to a report on his adventures on Monday morning.

Thursday was Melbourne Show Day, a public holiday. Instead of visiting the Melbourne Show Grounds, his day off was spent with Pascaline driving into the countryside. The weather was fine for escaping the confines of the city and breathing in fresh air. They drove into the Dandenong Ranges, stopped at a picnic ground by a lake and took a ride on a mini steam train along twists and curves through green hills and valleys. They found a small café and had lunch on a terrace overlooking the water. Family parties were out, too, taking advantage of the spring sunshine. The sun was warm but not hot, a gentle breeze fanned their faces and he had Pascaline beside him. Children were in small canoes, paddling furiously and getting nowhere with shouts and laughter. He enjoyed the sense of freedom, a brief respite from The Champions. It seemed a world away, yet he was looking forward to getting to work and to hear how Tim had fared.

'We should do this more often and get you away from the company,' was Pascaline's comment on the way back into the city late afternoon. Back home, he turned on the television and shared a drink with Pascaline while they watched the evening news. A small plane had crashed in North Queensland on the way to Townsville from a mining town. No survivors. He froze. Pascaline dropped her glass. This could not be the plane that Tim was on. He muttered, 'Please God! No!'

He raced to the phone and rang Rob in case he didn't know. Rob's wife, Margot answered. She was crying.

'This is terrible,' she said. In between sobs, she said they heard early afternoon, and both Rob and Sid had gone to Tim's place to be with Amily. 'That's where they are now.' She hadn't heard any more, and she thought Felix's call might have been Rob's. He got off the phone and back to Pascaline. She was crying.

'Horrible! Horrible! Horrible! Poor Tim! He was such a lovely man. And you wanted to take his place. You could have been on that plane. I feel sick.'

Felix felt foolish and ashamed. Pascaline did not want any dinner and retired early, and he muddled through a simple meal, somehow thinking that the best way to cope was to stick to a routine. He watched the late news and, although the item was repeated, there was no more detail.

With a heavy heart he drove to work on Friday morning, trying to convince himself that the day would be normal and that they would see Tim on Monday. In a state of delusional hope, he imagined Tim dropping in for drinks after work, eager to tell his story and everyone keen to listen. He stopped for red lights and on the footpath outside a newsagent was a poster for *The Age* newspaper with a full-size photo of Tim. No mistaking the smile and the curly black hair. It could have been his graduation photo. Underneath was the caption, *Melbourne Man Dies in Plane Crash*, which sent Felix lurching into a kind of numb fatalism. It was a stark reminder that Tim was no longer with them. Friday was the longest day. The gloom was heavy. The girls were crying. Tim was their favourite – a darling they were calling him. Aaron had only heard when he came to work. He was stunned. The rest already knew and had time to process the news. Felix tried to imagine Tim in his last moments. Did he realise he was about to die? His thoughts drifted to how he would have reacted if he had been on that plane. Too confronting to hold for long!

Sid had more news. Amily had handled the news reasonably well. Both families would be coming across from South Australia. Nine people were on board the fatal plane. Apart from Charlie and Tim, the wife of the chairman of Mt Hedley Mines was taking their two grandchildren back to their parents in Brisbane. The others were Mt Hedley Mines employees and the crew. Tragedy had reached out her cruel hand to many families. The airline had salvaged Tim's luggage, which was returned to the office. Sid showed them the case and the training manuals. The case had split open, and the thick folders of the manuals were buckled, silent testimony to the force of the impact.

Everyone was subdued, conversation no more than necessary and there was none of the usual chatter or banter. It was a relief to finish the day with customary drinks in the kitchen. Felix was sure this would be a sober affair and would not last long. Everyone would be pleased to get away for the weekend. The emotion that had been held back during the long day was released with the first sip of alcohol. They were shouting and laughing at the slightest suggestion of humour. Nothing joyous about the laughter; it was forced, intense, cathartic, a full throttle purging of the emotions such as they had never experienced before or after. An outsider would have been shocked, even sickened, at their mad, crazy reaction to losing not one but two of their colleagues. Then, as they washed and put the glasses away, the gloom returned and with heavy sighs they left in silence. But for the valiant efforts of a near exhausted streetlight strangled by the tree branches, they would have struggled in the dark to their cars.

Tim's father joined them for drinks one afternoon at Sid's invitation. He was an older version of Tim, small and compact in stature, wiry from a life of farming. He showed them a photo of himself, as a young man, holding a baby boy who looked likely to grow into the man holding him. The meeting was awkward, but they made him welcome.

'My heart bleeds for this man. I can think of nothing worse than losing your own child,' he said to Pascaline that evening. She was grieving, too, for despite the company's claiming too much of his time, she felt close to his work colleagues, especially Tim.

Life moved on. The office returned to its routine and the company continued to prosper. Felix felt himself being sucked into The Champions as he grew in experience and confidence. It became his major focus, his source of identification. Other consultants were recruited, and he became a senior, involved in their induction and continuing supervision. He had begun the halting crawl towards the mirage of success, which veterans of the corporate life knew would always be just out of reach.

He had begun to climb the ladder.

PART TWO

DAYS OF DISILLUSION

Chapter 6

Felix knew he should speak to his silent neighbour. He was on Ansett flight 7.30 am Sydney to Melbourne, presented with an opportunity his fellow managers would die for. Next to him in the window seat was Sir Ian Turner whose face he recognised from its regular appearance in the financial pages. In the flesh he had a definite presence, Sir Ian was two metres tall and had an air of confidence as if used to moving in high circles, yielding great power, intimidating others, making big decisions. He was not a knight of the realm for nothing.

Rob travelled first class because he loved its roomy comfort and the extra attention from the hosties made him feel like a top business executive, but in a memo to his managers he suggested they, too, should travel first class for *the informal opportunity presented to meet captains of industry and commerce and promote to them the company's services.* Felix, too, enjoyed first class and glowed in the extra attention the hosties gave him. But sitting next to such a heavy this morning gave him a touch of the guilts ... a partner in a stockbroking firm and chairman and member of several boards. If ever a person was influential in company decisions and needed to be introduced to the business, this was the man. He should have penetrated the barriers and been at his sociable best, but an invisible hand restrained him and prevented him from turning to Sir Ian. He was absorbed in his documents, marking the occasional item in the margin and giving no hint at all that he was interested in small talk or even aware of his fellow passenger.

Felix had no problem in charming targets and seizing the occasion to market the company but this morning, while the captain piloted his way through the dreary July weather, he continued his journey in solitude through *The Sydney Morning Herald*. He read an item from the finance news about his mute neighbour, which included his photograph, younger looking than the man next to him but handsome and distinguished. In his role as chairman of Consolidated Holdings, Sir Ian was forecasting a twenty per cent increase in profits. The article would have presented an ideal opportunity for comment. He could have congratulated Sir Ian on the splendid way the board had managed the company and advised him how The Champions could help with any expansion. He would have accepted the compliment and replied that staff recruitment was the job of the human resource manager, leaving Felix with a wonderful opportunity to ring the incumbent with a message that his chairman Sir Ian told him to talk to him (or her).

Instead, they continued the early morning flight as strangers, ships remote from each other on a high sea. He didn't even take advantage of the captain's announcement that the plane would be late in landing because early fog had disrupted traffic.

Moody anticipation of the day ahead kept him silent. He wasn't looking forward to the meeting. One half of his mind concentrated on *The Sydney Morning Herald*, the other was on the agenda and a foreboding he would come under the screw. State managers were responsible for achieving income objectives and making a profit and travelled to Melbourne monthly to review operations for the preceding month and to give an account of themselves. At most meetings he got off scot-free because his state, New South Wales, had met or exceeded its budget. He was able to sit back and listen to the criticisms directed at the managers whose states had failed to reach budget. The latest month had been difficult as one of the major clients was in serious financial difficulties. Felix guessed they had expanded too rapidly, borrowed short term for long-term investment, a popular mistake in a corporate world bent on measuring success by growth. The last thing they needed at this time was a management consultant firm offering recruitment services.

He tried to read an article related to the previous year's High Court Mabo decision, which recognised native title and put an end to the doctrine of terra nullius – the legal pretence that Australia belonged to nobody before white settlement. The ruling had raised the ire of the mining industry, which set itself up as the gallant defender of business and everybody's backyard. Felix was aware the topic was important to The Champions as the mining industry constituted a substantial slice of their client base. He'd read the same paragraph three times about certain politicians receiving a heaven-sent opportunity for a fear-and-loathing campaign, so he gave up, folded the *Herald* and pushed it into the seat pocket, to be retained, read and digested when his concentration had improved. Alongside, Sir Ian was immersed in his documents. They could have been thousands of miles apart, instead of just a few inches. As the plane began its descent to Tullamarine, Felix closed his eyes. He was tired and had risen early to catch this plane. The budgets Peter set for Victoria and New South Wales were enormous. He must have spoken aloud for he detected movement on the left. He opened his eyes. Sir Ian's eyes flickered and threw a quick glance in his direction, the first time he had acknowledged Felix's existence.

'It's a nightmare!' he found himself muttering. Sir Ian stirred again and lifted his eyes to stare out the window. Next to him was a nut whom he didn't need to know.

Up to Peter's appointment, management controls had been a homespun affair with Sid and Rob grateful for whatever contribution each of the states made. But the company had grown from its humble beginnings in St Kilda Road and the founders realised that financial management should extend beyond the activities of an accounts girl, Julie, who operated under the guidance of an outside accountant. Felix had to admit Peter arrived in the nick of time for the company's good. The job had outgrown Julie and the company had outgrown its founders. Management accounting practices, such as budgeting, made Rob and Sid aware they could make more money than they ever dreamed possible.

'Sorry for the delay, ladies and gentlemen,' came the captain's voice. 'We'll continue to circle until air traffic control calls us.'

Sir Ian stirred as if frustrated, impatient to get to his meeting. Another opportunity missed. Sir Ian ploughed on undeterred through his papers while Felix continued to brood, fixed stare boring into the back of the bald head in front.

'The company's no more than an accounting exercise,' he had complained to Ron Bell over their airport drinks in Melbourne. 'This process is supposed to make us managers feel we own our own budgets, that we're responsible for their achievement, and we'd work harder and put more pressure on our staff. I always feel my budget's been dumped on me and that the consultation process has been pointless.'

'No surprise Sid and Rob always agree with Peter's calculations,' Ron had added as he finished his drink to catch his plane.

'We have the okay to land. We'll hit the tarmac – land I mean – in approximately ten minutes.' The captain laughed at his own joke.

Sir Ian stirred again, as if the notion of hitting the tarmac raised some anxieties. An opportunity to reassure him with small talk, to reassure him that, even though he was chancing it with Ansett, this flight was not a white knuckles job. As a distraction, he could even have sought Sir Ian's view on Mabo; Consolidated Industries held substantial mining interests. Instead, he pondered over the likely outcome of the day. At previous meetings he felt sorry for his fellow state managers who had been placed naked on the rack. He wondered, too, if he would be stripped. Would they experience the same feelings for him as he faced Peter's inquisition? Peter would use terms such as 'you promised' as if he had given a personal guarantee of achievement when he reluctantly accepted Peter's estimate, as if he had control over every factor that was likely to influence the state's income. Peter would trot out his statistics, his running monthly averages and other devices from his bag of accountant tricks and demonstrate that New South Wales was on a downward slide.

A stream of business suits left the aircraft. Some paused to thank the smiling hosties waiting at the door and smiled in return. Others, including Sir Ian, brushed past them and hurried up the walkway bridge. Felix followed him into the arrival lounge. Taller than everyone else, his presence dominated the room. Outside in the chilly Melbourne morning, Felix watched Sir Ian's expensively clad back disappear into a chauffeur-driven limousine. He regretted the wasted opportunity. Peter would ask what steps he had taken to rectify the budget downfall. Having run out of plausible cover he could have invoked Sir Ian as his fig leaf. He could have told the meeting he'd met Sir Ian, described his presence as charismatic, reported his strong interest in the company's services and with a little harmless exaggeration elaborated on his many questions.

Whether or not Sir Ian would put business his way was beside the point. He had an answer for Peter.

Chapter 7

Felix collected his bag, walked out of the air-conditioned warmth of the airport into a blast that came straight from the Antarctic. His light suit was fine for Sydney's benign climate, but he shivered his way to a bleak Melbourne taxi queue. No chauffeur-driven limousine for him. The wait seemed endless as the queue disappeared into the line of cabs edging forward. The wind chilled his bones. A frozen Felix might have to be carried off stiff before it was his turn. He wished for an overcoat. He didn't even own one. He promised himself before the next visit south he would buy himself an overcoat and thermals as well.

'Bloody cold here, mate,' he said to the driver.

The driver grunted. He was cold and tired, having worked from the early hours, busting to get home to his warm house.

'That wind reminds me of when I lived in Melbourne. I used to turn on the heater in May and off in September.'

Another grunt. He was weary of every interstate visitor talking about the weather. He drove in silence along the Tullamarine Freeway and across the city to suburban Hawthorn.

Despite the freezing wind Felix paused to gaze at the office building, a modern two-storey premises with windows evenly spaced at the front and sides, a far cry from the dowdy affair in St Kilda Road that Felix first knew as The Champions. He allowed a young woman in a scarf and heavy coat and with a pram and crying baby push past him. Perhaps the infant felt the cold, too.

Inside in the warm foyer, Cressida was waiting. Cressida had many roles. She was secretary to Syd, Rob, and Andrew. She managed to fit in secretary to Kelvin Brophy, the Victorian manager, as well. She was a woman of influence with her finger on the pulse. Company gossip, which travelled faster than formal news, had linked her romantically to Kelvin. Felix could see nothing exciting in Cressida although he had heard from malicious sources she was a different person after a few drinks.

'Everyone's here,' she said.

Felix bound up the stairs to the boardroom where the management team was already assembled, Cressida in the rear. The smell of stale cigarette smoke drifted into the passage, and entering the room was like walking into a fog. Every face turned towards him in the heavy air.

'Sorry, my plane was late.'

He sprang to defensive mode because he had expected Peter to pounce and imagined the conversation:

'You're late, Felix.'

He would respond with guns blazing:

'I have absolutely no control over what the airways do with their planes, Peter. If they want to circle about the airport, I can't stop them. I can't clear the fog.'

'You could have taken an earlier plane or came down last night to make sure you arrived on time.'

Instead, Peter ignored him as he peered over his half-rim glasses at the people seated around the table. Felix took a moment to acknowledge the management team of The Champions. Sid, his brother Rob, then Sid's son Andrew, and Peter. They were head office, in the roles of chairman, managing director, general manager and accountant. Kelvin Brophy was the Victorian manager, Nigel Mernagh from South Australia, Sam Rayment from Queensland and Ron Bell from Western Australia. Felix Schmidt joined them as manager New South Wales. Ron invited Felix to take the seat next to him. The others acknowledged him with a nod. From the stack of files he had placed before him on the boardroom table, Peter was well prepared. In her role as confidential secretary, Cressida joined the meeting to take the minutes.

The room itself was impressive. The table was a large affair of polished oak, fit for the boardroom of the largest corporation, a sign to the world that the company had arrived. Rob justified its purchase with the comment that clients would be impressed and realise they weren't dealing with a tin-pot outfit. Two prints decorated the wall; one was of William Dobell's *Dame Mary Gilmore* at her scrawniest, the other, Rembrandt's *Portrait of an Old Man* with lace collar and white droopy moustache. It was a puzzle who they were supposed to impress. Companies often have portraits of their founder/s in their boardroom. Cressida had the job of choosing the decoration. She may have seen them as Sid and Rob. The other touch was framed motivational one-liners, such as: *Good is not enough if you can do better*; *Nothing works unless you do*; and *You can always do more than you think you can*. Andrew added them when he became general manager. His aim was to motivate the consultants and, no doubt, impress the clients that they were dealing with a mob who were enjoying the trappings of success but ready to work their butts off on their behalf.

In his role of company chairman, Sid opened the meeting, 'Welcomed to our interstate travellers,' he began. 'Today and the weekend will be significant, for it's the first time we'll be bringing the whole company together. As you know, the rest of the staff will be coming from interstate later today for a national conference up at Eildon.'

Felix was very aware of the conference for the logistics of bringing his consultants to Melbourne whilst adhering to the company policy of no more than one consultant per plane (an outcome of the plane crash in the early days) had verged on the nightmarish. His secretary, Janice, had managed to book flights throughout the afternoon and their return flights on Sunday evening. There were thirty from Melbourne and thirty-three from interstate and all would be converging on this lake-side resort to the north of Melbourne.

'Out of dissatisfaction with our employer, one of the leading management consultant firms at the time, Rob and I established the business in a small office on St Kilda Road with barely any finance. It was touch and go for a year or so, but we persevered. And steadily we continue to grow.'

Felix, having heard this story many times, found his attention wandering and studied the portraits on the wall to see if he could detect any resemblance to the founders.

'We moved because we outgrew the office. We decided we should have our own building. Nothing like bricks and mortar for security. I used to say to Rob, if the business goes down the tube, we've still got the building. We purchased this suburban block, just rezoned for commercial purposes, demolished the old Victorian house, and erected this two-story office building.'

The management team listened patiently to the preamble, waiting for the real meeting to start.

'At first Sid and I thought that owning our building was part of our judicious planning for our families' security,' Rob interrupted, 'but when Peter arrived, his comment was that so much capital was tied up in the building that could be directed towards further financing the business.'

'I had a lot of misgivings,' Sid continued, 'about giving up our security, but we listened to Peter and agreed to sell the building to an insurance company on a lease-back arrangement.'

Peter shuffled his papers and smiled, bathing in Sid's praise for his good advice. Felix detected a smirk.

'You'd have to agree with me that our families had been waiting patiently for years to see benefits from the business into which their respective dads had put so much time, effort, and money. They knew that they were wealthy enough on paper, but they never saw any cash as it was all tied up in the business. Now each of the kids has received a share of the building's sale. We made sure sufficient funds were held back to finance company expansion.'

Sid and Rob each had three children. That cash distribution was their first real taste of wealth. It wasn't hard for Felix and the others to believe they looked forward to receiving more. The first seeds had been sown.

'At the moment, the company has a staff of over one hundred in five states. It's fitting that the consultants come together, to meet each other and to celebrate this stage in our journey. It's a costly exercise but Rob and I believe it's worth it.'

Sid leaned back and lit a cigarette. He took a drag, his cheeks hollowed and pulsed out three, four smoke rings, perfect circles rolling in the dead air.

'And we're going to get bigger,' said Andrew, still in his twenties, with an emphasis that suggested he should be the one to lead the company into El Dorado and that, although they had done a great job in bringing the company up to this point, it would soon be time for his father and uncle Rob to either die or step aside.

Sid had already retired from full-time work. He moved to the north coast of New South Wales and was not involved in the day-to-day operations, but he chaired the monthly meetings and, from time to time, an old client enticed him out of his hobby farm to run a training programme. Sid saw himself as a mentor for the 'young blokes'. He was full of wisdom and ideas. He had a good intellect and Felix enjoyed their discussions. Sid liked to challenge his antagonists' thinking to ensure they were arguing from a sound basis. On the surface, he accepted the changes that business growth and the arrival of Peter had brought, but his reminisces suggested that he hankered for the old days.

By contrast, Rob remained involved and immersed and endeavoured, as he put it, to 'keep up with the times'. Keeping up with the times meant accepting Peter's methods. Peter believed that the way to motivate people was to set up competition. The earlier practice was group bonuses in good times. Peter reckoned consultants should be given individual income targets and be rewarded as individuals rather than as a team. That's what happened.

Andrew was still at school when Felix joined the company. Andrew arrived straight from university. No carefree backpacking days for him. Sid insisted that Andrew start at the bottom, as it were, and that he should serve an 'apprenticeship' in all facets of the business before being allowed into management. He carried the title of general manager. He was keen, busting to do well but, unlike his father, he was practical rather than visionary. Sid had his eye on tomorrow. Andrew thought about today.

'Okay,' said Sid. Rob, too, lit another cigarette and the air was thick. 'Let's get on with business. Over to you, Peter.'

Everyone stirred in their seats. Peter opened his folders, produced a pad of photocopied papers, and passed them around – last month's results. If he were a more extroverted character, he would have done so with a flourish. Like a ham actor playing Shakespeare he would have flung his cloak over his shoulder before distributing his booty. But he was Peter, a bean counter, plain matter-of-fact, the-facts-are-the-thing-that-matter Peter.

'June's results complete the financial year, gentlemen,' Peter began, 'and you can see the results overall have been good and, in fact, have exceeded budget.'

Everyone scanned the page of figures. The results were exceptionally good, indeed, and reflected the sturdy growth the company had made during the financial year. No one got up to dance on the board table. No one sang *We Are the Champions*. No one congratulated or pat anyone else on the back. Each studied the figures with restraint without a trace of jubilation.

That was the good news. Felix was waiting for the bad. He didn't have long to wait.

'There has been a dip in New South Wales figures, you will notice, although overall, the state has exceeded its budget. I trust that is not the beginning of a trend, Felix.'

The anticipated grilling was about to commence. He felt vulnerable, standing naked before his colleagues.

'Of course not.' He rose to the defence of his state. 'That was because of the departure of one major client.'

'What have you done to replace them?'

He wished he had spoken to Sir Ian. What a story he could have told them.

'We'll have a meeting of all Sydney consultants next week to discuss our marketing strategy for the coming financial year.' His defence was tame, he had to admit.

He reflected on their company accountant. Peter had far too much power for a bean counter because he had the ears of Sid and Rob, who regarded him with awe for his stream of financial wisdom, scattered like breadcrumbs to sparrows in a public park. Peter was a strident critic; his mission was saving the company from impending ruin by whipping indolent state managers with tongue and figures. Western Australia was regularly hit the hardest because it was a new branch struggling to break even in a resistant market and income rarely covered staff costs let alone reached budget. Its manager, Ron Bell was always in trouble. Queensland was in trouble, it seemed, on alternative months and the market in that state seemed as volatile as its manager, Sam Rayment. Not much was expected of Nigel Mernagh of South Australia as the market was small and had stiff competition in a former employee who deserted the company, set up his own show and pinched the clients.

Peter made no comment. Last year's results were already history. Time to turn to another set of papers.

'Gentlemen, I want to present to you the budget figures for the coming year.'

The mood around the table changed. People stirred in their chairs. Budgets raised temperatures and launched impassioned discussion.

'I have taken the estimates you presented during the month and have worked on them after I discussed them with Sid and Rob. We all reckoned that you had been too conservative, and I have adjusted them accordingly.'

The room was silent as state managers absorbed the information and compared their estimates with Peter's adjustments. It would be fair to say the earlier restraint turned to a silent astonishment as if everyone was too amazed to speak. Sam who had the shortest fuse was the first to explode.

'What!' screamed a strident voice inside the hollow of his mind. In no time, he found the moral outrage button. 'This is ridiculous! Peter, you've increased my estimates by twenty per cent.' The frown marks above Sam's eyes drew attention to his clear, intense pupils. He was fierce, indeed, projecting an image of his weekend role as a lay preacher, striking the fear of the Lord into straying members of his flock.

'You'll notice, Sam,' said Peter calmly, refusing to be intimidated, 'that Queensland exceeded budget by fifteen per cent last financial, so last year's budget figures were an underestimate of the state's potential. Based on last year's results, you should reach budget with just a little stretching. You have to set a budget, you know, that's hard to achieve to stretch you and keep you on your toes.'

'No need to patronise me, Peter.' Sam snapped. 'I know what hard work means.'

'Okay, okay,' intervened Sid. 'Let's just discuss things calmly.'

Sam was silenced and, over an intense frown, returned to studying his state's figures.

'Do you mean to say that every time we achieve budget, you're going to lift it? That's a real laugh.' Felix expressed concern with a humourless grunt; the estimate that he had presented to Peter had also been increased by twenty per cent. His sarcasm failed to make any impact.

'I reckon the targets you set for yourselves last year were too easy,' continued Peter.

'These figures are flying in the face of reality. You don't appreciate just how tough the Sydney market is.' Felix's acrimony left Peter unmoved.

'New South Wales represents forty per cent of the Australian market,' Peter contended. 'So, the state should contribute a similar proportion of the company income.'

'The Sydney market's far more competitive, more fickle, far less loyal, than Melbourne's,' Felix argued. 'Melbourne's the home market. Sid and Rob started the business there. You've been trading longer.'

'You've got to think positive, Felix,' was Andrew's contribution.

'Well, if we all pull our fingers out, we should be able to reach them,' said Kelvin Brophy who had the biggest budget – brown nosing as usual. Felix was tempted to comment. At the same time, he did not envy Kelvin having to share the same building with head office breathing down his neck. While Kelvin lived under the shadow, other state managers had the autonomy of long distance.

'All very well for you, Kelvin,' said Sam, 'you have the distinct advantage of having Sid, Rob, and Andrew all active in your state. We have the problem in Queensland of constantly having work poached by other states.'

'What do you mean by that, Sam?' Felix was back on the defence. His mouth was dry but under his neat white shirt the perspiration, like his anger, was building up on the ridges of his spine.

'You know what I mean, Felix. I can mention occasions when I've found your consultants working in my state. You know what the company policy is.'

'Sam, I know exactly what the company policy is.'

'Okay, okay, just calm down, you hotheads. Let me restate company policy,' Sid intervened. 'So there's no confusion. The policy is that any work generated within a state should be conducted by the office in that state. That helps the smaller states establish their market.'

'The problem is that negotiations are frequently conducted at head office level in either Melbourne or Sydney.' Felix had calmed down enough to be articulate. 'For example, last month, one of the Sydney consultants, Viviana, won a big expansion job involving several positions in Queensland. The client wanted her to handle the work. Why? Because he knew her. She had gained his trust. So, who do we please, the client or Sam? Can we blame Viviana for being upset? Like every consultant, she bears her own income budget. She worked hard to get the business. She's reluctant to give up work she's won by her hard marketing and enthusiasm, and have the income credited to another state, just to please you, Sam.'

'Sydney consultants are always sniffing around Queensland clients.'

'That's because my consultants are hungry. Sydney used

to handle the Queensland market before the Brisbane office was established. Sydney consultants were dismayed to see the fruits of their arduous marketing efforts passed over. Their old clients still contact them.'

Sam's face reddened but Sid intervened before he could explode.

'We have to thank our Sydney colleagues for laying the foundations, Sam. There's no need to wage war across the Tweed River. Rob and I saw it a good move when you approached us about taking over your business and bringing an established clientele into the fold.'

'That's not how the Sydney consultants saw it.' Felix knew he should shut up, but he had problems with Sam who brought out the worst in him. 'Sam's share of the market was pretty small.'

'It suited our plans to open a Brisbane office, Felix.' This time Rob intervened.

'What gives me the shits whenever Sam thinks someone from Sydney has trespassed on his patch, is that he's on the phone to Andrew. It'd be nice if he spoke to me first so we could sort it out between us.'

'Brisbane was a good move for the company. You Sydney consultants should think company wide.'

'Thanks a lot. It's not easy to think globally when you have individual income budgets to achieve.'

'That's enough, gentlemen,' intervened chairman Sid. 'This is no better than dealing with unruly schoolboys. Let's not fight each other. We should be out there fighting the market. Give Peter a go and let him get on with it.'

Tempers cooled and Peter continued with his presentation.

Each state's revived budget was discussed in turn and comparison was made with last year's results. Because last year's achievement was ten per cent over budget, Peter argued that this year should reflect twenty per cent increase over the previous year's results.

'Admittedly, we've had a pretty good year. Times are buoyant, but can they stay that way?' Kelvin asked, an unusually challenging question for Kelvin who always seem to agree with the powers.

'You've got to go forward. You've got to think positive,' was Andrew's contribution.

The smaller states also saw increases. More was expected of Western Australia, but South Australia got off lightly. Sid and Rob made no further comment, allowing Peter and Andrew to make their mark. If Felix were asked why they were silent, he would have said they were listening to the ring of cash registers.

'Okay,' said Sid by way of winding up the meeting. 'What you must do now is go back to your staff, work out each consultant's individual target and how they're going to achieve it. Hit the ground running!'

The meeting wasn't exactly boring, but Felix was happy to see it end, relieved to retreat from the stench of tobacco smoke. After Rob's and Sid's third cigarette, he lost count.

'You've got to go forward. You've got to be positive,' was Andrew's final comment.

Chapter 8

'Good to see you, Felix.' Ron Bell turned to Felix as soon as the meeting was over. 'How have you been?'

'Good, Ron.'

'You and Sam were having quite a barney.'

'Sam's a puzzle. He's fiercely protective of his patch. I hear he's a religious man, a zealot. He seems to regard Sydney as the kingdom of the devil. No matter what initiative the Sydney office takes, Sam seems to regard it as evil.'

Ron laughed, looking in Peter's direction, who was gathering his stack of papers. 'At least, we didn't have to put up with Peter patronising.'

*　　*　　*

Sid and Rob hoped for much from Western Australia but results never met Peter's expectations. Based on his own involvement, Felix's assessment was that the west lacked the market size and depth.

In the early days, Sid was a regular visitor to the west because of his connections with the mining industry.

'As part of our national expansion we should have a Perth office,' Sid commented at one of the family meetings. 'I know the west. The Perth market's parochial and doesn't respond to 'wise men from the East' coming across to tell them how to live. Rather than send one of our eastern states consultants to manage the office, we should find a local man for the job.' Rob and Andrew nodded their heads in agreement and expectation. Rob grabbed another cigarette. Andrew just looked at his father. He had never taken up the habit.

'I've asked around and found Ron Bell,' Sid continued. 'He's got a background in consulting and in running other businesses. On the other hand, we don't want a repeat of the Adelaide debacle on our hands. We made the mistake of giving Claremont too much freedom from the start.'

'We could send one of the company's experienced consultants across to sit with Ron for six months and teach him the ways of The Champions,' Andrew suggested. 'In that way we might engender a company loyalty in Ron which we were never able to accomplish with Claremont.'

'Who do you have in mind?'

'What about Felix? He's an old lag.'

'Consultants have come and gone, but Felix's been with the company going on ten years. He's the longest serving consultant. He's seen the company grow around him,' Rob added. 'He needs a new challenge. He's a worry. He's been disengaged and languishing since Pascaline left him.'

Good old loyal Felix was happy to accept the inconvenience and the challenge. Instead of taking the plane which would have delivered him to the west in four hours, he took the train. Over three days, he enjoyed time out in a piece of Australia he had never seen before. The Nullarbor Plain was a vast, treeless stretch of semi-arid land, which contained the world's largest exposure of limestone, he read in the brochure. The train stopped at sidings named after early Australian prime ministers where small towns struggled to survive in not the most welcoming or habitable country. The journey itself was an odyssey of self-discovery and Felix admired the residents' courage and endurance against the loneliness and extreme summer temperatures. At one of these sidings, named Cook, he had enough time for a brief stretch of the legs and to appreciate outback humour in the crude sign outside the local health centre: *'When you're crook, come to Cook. Support our local hospital.'*

Ron found space in one of Perth's massive office towers and the Perth branch of The Champions was on the way. Ron found Felix capable and intelligent. He was literate, wrote persuasively and could pen an excellent report. A good person to have on side, his manner was usually quiet and conservative although he could burst forth after a drink or two. Rob told him Felix was not a good salesman because he lacked the outer exuberance of the stereotype, but Ron found he did not fit the typecast. More than once, he went out into the wilderness, the wild west as it were, like a stone-age hunter, and brought back the trophies. In turn, Felix found Ron an impressive colleague, ready to celebrate the occasion. He had an infectious enthusiasm and, with his contacts, knew the Perth market. Together, they began to build the business.

Apart from the mining industry, Perth was a branch town and Felix could understand how many of the head offices in the east found their Perth operations ungovernable. He'd heard the same story from other branch managers. For most of the year, they did their own thing and, as long as they made a reasonable fist of things or concocted plausible explanations when they did not, they were left alone. Perth was a long way, and travelling to the west was a significant expense, but every so often, probably once a year, head office made a visit. Head office brought a wife or girlfriend with them and stayed a day or two, so the branch manager had the extra task of entertaining them and taking them to the local hot spots. Head office made a few suggestions, the branch managers listened, nodded their heads and agreed to change things but, as soon as head office boarded their planes, enjoying their drinks and satisfied with their job of management, the branches went on with their old ways.

The Champions were no different. After Felix had been in Perth for a week, both Rob and Andrew travelled across with their wives for the official opening of the branch. By day, Rob and Andrew discussed business plans while the girls, Margot and Frankie, visited the shops of Perth and toured the countryside for wildflowers. At night, Ron organised a cocktail party to meet potential local clients and afterwards they ate lobster at an exclusive restaurant where the raw marine odour seeped into their nostrils as they chose their own from live creatures rattling against the glass of cloudy tanks. They departed happily, leaving Ron with the task of recouping the money the expensive visit had cost them. Peter wanted to load the branch with the costs of the launch, but Ron argued they should be tabbed as development costs and charged to head office.

Felix enjoyed his days in Perth and was sorry to return to the east. They worked well together, and Ron wanted him to stay. 'We make an effective team,' he argued.'Perth's isolated, I'm afraid,' Felix replied. 'The odd railway, pilot or traffic controllers' strike demonstrates how isolated the city is.' Felix never had time to identify with the spirit of the west, but he learned its wily ways, particularly how to deal with head offices in another city.

'You're a colleague I feel I could trust,' Felix said at their farewell drinks. Ron and Felix became good mates.

Chapter 9

With the meeting over, the process of moving the company to Eildon began.

'How'll we get to Eildon?' Sam asked Andrew when planning was discussed at the May meetings.

'We'll rope the Melbourne staff into a carpool.'

Felix shuddered. 'Why pick Eildon in freezing July? I grew up in regional Victoria and know how cold the highlands can get. It's a miserable place in winter.'

'The Lakeside resort's never busy in winter,' replied Andrew. 'I know the owners. I booked the whole resort and made a special deal. They grabbed the opportunity of accommodating and feeding our mob in what's normally a dead time.'

Peter pulled out a blank sheet of paper and wrote down some figures.

'Do you realise how much it's going to cost?'

'It's been an excellent year financially, the best ever,' Rob said, lighting a Camel cigarette and leaning back. 'It's an opportunity to reward the consultants.'

'They'd prefer the money in their pockets,' Peter replied.

Felix nodded in agreement with Peter. 'The family's helping an old mate.'

'Don't be a cynic, Felix. It'll motivate the consultants to work their guts out and make lots more money. They'll hit the ground running,' said Sid. 'We'll recoup the costs in no time.'

During the afternoon staff arrived from interstate. The weather grew colder as the hour advanced. Still wishing he had an overcoat, Felix travelled with his Victorian counterpart, Kelvin, in the front passenger seat while Nigel from South Australia sat in the back.

Felix knew Kelvin Brophy from Family Welfare. Like him, he became disillusioned. Felix recruited him, and in his early days, was his mentor. Kelvin's ambition soon brought him out from beneath the umbrella into direct competition for Rob's approval. Kelvin regarded Felix as a friend but, at the same time, they were in competition. They sometimes had a drink together after these meetings at which they exchanged confidences and opinions. Felix approached these drinking sessions with caution for he was never sure how much of what he said to Kelvin was passed on to Rob.

Not much was expected of South Australia. Nigel Mernagh ran a one-man show and operated as a service to the other states. The market was small and most of it had been captured by John Claremont, once the Adelaide branch manager. Claremont was an entrepreneur and was successful in building the business but insisted on a larger reward and when he met resistance from Sid and Rob, resigned and set up his own organisation. Sid regretted they hadn't looked after Claremont well enough, for his departure was a setback to their expansionary plans. Sid could think of nothing good to say about him, and although he has praised him effusively while within the company for his business acumen and held him as a model for others to emulate, Sid now regarded him as unethical and dishonest even though ironically Claremont had done no more than what they did. Sid and Rob decided to remain in Adelaide but to take it quietly. Nigel was recruited to the Melbourne office and asked to return to his home state. They appointed Nigel, a quiet bloke, who they regarded a safe bet, unlikely to be a business builder but nevertheless a sincere man who would do his best for the few Adelaide clients who remained loyal to The Champions. Nigel had as much to say on the trip as at management meetings, which was little, and only responded to the few questions from the front.

On a dreary, cold and miserable Friday afternoon, they drove through the eastern suburbs and rain showers into a countryside of undulating hills covered with orchards of leaf-less trees, in recession, waiting for the spring to return them to life. Felix, Kelvin and Nigel still had a winter to endure before they could enjoy a return to warmth. As they approached Eildon, the day darkened and slipped into nightfall. At Eildon they left the warm car to walk through the freezing carpark swirling with snowflakes. At reception, mine host was hover-ing, greeting his guests. The resort was comfortable enough with a décor that was fashionable a decade or two ago and had reached the stage of needing refurbishing. Felix, Kelvin and Nigel appreciated the warmth although they had to brace themselves for the cold again to get to their allocated rooms, laid out in motel-style. Felix had an individual room, Room 14. By dinnertime all the company had arrived.

Only income-earning consultants from interstate offices had been invited to the conference. Their support staff stayed home but all the Melbourne office staff had been included because Sid, Rob and Andrew knew them. They were hard working girls and nice to look at, Sid claimed. They should be rewarded too. Besides, they incurred no transport costs and their accommodation had been severely discounted in the deal Andrew made with mine host. Excursions had been planned to local sites but because the weather was so foul, their programme was abandoned, and they joined the consultants in the warmth.

*   *   *   *

After dinner, the first session of the conference commenced. Firstly, there were a few words of welcome by chairman Sid who repeated the afternoon's speech, reminiscing on the beginnings of the company. He felt a deep sense of satisfaction from the opportunity he and Rob had received to contribute to the country's economy and to provide employment to such a large number. Rob sat back smoking his umpteenth cigarette for the day, nodding in agreement at his brother's sentiment. He looked over the faces of the audience. They were bright-eyed, reflecting an enthusiasm and an excitement to be included. For some, this was their first visit to Victoria. A large log fire at the front of the room cast a cheerful and welcoming light.

Andrew followed, this time as the heir apparent, (the *Dauphin,* as Pascaline used to call him) to strut the stage before the entire company. He had prepared an overhead depicting the company's income growth since its inception. He presented a graph, income level at the side, calendar year at the bottom. The graph showed a steady rise as a thick black line from the left-hand bottom corner. The incline was the steepest in the last two years and continued as a dotted line for the current year, continuing just as steeply for the following five years in geometric progression right up into the top right-hand corner.

'Our exciting future,' he said. 'There's nothing to stop us from reaching these heights except ourselves.'

Andrew was like a sales manager motivating his staff to great heights of achievement, a football coach urging his team to put in a supreme effort in the coming struggle. But he was not speaking to a sales or football team full of unbridled optimism, which might accept whatever they were told. He was speaking to a group of professionals most of whom were university educated and used to critical evaluation. Instead of a wild enthusiasm, they responded with raised eyes and side glances. Andrew detected the touch of scepticism in his restless listeners and concluded: 'You've got to be positive. You can always do more than you think you can. You've got to get out and fearlessly pursue your goals.'

'This is pie-in-the-sky stuff,' Felix muttered while having a drink with Ron afterwards in front of the open fire.

'Don't take it too seriously,' Ron agreed. 'It's good to be positive but you've got to be realistic. He's just stirring up the troops before they go over the hill.'

The bar closed at 11.30 and the company was encouraged to retire early in preparation for a busy day of conferring. They left the warm conference room where the fire was still glowing and faced the cold to get to their beds, saved from a freezing night by heaters and electric blankets.

They woke to a gloomy Saturday morning. Snow had fallen during the night and left a slushy covering. Misty rain obscured the grey uninviting lake as they made their muddy way to breakfast. Consultants were happy to stay inside the warm resort and no one, not even as a joke or a dare, suggested a swim in the lake.

The day saw them involved in a series of sessions covering the activities of the company. Presentations were made on successful consulting assignments. The various divisions of the company met to discuss ideas on developing business. Zachary Evans, the specialist salary consultant who ran a one-man band from the Melbourne office, had developed a new method of job evaluation. Job evaluation is not an exact science but a systematic way of determining the value/worth of a job in relation to other jobs in the organisation. Its task was to minimise subjectivity and enable rational, consistent and transparent decisions to be made about roles and salaries. Zachary had shrouded his product with a quasi-scientific mystique that impressed Sid and Rob, and Andrew had hopes that this area could take off in competition with strong players in the field. The afternoon was devoted to teaching the consultants this method in order that they could promote it as an extra service.

Consultants were weary after an afternoon of calculations and mastering unfamiliar jargon, but, with the business of the day concluded, it was time to relax. A concert followed dinner. Between the last session and dinner, consultants involved themselves in preparing scripts, writing lines and organising impromptu costumes. While the rest adjourned to the bar and to the fire for what they regarded as well-earned drinks to wash away the tedium of the day, the creative types were engaged in secret rehearsals in the rooms. The wines flowed freely during dinner and mine host and his staff, locals recruited for the evening, did their best to keep up with the demand. Laughter was loud and raucous, people had to shout against the general din and by the time dinner was consumed, most of the company were well on the way. Alcohol continued to be served during the concert and the audience was prepared to laugh at anything. Some items were solo, but others were groups representing the states. For some, scripts were still being written as they mounted the makeshift stage. Felix joined the Sydney staff, all dressed in T-shirts bearing the slogan 'New South Wales – the Premier State', which his secretary Janice had organised. New South Wales was polished. Many of the lines, which were clever and witty sendups of Sid and Rob, had been written the week before and if there had been any formal judging, New South Wales would have been the premiers.

'A pity Sydney didn't put the same effort into their results for the last month,' someone heard Peter mutter into his beer. Peter was a quiet, steady and consistent drinker and no one saw any changes in him over the evening. He kept closed the shutters on his soul should his spirit escape. But the remainder threw open their windows, let their manic out and jubilation in and plummeted into the evening. The freeing spirit soared as the company relaxed and restraint dissolved in alcohol. Felix had a mild interest in how Cressida behaved under these conditions. Sad enough on the job, she was reputed to be the genuine party animal after a few drinks.

A sober drop-in coming in from the cold would have found a mob thoroughly engaged in the process of enjoying themselves. They were spread over two rooms. One room was the training room where they had assembled all day. It housed the fireplace and a large video screen for which mine host had found an old film, a sloppy romance, which no one was watching. In the other room was a sound system and for that, mine host had found music to which many of the younger consultants and others not so interested in getting drunk were dancing. Cressida was among the most vigorous of the dancers and in no time she led a conga line around the dance floor, out into the TV room, weaving around the tables and chairs, whooping and encouraging everyone to join. Before long, the whole company, even Peter, was snaking its way through the resort. Some of the Melbourne girls learned belly dancing and soon their colleagues were calling for a demonstration. They obliged but then demanded that others join and in no time most of the company were shaking their midriffs. As the inhibitions faded away, secret yearnings revealed themselves and the dullness of office respectability was turning to high gloss as consultants manoeuvred into the preliminary stages. Behaviour at the office was governed by definitions of what was 'appropriate', but tonight the rules were undergoing transition. The attention that some were giving to others was more than enough to keep the gossip wheels turning for months. Kelvin Brophy was paying close attention to the dancing Cressida, which was expected as they were already linked in an affair. Others were conscious of peering through a different lens at their colleagues, relaxed and giggly, swinging their bodies around, wondering about their willingness in other areas.

For one fleeting moment, Felix had an image of a comforting female body warming the bed in the cold motel room he would have to face some time later that evening. He found himself dancing with one of his consultants more than once. Viviana was behind him in the conga line, and they were swinging their bodies together in the belly dancing. She grabbed his arms twice when he was taking a breather.

'Come on, boss. Let your hair down.'

'I thought I was doing that already,' the breathless Felix shouted above the din. Alcohol was doing its job of dissolving his inhibitions. But not enough for Viviana. It dawned on his soggy brain, like a light piercing the fog, that she, with her fluttering eyes, could have been making a pass.

He had worked with many women during his career. Most of them were hard workers and he respected their skills and competence. He did not share Sid's view (offered after a long night in the cup) that women had two functions. He liked to think that he had made some good friends among the women he'd worked with. Occasionally, he might wonder what they were like in bed as every male must think from time to time about their female colleagues. Females thought that about their male colleagues, too. While some had been enticing, he'd never succumbed to the temptation of having sex with a colleague. There were enough problems to deal with, without adding a liaison or two.

Viviana was his best performer. She had her loyal clients who always turned to her. She flattered them. Her monthly figures were always good. She was highly regarded by Andrew. She could do no wrong. But Felix believed she conformed to company rules and policies as it suited her. She played the game to her own rules. She seemed indifferent to people who might be less skilled or less fortunate than herself. The thought of a sexual liaison with Viviana sobered him up as if someone had thrown a bucket of water over him or pushed him out of the Lakeside Resort into the freezing night. As manager of New South Wales, he had enough headaches as it was managing his maverick staff without adding someone with a hold over him. He wasn't sure if Viviana really had her eye on him, or if he were just deluding himself, but he played safe and, for the rest of the night, avoided her.

Others did not have the same inhibitions. Without the restraints of an office routine and fuelled by alcoholic vapours, the girls of the Melbourne office became an attractive target for predatory males among the consultants both from Melbourne and interstate. In turn, the girls flickered their eyes and sent invitations to the same males to check out their stuff. The dancing continued and bodies, which in the office maintained a respectful distance from each other, pressed closely and groped for each other. Among the males was a relaxed Nigel Mernagh who knew most of the Melbourne girls from the time he worked in the office. Alcohol had loosened his limbs and he was a sought-after partner. Felix knew some of the girls, too, and joined in but was soon tired and sat out the dances with the drinkers.

Mine host continued to serve drinks and to turn up the volume as if he were keen to ensure that if his alcohol did not batter the company insensible, the racket would. The bleak winter had turned customers away, but a profitable weekend would cover the loss he had endured so far this season. Those of the company who weren't dancing were consuming with enthusiasm, while the dancers, thirsty from their exertion, regularly joined them. Although mine host would be exhausted by the end of Sunday, he wanted the drinking to continue into the night. He would have weeks to recover. It was midnight and already some of the consultants were leaving, among them Kelvin and Cressida. One successful strategy mine host had found in the past to keep the customers' attention and the drinks flowing was to play porno films on his large video screen. Indeed, some of his former clients, sales managers with groups of randy male salesmen separated from their beloveds, demanded such showings as they argued that they helped to bond their teams together, like naughty mice playing while the cat was away. To date, these groups had been all male and The Champions was his first group with a sizable number of females. Accordingly, he placed his copy of *Deep Throat* in the machine. No one noticed at first for the video had been operating all the evening and the soundtrack had been drowned by the dance music but, as the well-worn images of Linda Lovelace endeavouring to swallow innumerable penises appeared, the screen demanded attention.

With a male sales team or a football club, there would have been much cheering and encouragement of Linda at her performance and shouts of appreciation at the size of the male tackle confronting her. There might even have been discussion among the viewers whether any of those present could match the male actors in their dimensions and, in extreme cases depending on how far the night had deteriorated, a competition and 'short-arms' inspection could have been mooted. But the presence of the ladies dampened any enthusiastic response the males might otherwise have shown. If the males had been with their sporting clubs, they might have welcomed Linda with metaphorical open arms. But the reaction was more one of embarrassed silence. What gentle seduction may have been going on was in the early phases – subtle game-playing, quiet and manipulative, like lifting the skirt just a little above the ankle or fluttering the eyes. But the room was raging with full frontal nudity and outrageous sex games as if all the stages between one and ten had been bypassed. Bright, hard, garish light had replaced soft, sweet, seductive tunes. Instead of a turn-on, *Deep Throat* was a put-off. Some of the ladies who had never witnessed a blue movie couldn't control the vigour of their exhalations, which were equal parts of carbon dioxide and disgust. Others turned their backs, decided that their male colleagues, tolerable in the office, were creeps under the grog, wondered what the heck they were doing there and called it a night.

Righteous Sam, the lay preacher, approached Andrew.

'What would our clients say if they knew we were watching porn at our conference?'

'They'd say we were human,' slurred a half-sloshed Andrew. He did not back off. He had to justify the choice of the venue and to defend mine host's selection.

'That actress, Linda Lovelace, has been saved for Jesus,' said Sam, the churchman concerned with the redemption of sinners and rescuing them from the clutches of Satan. 'She saw the error of her ways and is now a devout Christian.'

Like most of the company, Felix was not impressed. The chances of emulating the actors in this cold hole were zero. He needed a much more temperate climate to remove his clothes and prance about naked. The sight of all that bare skin gave him shivers and drew him closer to the fire, which was one of the tasks mine host had neglected. While others continued to watch the screen, Felix found a log in the firebox and threw it in, sending up a shower of sparks, and the intense deep heat soon had the flames licking their way along the log and the warm glow quickly spread itself across the room. He should go to bed as they had another day of conferring but did not relish running the freezing gauntlet outside to get to his chilly room. He remained by the fire for a few more drinks.

To mine host's disappointment, the impact of *Deep Throat* was in breaking up the party rather than restoring it. He had poured water on the fire rather than petrol. People began to drift off into the night leaving the hardcore drinkers snug by the fire. Felix did not hear much of the conversation as he stared into the fire. Sam, despite his Godliness and its now being the Sabbath, had remained and was trying to convince Ron from the west that the larger states such as Victoria and New South Wales should do more to support the smaller states, but Ron was arguing that each state was able to generate its own business. Felix was pleased when Sam decided to retire, leaving his trusted friend, Ron.

'You've seen a lots of changes since you've been with the company, Felix?'

He was in a drowsy reminiscing mood.

'For sure, Ron. I often think of the time when we were only a small office in St Kilda Road. Andrew was still at university, but he worked for the company during vacations and I had the responsibility of looking after him.'

'Andrew's young and learning the job,' said Ron as he took a confidential sip. 'He's not as visionary as his father, but he thinks he has to prove himself. His father would be a tough critic.' They kept their voices low as Andrew was on the other side of the room playing billiards with Sid.

'Andrew reminded me of a labrador pup, the way he'd darted around the place, full of questions and enthusiasm. He was a bit of a nuisance, but he was eager to learn and make himself useful. Sometimes, I'd get into trouble with Sid.

Andrew would make some statement at home to his father. He'd disagree and ask, "Who told you that?" Andrew would reply "Felix", and, next day, Sid would tackle me for my erroneous thinking.'

'Sid would put you right.'

'I didn't mind. That was Sid's style – to challenge and debate. I always felt Sid was straight. What he said to you face to face was the same as what he'd say behind your back.'

Felix fell asleep in the middle of their conversation and Ron poked him in the ribs. Time to end the day. At other times he remained with the stayers and drank the well dry. He left the warm fuggy room for the sub-zero walk to his room. Although it was not snowing, the ground was icy, and he had to tread with care. The room was freezing. He thought of the time he had shared a bed with Pascaline. He had chosen work and career, which offered no comfort on a chilly night. No time for regret. The alcohol had anaesthetised him from the cold, and he was asleep and snoring as soon as he hit the sheets, just managing to turn on the blanket.

Mine host was the last to retire. He was having a good weekend and was grateful to his old mate, Sid Champion and young Andrew, for putting the business his way. Sid owned a weekender just down the road. The resort bar was their regular watering hole. He enjoyed Sid's visit; he was full of tales especially of his trips to remote mining towns. He'd left the bargaining to his son. Andrew was a good negotiator and businessman. He said the company was a group of professionals but, as far as he could see, they were no different to any other group that stayed at his resort. His usual clientele was sales teams or sporting clubs. Andrew's mob drank just as much grog as other groups, judging by the empties. He watched as they flirted with each other. He wondered how many shared a bed – a challenge for most as only the managers had a room on their own. Every bed was taken in the shared rooms.

He waited until no one was left in the resort. He was keen to retire as he would have to rise early. Usually, his last job was to check the accommodation for any irregularities. Some-times, drunken sales-types wanted to fight colleagues over long-held grudges. He rugged himself up and walked along the path outside the rooms. All was quiet on the western row. He turned the corner into the next row and stopped in the shadow when he saw a couple covered with a blanket trying one of the doors. He wondered if they were locked out or looking for an empty room to pursue their liaison. Sid's room was empty because he decided to sleep at his own place, but he wasn't going to tell them that.

'Can I help you?' he asked from the darkness.

'No,' a male voice answered. The couple moved to the next door and disappeared inside. Happy that he didn't have a rape case on his hands, mine host continued his rounds. He gave room 14 the prize for the loudest snorer.

Sunday was one of those days Felix would prefer to forget. Once upon a time he could bounce back like a rubber ball after a night of drinking, but age and years of knocking himself around had robbed his body. An evening of alcohol couldn't be cancelled anymore by a good night's sleep and a hangover could stretch beyond the day. He would have been happy to remain in bed for the morning but, conscious of the need to be seen as a stayer, and mindful of the jibes that latecomers and those looking the worse for wear would receive, he rose from his bed to shave. He looked at the image in the foggy mirror. Wrinkles, which at one time would have disappeared with a refreshing shower, seemed to have set and hardened. Struggling with both weariness and the weather, with bright brittle face concealing the pain, he appeared at breakfast at the appointed time.

He caught Viviana's eye as he entered the room. As she approached the bain-marie for a serving of scrambled eggs, she seemed to turn and toss her shoulder as if she wanted him to know she did not wish to sit near him. His faculties were depressed but he was not deaf to the point she was making. Did she really make an offer the night before, or was it just his imagination? In his present state of mind, he couldn't care less. He sat next to Ron who, seeing he wasn't a hundred per cent, didn't press him for conversation. Not everyone turned up for breakfast but everyone managed to make the first session.

Andrew had been toying with public relations and had arranged for a Jon Christie, a public relations consultant, to attend, to explain what public relations consultants did and how their services could contribute to promoting the company's services.

'Such consultants have their contacts in the media and know which ones to use to promote particular stories,' Andrew explained by way of introduction.

'PR is a set of techniques and strategies related to how information about a company is disseminated to the public and especially to the media,' Jon Christie explained. 'Its primary goals are to disseminate important company news or events, maintain a brand image and put a positive spin on negative events.'

That last comment stirred Felix and forced him out of his lethargy.

'That makes public relations sound like just another form of manipulation,' he ventured.

'Sure,' agreed the consultant.

'There's nothing wrong with that,' said Andrew.

'What makes you think our company should use you?' asked Adelaide's Nigel Mernagh. He had plenty to drink the night before but was among the fresh faces.

'Well, I've got to eat.' Jon Christie was overweight and overbearing. He had meant to make a joke but his attempt at humour fell flat, his inadequate answer woke everyone, and Nigel's reply voiced the common concern.

'You'll have to do better than that.'

Andrew rushed to his defence with the comment that he had a project in mind and would test the effectiveness of public relations within the next few weeks.

The company began leaving the resort from after lunch. Flights had been booked through the afternoon and evening for the interstate consultants. Again, the local consultants drove the visitors to the airport. Kelvin Brophy took Felix. Nigel rode in the back seat. There was little conversation as both Felix and Nigel slept.

Felix was not unhappy to leave freezing Eildon. If they stayed much longer, they could be snow-bound. He must be getting old; he was feeling the cold. He was equally pleased to leave chilly Melbourne. Relaxing with a beer in the comfort of his first-class seat on the Ansett flight to Sydney, he was surprised to find himself agreeing with Peter that the conference was an unnecessary expense. Bringing together the whole company was supposed to be a motivating experience to go out, refreshed and enthused, into the market to fight the enemy, whoever they were. He did not feel motivated or refreshed. He was feeling sour, at the tail-end of a hangover, and saw before him a hard slog to achieve the budget set for the coming year. Despite the optimism displayed by Andrew, he could hear the distant rumbling of a down-turn on the horizon in politicians' unease about high inflation figures. Andrew's optimism – or was it self-deception? – worried him. Andrew wanted to increase staff to handle the influx of predicted business, which would be necessary if the budget figures were to be achieved. The increases were based not on solid economic forecasts but on imagination, which Andrew's optimism had allowed to run loose. In fact, the pundits were pessimistic. Felix preferred the business to come in first and then worry about how they would resource it. Andrew saw that as lack of planning. Felix believed it prudence to keep fixed costs, such as staff, as low as possible, to wait to see what the year might bring.

He was not enjoying this management caper. After his stint in Perth, with nothing to hold him in Melbourne, Rob invited him to join the Sydney office to strengthen its technical expertise. When his predecessor, Horsey, resigned to join an opposition firm, he expected to move into his shoes. But Andrew hesitated. He advertised outside. Why? Felix asked him. He was a valuable member of the company with loads of technical expertise and a good bloke to work with, etc., he replied, but he wondered about his management skills. Felix was so incensed that he accepted Horsey's invitation to join him and resigned. Luck was with Felix, for two of the Sydney consultants resigned the same day to form their own consulting firm – one of the hazards of the industry. That left Andrew with an enormous hole in the Sydney staffing. Andrew gave him a massive salary increase and appointed him, with the attitude 'Let's see what happens'.

He had a staff of thirty in two offices. Even in the time he'd been manager, the numbers had grown. He shuddered at the thought of what would happen, of what he would have to do if business took a dive. Conditions had been bountiful in the last few years. It had been too easy. Bad times must follow, like the seven years of famine following the seven years of bountiful harvests in Pharaoh's dream. Had the company followed Moses' advice to store food in the granaries for the inevitable famine? Had the company put aside reserves to cope with bad times? He feared not. Now, after years of nothing, prosperous times had arrived to allow the families to cash in on their good fortune.

Felix would be lying if he did not admit he was a reluctant progressive. He cast his mind back to the early days when he joined the company. Life was less complicated. They were close to each other, they shared in each other's successes when business was gained and commiserated when bid-for business went elsewhere. Each new piece of business was a challenge overcome, a source of great joy and satisfaction to all, an opportunity to sing the company's theme song, *We Are the Champions*. Any individual achievement was common to all, a situation that changed with Peter's introduction of individual income budgets.

They were once a family. They enjoyed each other's company, saw each other socially and invited each other to their homes. The business invaded all aspects of their lives, and they loved it. The company gave them meaning. They had a joke that their business success was better than sex. For a time, it did not compete with the sex, excitement and emotion of his life with Pascaline, but it came close. Eventually, it began to push away love, deadened his interests. His passion was transferred. The company took over his life. It was fulfilling and empowering. He looked forward each morning to getting stuck into work, but it drained away his energy, time and desire for intimacy with Pascaline, his beautiful French *'petite amie'*. Those chaotic golden days were gone. Now the company was secure, business was booming and income was pouring in, but he had paid a price for his new love affair.

As the plane began its descent, he wondered what issues might face him that week in the office where another cast of players was waiting for its cue.

Chapter 10

Felix collected his car from long-term parking and after paying a mind-blowing fee, drove to Cremorne. Not much traffic late Sunday night. He parked his car in his allotted spot under the building, walked up the stairs to the foyer and collected Friday's mail from his box. Nothing of interest in the usual pile of junk mail. The envelope that took his attention was from France and addressed to him in Pascaline's handwriting. She wrote occasionally, sometimes in English, sometimes in French. He opened and began reading the letter (this one was in English) as he walked up the three flights of stairs. Nothing to get him excited, just ordinary news. She was enjoying everything about her new job at the language school. She liked her boss, her new work mates, the teachers, the other secretaries and helping the students with their problems. He stopped reading to concentrate on the climb. On the third landing, he paused for a breather and continued reading. 'We are looking forward to Bastille Day celebrations,' she wrote.

Who's we? A new boyfriend? That thought made him wince, his woman with another bloke.

He opened the door to his lonely unit, a dull cheerless affair, with a combined living room/kitchen, one bedroom and space for one car under the building. Not as modern as many but no different from thousands of other units in Sydney. Nothing special to call it home. Just a place to sleep – cold and empty, a spiritual as well as physical vacuum. Nothing extraordinary about the furnishings, what you would see in any run-of-the-mill retailer, or Salvo's op shop. He hadn't even bothered to find any wall coverings. He remembered the times he used to come home from a trip to be greeted by Pascaline's kiss. Their home, an apartment back in Melbourne, was inviting, warm and loving. She had taken care in selecting the furniture, paintings, ornaments and vases of all sorts. She visited the market for fresh flowers. Pascaline usually had a cold beer ready and something ordinary for dinner like lamb chops, not a favourite of the French. How he appreciated a simple meal after a week or so of restaurant meals with all their sauces and spices. They would tell each other what they had been doing, and later, make love.

He turned on the television to break the silence, sat on the couch with a beer, which, because there was no one else, he had to get for himself.

He switched to a film but failed to follow the plot for the intrusion of these memories of better days. He had to think how long they were together and how long they had been parted. He was tired from the weekend. Four years? Or was it five? Just before he went to Perth and then Sydney.

Back in the Melbourne days, they used to gather for a few beers after work. He was always in conflict, endeavouring to maintain the balance. He wanted to get home to his Pascaline but also stay with the boys, to share their day's work and the thrill of their achievements. Work was a pleasure; he thrived on its adrenalin peaks and was inspired when it all came together. His sense of achievement made him feel complete and threatened to block out everything else. A key to his identity, work competed with his life of excitement, emotion and sex with Pascaline, a constant threat to the energy and desire that made their intimacy happen.

One evening that he will never forget, he stayed much longer than intended and came home after 8 pm. As he entered the apartment, something was different. Pascaline was quiet, stiff, as if she were holding something within. He tried to kiss her, but she moved away with a shrug of her shoulders to the other side of the room.

'What's wrong?' he asked.

'Oh, Felix! Can't you see?' She covered her eyes with her hands. Unsure what he was supposed to see, his anxiety jumped off the scale with a feeling in his guts that shook the foundations. He said nothing and waited for her to continue.

'I want out.'

'What?'

'Je veux sortir.' She resorted to her native French as if that might make her thought clearer. He was speechless, unable to believe what he was hearing. His life was ready to collapse, like a building teetering on the brink of an earthquake. He felt a combination of fear, frustration and love and moved to embrace her, but she turned away.

'I am sick of being half a couple. I need to find my own self,' she returned to English.

Only after he sucked a deep breath was he able to speak.

'What do you mean?' He thought he knew what she meant, but he couldn't believe it.

'Do you really love me?' she asked.

'Of course, I do. You're my beloved, the person I love most in the world.'

'You do not show it. I've lost you to the company. I had you when you worked for Welfare but since The Champions, you are a shadow of what you were. The company is your lover. It has seduced you and left no time or energy for me. You do not need me anymore.'

'Oh, Pascaline. I cannot believe you're saying this.'

She spilled it all out with unusual vehemence as if a wall holding back a reservoir of resentment had collapsed.

'You have lost your balance. All you can think about is your work. That makes you dull and boring. Once upon a time, you were passionate, alive, exciting. You had lots of interests and time for me.'

'I've always got time for you,' he protested.

'You took me for granted that I would always be there, waiting for a scrap of your time.'

He tried to speak but his mouth was dry and choked his words.

'When did we go to the theatre together?'

He couldn't remember. She had a point. That there was never anything on that he wanted to see didn't wash with her.

'You used to be an avid reader. When did you last read a novel or anything that was not to do with business?'

She had another point. At one time, he could never pass a book shop without entering and buying. He was a regular at the local library. Nowadays, he never had time. He didn't think much at that moment about whether her accusations were true, about what sort of person he had become and whether his infatuation with the company had blocked out everything else, flattened his horizons and narrowed rather than broadened him. He left that to later, much later. Instead, he was confused, one thought tumbling after another, bewildered that she was slipping away. He wasn't sure what language they were speaking. The meaning was clear enough.

'*As-tu trouvé quelqu'un d'autre?*' (Have you found someone else?)

'*Peut-être!*' (Perhaps!)

'*Qu'est-ce que tu veux dire par ça? Peut-être?*'(What do you mean by that? Perhaps!)'

'I met a nice man at the Alliance Française. He's very charming.'

Pascaline had been tutoring.

'What's his name?'

'Jean-Claude.'

'What does he do? How did you meet him?'

'He works for a French company that sells wines to Australia. He had a wine tasting at the Alliance. He's due to return home. He asked me to come back with him.'

Felix instantly disliked this Jean-Claude. He had visions of confronting this smarmy Frenchman, smashing in his face and kicking him as far as Paris.

'Have you slept with him?' It was a foolish question. His anger was rising, and he wasn't sure of his reaction if she answered yes.

'Jean-Claude wants to.'

'We should try to talk and work things out. We should go to a counsellor.'

'No, I do not want to talk to anyone. I want you the way you used to be.'

She hadn't ditched him entirely. There was hope yet.

'Perhaps, I should take a few days off and we could go away on a holiday, just the two of us.'

'If you could only spend more time with me.'

He tried to speak but found no words.

'Felix? You are just *un bourreau de travail*, a demon for work, a workaholic.'

Pascaline did not know much about the sociology of the corporate work ethos. She was aware that organisations wanted their people to be content and proud of where they worked, but she had never given much thought, if any, to values such as dedication, integrity, accountability and collaboration, which every organisation tries to foster. She was unambiguously aware of their impact on Felix. She had never heard of the Japanese word *karoshi*. Just as well. It means working oneself to death, once considered unique to Japanese work culture, but later recognised as worldwide.

Pascaline was in no mood for love that night. Her heart hurt after telling him that she had to let him go. She did not want their love to end. She did not like the pain, but she felt she had to leave. She did not lose him suddenly or unexpectedly. She began to lose him piece by piece the moment he joined the company. Now, there was little left. Once, their love affair was enriching but now it was distressing. Equally upsetting was the pain she was inflicting on her lover, but she had to tell him that once he was welcome but that did not mean he should remain in her life for ever.

The next day, he approached Rob and stressed he needed to spend time with Pascaline. Rob liked Pascaline. He liked having a lovely French lady around. He knew, too, that while this potential disaster hung over Felix, it would affect his productivity.

Felix took a week's leave, and they had a holiday together.

They quit Melbourne and drove through Gippsland right to the border of New South Wales, taking their time to look at the country. They did not book anything, just went with their fancy. He tried to relax but the apprehension of losing her never left. They came back to Victoria through the Snowy Mountains, not before stopping for three days in a neat little cabin by the side of Lake Jindabyne. They enjoyed a day's skiing in the mountains. The winter snow had arrived, and the air was fresh and invigorating. It reminded Pascaline of home. She was fascinated that the beautiful lake was not natural, but was man made, formed by a dam wall that flooded the valley. The islands were the tops of hills, and the old town was lying below the water. She wondered if the old ghosts were drowned, too, or did they appear now and then, in the vapour rising from the surface.

On their last afternoon they walked along the lake shore. Seagulls landed in the water and pink and grey galahs settled on the grass. The air was cold, a chilly wind blew off the snow-covered mountains, but the sun was bright off the water. He wished it were mid-summer and warm enough to wade out knee deep. He had visions of Pascaline leaning down, dipping her hand in the water and splashing him. She was running away from him, lifting her feet high out of the water and giggling. He chased her, skimming a handful of water at her and splashing her with every step. He caught up, scooped her up and held her over the water as if about to drop to her.

'*Dis que tu es désolée.*' (Say you're sorry.)

She struggled and tried to put her feet down. She managed to escape, squealing like a child, and he followed. Her little game gave him hope of a change of heart and he was ready to play. If she were reverting to her childhood, she would splash him again. The water ran down his face and he followed as she sprinted back to dry earth. She did her best to stay ahead but he caught her, held her tightly and kissed her. Alas, it was only a daydream as they walked in silence.

It reminded him of an earlier time, in Spain, after a hot day's walking. Their relationship was just beginning, and he was re-enacting the game they played that warm afternoon. He asked Pascaline if she remembered the refuge next to the stream.

'Oui, on se connaissait.' (We were getting to know each other.)

They sat in silence outside their cabin and gazed at the still waters, reflecting the mountains. They followed the breezes across the surface as they left behind them the gentle distur-bance of their ripples.

'I could live in this place. It is peaceful and serene.'

She gave him hope. He, too, could live here. Could she live here with him? He felt resentful that back in Melbourne, the company was waiting, a stern lover commanding him to return. The company, made up of the founders, their families and the staff, had developed a mystical entity of its own that entrapped and held on as tightly as any lover.

Their last night in the cabin was full of carnal passion. They clung to the fires as long as they could, desperate the flame would soon be extinguished, and they would have to square up to a winter of the soul. In his mind he heard the words of *Bésume mucho*, a beautiful lament he learned while in Spain.

Bésume, bésume mucho Como si fuera esta
noche La última vez

Kiss me more, kiss me many more times as if this
beautiful night is the very last time.

They drove back to Melbourne in silence. He prayed that
she was playing a game to win him back, was happy with their
holiday, brief was it was, and life would return to normal. She
was playing no game. Nothing had changed. He faced the
same conversation, the same accusations. She was dead serious that she was leaving.

They had no children. Pascaline always said she should get
married first. She did not like the idea of a family born out of
wedlock. That was her Catholic upbringing. At one time, they
discussed marriage, but she said, 'not yet.' At another time
she said they should get themselves checked out before committing themselves. In a last bid to save her, he promised her
he would lay himself bare to the medicos and have his semen
examined. Too late. She had made up her mind.

He was bewildered. He had no notion anything was wrong.
Pascaline asserted that she had been trying to tell him for ages,
but so absorbed was he with himself and the company that
he may have listened but didn't hear. He wanted to tell her
that if he didn't listen well enough, to tell him again in a way
he'd understand. If he were insensitive to her needs, to her
desires, or to her thoughts, communicate in a way he would
understand. If he had hurt her feelings, make him aware of
it. Too late. He watched her as she walked away. The words
'Stay please' (*S'il te plait, rester*) escaped his lips, barely audible,
but she was gone. Back to France she went with Jean-Claude.
Their last good-bye was the hardest. He couldn't imagine it
ever happening, which made him all the sadder.

He could not stay in their unit. He moved into a nondescript flat in East Melbourne and when the company opened a Perth office, seeing he had no ties, Rob asked him to work in the west for six months. He did not want to return to Melbourne. He transferred to Sydney, primarily for the company's needs but also for his need to get away and find a new life. He did not let on to his colleagues how he was hurting, but Rob and Andrew were supportive. They thought he had survived her leaving, but what they didn't appreciate was that he had to relearn how to survive each day because each day she was still gone. Just as well he had total involvement in work to distract him.

Added to his confusion was a feeling he had let her mother down. Before they left France, he promised Ghislaine he would look after her daughter. Torn between addiction to the company and responsibility to Pascaline, he had neglected her and failed Ghislaine's trust. What did she think of him now, her daughter back in France?

He was leading a double life. By day, he was the business executive in charge of himself and dealing with his challenges in a rational and logical way. By night, he was fragile and perplexed, unable to understand why he was so vulnerable to his emotional hurt. He twigged to a major deficiency. He could not read subtleties. Pascaline's disillusion was staring him in the face, but he did not see it. He relied on her to tell him what she was thinking and feeling and when she did, he was sort of able to understand what she was saying, but he wasn't enlightened, not emotionally.

He re-read her letter. When she wrote 'we', did that mean she had found another man? She mentioned in an earlier letter she had ditched Jean-Claude shortly after arriving back in France. Serve the bastard right. Was she working her way through half the men of France? God knows what sort of bizarre relationships she was going through to get herself her 'freedom'. He did not want to think ill of her. *Arrete cette bêtise,* he reprimanded himself. Stop this silliness!

What made her beautiful lay not in her appearance or what she might have achieved, but in her love. She came with him to the other side of the globe. In her courage and audacity, she left her familiar world behind. She had a fire within her, the light of which dispelled any darkness in his life. He found her most alluring not when she was dressed up, but when she wasn't. When she was lying on the grass, hair tangled in a mess, laughing about something that had happened. When she had removed the wall she built for most people, he could not take his eyes off her.

He continued to feel connected with her on the other side of the world and was both puzzled and pleased she kept in touch. This glimmer of hope, like a tiny flame, stretched across the oceans, dim when it reached Australia's shores, but nevertheless, it arrived. He might have never heard from her again, but she gave him hope that their paths might converge again. He wrote back. Not that he had news, only about the company, which she would not want to hear.

One of these days, she wrote, she might revisit Australia because of the country she loved, particular the Snowy Mountains. She could live there because the country reminded her of her mountains in France.

Although she had left him, she wanted to maintain the contact. The bond remained unbroken, the footbridge *(la passerelle)* they built together was still intact despite a bad shaking. On the other hand, she wrote that they were probably incompatible and not suited for each other. He should forget about her and find another partner. The contradictory message she was sending confused him, too subtle for him. Was she displaying the illogic inherent in humans falling in and out of love, or was there something else she was not telling him? They were never legally married, and he wondered that if they had tied the union in church and had children, he might have kept her.

He got up from watching mindless television and his own reverie, to find another beer. Only one left. No problem. There was a bottle of whiskey in the cupboard. He opened the last beer and settled back into the couch. He found himself something to eat, but then realised they had fed him on the plane. A little food might absorb the alcohol and leave him in a better state to cope with whatever tomorrow produced. He emptied a tin of spaghetti into a saucepan and finished the beer with the meal. He thought of a nightcap but was knackered from the weekend. If he drank whisky, he would want another. He knew that he should rest to be ready for the chaos of Monday at the office.

It would be nice to quit this soulless place, he mused, as he settled down to sleep. The lease expired next month. He should find something less dreary, a unit with more character. He should reward himself with nice ornaments and paintings, too.

Chapter 11

A tear rolled down her cheek as the train slowed upon entering the suburbs of Chambéry. The lady sitting opposite with whom she had been chatting off and on during their journey leaned forward and took her hand. An older lady, someone's grandmother, she had short grey hair and bright caring eyes that had seen it all before.

'Are you coming home?' she asked.

'Yes,' replied Pascaline.

'How long has it been?'

'Too long, but not long enough.'

The lady smiled and asked no more questions. They gathered their belongings in readiness and wished each other *au revoir*. The train came to a halt at Chambéry Challes-les-Eaux. They descended, Pascaline helped the older woman down the steps and walked the length of the platform to the entrance. Ghislaine was waiting at the gate. She embraced her daughter and ushered her and her luggage to the car, and, in no time, they were out in the country driving towards the farm. Leaves and bunches of grapes covered the vines climbing above the courtyard, but the sun managed to shine a welcome out of a clear blue sky and a gentle breeze set the dappled shade dancing. They sat on the benches under this canopy. Little had changed since Pascaline last saw the courtyard. Ghislaine had added a small statue of a grinning Bacchus, his gleeful smile anticipating the coming grape harvest. Pascaline leaned over to stroke his head.

'I like your new friend,' she said to her mother.

'That was a gift from Anton. He bought one for his vineyard museum collection and another for me. He thought it would be company for me under our vines.'

Ghislaine laughed and Pascaline joined her. Her expression changed as the adrenalin rush subsided and the excitement of coming home was wearing off. She remembered she had serious matters to consider. She turned to her mother.

'Maman, I am happy to be home, but have I done the right thing?' asked an ambivalent daughter.

'Pascaline, my dear.' Ghislaine took her daughter into her arms and stroked her hair. Pascaline nestled into her mother and travelled down the years to the little girl who sought comfort whenever she was troubled. 'There will be times in your life, and knowing you as my dear daughter, many when you will regret the choice and feel guilty you made it. We are all of us only human. We would like our decisions to be unambiguous and clear cut, but it is seldom so.'

The afternoon had advanced; the breeze developed a cool edge. They moved inside to the warm cosiness of the kitchen, which looked the same to Pascaline as when she left for Australia with Felix. Pots and pans hung on the same hooks; the large scrubbed table and chairs were in the same place. Perhaps, a newer, larger model of TV sat at the end of the room. She wasn't sure.

'You should rest while I prepare dinner,' Ghislaine suggested as they carried her bags to her old room. It, too, looked much the same as she remembered it. She picked up the patchwork quilt and held it to her cheek as if cherishing a childhood under its warmth.

Back in the kitchen Ghislaine peeled potatoes and struggled with a paradox. She was enthusiastic in her welcome and pleased to have her daughter home but, underneath, she believed Pascaline could have been more resilient, stuck things out and stayed with Felix. She placed the potatoes in a casserole that she deposited in the oven. No way did she want to condemn her for leaving, no way did she wish to accuse Felix of neglect. She did not believe him to be a cruel man; in fact, he seemed a caring person, while she had no appreciation whatever of the pressure his enterprise might have placed on him. She turned to prepare the rest of the meal.

Pascaline seemed refreshed and relaxed after her rest, and together, they sat at the scrubbed table to enjoy her first meal back home.

Ghislaine was curious.

'Do you feel rested enough to talk?'

'Yes, Maman, I think so.'

'How did you find your Felix?'

Her daughter paused as she ate the last of her meal. She pushed her plate to one side and brushed her hair back from her eyes as if to see more clearly her former lover.

'At first, we passed happy hours together. He accepted me for what I was, and I accepted him. Gradually, the company came between us. The long hours he spent at work deepened the chasm. It became a gruelling and bewildering experience for me to see him spend so much energy devoted to his work that he had none left for me. When you love someone, you should not offer them second place.'

Tears returned to her cheeks. Ghislaine pushed her empty

plate aside and stretched across the table to take her daughter's hands.

'Perhaps I should have fought to win him back,' Pascaline continued. 'Different if my rival was another woman. I loved him and he still loved me, but our love got in the way and made me unhappier than when I was not in love. I failed to adapt to the demands of our life. I feel like I have returned from the ruins of the Promised Land.'

She sighed deeply as if she had just made a reluctant admission.

'He was an old-fashioned gentleman, not in the sense of being a man of property or of distinguished descent but in the sense of a gentleman of integrity who possessed strengths he himself did not know he had. He was intelligent, honest and compassionate. He tried to understand me and was willing to accept my faults, willing to look past everything and just love me for who I was. But he was humble and did not shout about his success or draw attention to himself.'

'What was the difficult part?' Ghislaine asked.

'The hard part was when I was alone, when all the memories hit me of how he used to be before the enterprise took him over. I missed his full attention, the excitement of having his arms around me. I missed how his touch could speak when words were not enough. I missed how he made me feel alive.'

'Letting go might sound easy,' said Ghislaine, speaking with a mother's wisdom, 'but it's one of the hardest things we will ever have to do. It takes an immense amount of courage to be able to say goodbye to someone who meant a lot to you.'

Tears rolled down both their cheeks. Ghislaine suffered at the story of distress unfolding before her. She looked across the table at a fragile daughter whom she needed to reassure.

'It was hard for you to let go of Felix, not that easy to move on. And starting over can be devastating. Finding someone new can be such a scary thing to go through. But, my dear, you could not keep holding on when it made you so sad, feeling like an old coat, waiting hanging off the hook. If you did, the misery would have built up in your heart and ran through your body until it ate you up. You had the strength to say goodbye.'

Together they left the table and placed their plates in the sink. Ghislaine washed while Pascaline dried and put items away. She was pleased she remembered where everything went. She was back in the swing of being home. Their conversation was more light-hearted as Ghislaine related local gossip about their neighbours.

They finished the tidying-up and sat in front of the television. Ghislaine fiddled with the remote, still getting used to its innumerable buttons. She turned the volume down and turned to Pascaline.

'You did not bring home your new friend?'

'My loneliness made me vulnerable to Jean-Claude. I realised he was a mistake even before we left Australia. He turned out to be an alpha male with a solid belief in his own worth, vain, obsessed with his appearance – one of those men who does not enjoy healthy food when he goes out to dinner because everything's bad for him. He drank too much of his own wine, I would say. His vanity is the first thing I think of when I recall his name. I left him in Paris. I know I am confused but one thing is clear: I will not contact Jean-Claude again.'

They watched the television, a cooking programme about cheesemaking. Ghislaine continued their conversation.

'I can speak to you from the heart, from the experience of your father leaving me. I'm not going to tell you tomorrow is another day, or that the sun will go on shining, or that there are plenty of fish in the sea. What I will say is this: it is okay to be hurting. I was hoping you would never go through the same pain as I did. What you are feeling is not only completely valid but necessary – because it makes you so much more a human. I cannot promise it will get better any time soon. I can only tell you that it will. For now, all you can do is take your time. Take all the time you need.'

'The confusing thing was finding someone I could not live without, and now living without him. I fear I will never see him again.'

'Maybe one day, you will run into him again. Maybe one day, you will be ready. You will be two people picking up right where you left off and you will be happy. Maybe one day. Somewhere, in France, in Australia, in the town, in the country, in the sun, in the rain. He will smile at you from afar and you will smile back. And you will just know. Like coming back home after a long trip away, after what seems a lifetime apart, maybe one day you will just know. You will just feel, and this time, you will be good enough to make it work. Good enough to stay together.'

Ghislaine paused to watch the next stage of cheesemaking. With the programme over, she hit the mute button and continued.

'If it's not your destiny to rediscover Felix, maybe you will find someone who contacts you in the middle of a busy day, not only when they are free. Maybe you will find someone who calls you beautiful even when you do not feel that way. Maybe you will find someone who calls you when they are around people, not only when they are lonely. Maybe you will find someone who sees you the best person even when you are feeling low. Maybe you will find someone who loves you in all your moods. Maybe he will say to you: "I want to love you in all the ways you have always wanted, the ways you have always deserved, in ways that leave no traces of doubt in your beautiful mind."'

'Maman, your message is so hopeful, so encouraging.' Pascaline wiped her eyes.

'Never let go of hope, my dear daughter. One day you will see that all has finally come together. If you pay attention to the pattern of your life you will realise everything works out. You have much to look forward to. Everything always takes you to a greater destination. You will grow and the things you think you cannot survive you somehow make it through. That is life. Always remember that.'

In bed that night, Pascaline lay under the quilt, made with love and tenderness by her grandmother, which had covered her slumbers for many years. She thought of the significant people in her life, especially her family. She thanked God for her loving and wise mother, for her brother Anton whom she would see the next day. She thought of her father, Pascal, whether she would see him or whether he was interested.

She thought of Felix. Should he remember her, it meant that he would carry something of who she was with him, that she had left some mark of who she was on him. It meant he could summon her back to his mind even though he was on the other side of the globe. It meant that if they ever met again, he would know her. It meant that he could still see her face, hear her voice and speak to her in his heart. Maybe she will wake up one morning with him beside her, spend her evenings looking at him across the table, sharing every mundane detail of her day and hearing every detail of his. Maybe she will fall asleep in his arms. Maybe. *Peut-être.*

She was tired and slept late. As she emerged out of her depths, her thoughts were of Anton. She would see him that day. She realised she was hearing his voice. Her brother was in the kitchen speaking to her mother. She had always been close to her brother and shared her secrets with him. Not that he always understood the workings of her female heart, but he listened attentively and made no judgments. She dressed quickly, emerged and they embraced each other with joy and laughter.

'I would love to stay with you, my children, but I must get to work. I will see you later.'

Now it was time for brother and sister to talk. Ghislaine had left a pot of coffee on the stove. Anton was tall and had the ropey build of a distance runner. He slid himself into the chair.

'I thought the Australian was a good guy.'

'He was. He is. I was in love with him.'

'What was it that made you feel this way?'

'I cannot really explain. I felt things with him that I had never felt before with anyone. When I was with him, I was the happiest. It was as simple as that.'

'Then why did you leave him? Why are you home?'

'I lost him to his work. He was a workaholic. I had to compete for his attention and that made me unhappy.'

Anton took a sip, removed his cap, and scratched his head.

'I can see that it is complex. Do not misunderstand me, Pascaline. I am pleased to see you home, but would you go back to him?'

'Not while the company is his mistress.'

Chapter 12

Felix was restless all night. Sharp violent nightmares that came in dreadful variations of the same theme broke his sleep. He couldn't even remember their detail – something about ornaments he'd brought home turning into monsters. He woke, ready to throw up at the thought of another working day. A vague apprehension seeped through him on the way to the office, located in St Leonards. He couldn't blame the road; the battle was no different to any other day, traffic that was barely crawling and sometimes less than that. The conference was supposed to fire him up, but he would have loved to detour up to the Blue Mountains for a day away from it all, or even the Snowy Mountains for a few days, except that the weather would be just as cold as Eildon. He tried to expel his anxiety. Begone! He had nothing to worry about. Cognitive behaviour therapy, a well-known therapy in the psychologist's toolbox, argued that humans feel the way they think. If he could change his thinking, he could generate more constructive feelings. He wasn't reassured. The change he needed was more profound.

He parked in the basement and took the lift to the sixth floor of the Sydney office of The Champions. He wasn't exactly ascending into heaven, more like purgatory, where he was expiating his cardinal sins – over ambition and neglect of Pascaline.

Natalie, the receptionist, wasn't at the front desk but his secretary, Janice, was arranging a vase of flowers.

'How was the weekend, boss?'

Janice always called him boss. She had been in Australia for years but retained her strong Welsh accent. She wasn't employed as such, but she was, by default, office manager, for she had the task of implementing his requests, which she did with gusto.

'Good. I caught up with my old mate, Ron Bell. Not sure if the meeting achieved much else though.'

They laughed as if the weekend was just another of head office's oddball requests. Their standing joke, *What's Melbourne up to now?* softened the demand. Their humour enabled him to offload his self-absorption. Time to dump his self-pity, time to remind himself he was the manager with two offices under his charge.

'I'm sure the consultants got a lot from the weekend. Meeting other consultants from interstate was worthwhile,' Felix said, feeling pleased. He was seeing positives already.

'Let's get down to work. Got anything urgent?' Felix asked.

'I think you should look at the cab charge dockets,' Janice replied.

Cab charge dockets were kept with the receptionist, Natalie, for consultants whenever they needed a taxi for company business. Natalie usually kept the dockets locked in her desk, although they were often left on the desk. Janice had the job of docket checking when the taxi company returned them at the end of the month. They were then passed on to Melbourne for payment.

'Some of the trips don't seem right.' Janice thumbed through her pile of dockets, pulled out two and laid them on the desk in front of her boss.

'Let me have a look.'

Until recently, there were no problems. Dockets were legitimate, signatures were legible, times recorded were within business hours, and the journeys were from the office to the city or inner city or reverse. Last month Janice noticed two dockets for late-night journeys with hard-to-decipher signatures, which would have been legitimate if a consultant were securing business after dining or drinking with a client. But no one knew anything.

'We'd better keep our eyes open for any others,' he had said to Janice, hoping that the strange dockets were a temporary aberration.

'Look at this one,' said Janice. 'The journey was late at night from Sydney airport to Penrith. That's over fifty kilometres. Here's another. Same journey, same indecipherable signature. I'm sure neither of these are legitimate.'

'How did this happen? Has someone stolen them? How many more are out there?' He sighed. He was about to face an unpleasant task. He wished for an intervention like a phone call from a new client with a truckload of potential business, which would offer a small relief in which to luxuriate and remove, for the time being, the arduous task from his schedule. But for the moment, the phones were silent.

'I better talk to Natalie. See what she knows. Ask her to come into my office.'

'Sure, boss.'

Janice said nothing else. She was confident Natalie knew a lot and her boss would suss out the truth.

The expression on Natalie's face confirmed that she knew tonnes. She was a sweet girl, chatty, easy to look at, had a lovely smile and liked to help. A graduate of June-Dally Watkins' Business Finishing School (or similar institution), her deportment was well suited to the role of receptionist.

'Natalie, sit down. I won't beat around the bush. There's been irregularities with the cab charge dockets. I'm wondering if you know anything about them.'

'No!' She turned her eyes, avoiding his direct gaze. 'How do you mean?'

She knew exactly what he meant. She had the look of guilt. He did not answer her question, said nothing and stared at her. She avoided his gaze, looked up to the ceiling and closed her eyes. He waited for his silence torture to work. When she opened them, it was clear they were glistening. A combination of fear and embarrassment had commandeered her body and changed her usual office-hours demeanour into that of a frightened young woman. Only after a tear or two had fallen on her cheeks was she able to speak.

'I only borrowed some vouchers because I had no money to get home and I was going to pay you back.'

'What about the ones from last month? They were late at night.'

She thought for a moment. 'My boyfriend and I were out at a hotel, and we had a bit to drink. I had the vouchers in my bag, so we used them to get home.'

'What about these ones for Penrith?'

'My boyfriend took a couple of the vouchers. I didn't want to give them to him, but he knew I had them.'

'Do you still have any?'

'No!'

Something about the way she answered made him ask,

'Are you certain?'

She did not answer but responded in lieu with more tears. He didn't expect a confession so early and at first was not sure where the conversation should go. Now he was certain.

'Where are the vouchers, Natalie?' he said quietly.

Natalie continued to weep.

'In my handbag,' she sobbed.

'Give them to Janice. I might have forgotten about things, Natalie, and just got you to pay back the company, but you've lied. I'll have to ask you to leave. You'd better collect your things. Janice will see you out.'

He felt like his dad, the schoolmaster, admonishing and expelling a naughty schoolgirl. He rang Janice on the intercom and asked her to come in.

'Natalie is leaving the company. She has cab vouchers to give you. Will you help her to collect her things and see her out?'

Janice nodded. In less time than it took to remove a nasty pebble from her shoe, she supervised Natalie's departure and escorted her out of the office, ensuring she didn't take anything else.

'The girls are saying that Natalie boasted about taking the vouchers,' Janice said after completing her task.

'I'd better ring Melbourne to get them to pay out Natalie and subtract what she owes us.'

Felix spoke to Peter. He guessed his reaction.

'Your security up there must be slack. Leaving taxi dockets lying around. How many more are missing?' His reaction didn't surprise. In fact, any other reply would have astonished him.

He sighed. He didn't know.

'I'm responsible for every little thing that goes on, do you reckon? Even the turds in the toilet?'

'You're the branch manager.'

He called in Janice and dictated a memo for all staff about cab charge dockets. Regrettably, things could not be as relaxed as he would like; security had to be tightened and from now on Janice would be responsible. Consultants could get them from her. He knew she would subject requests to scrutiny. She would take it on herself to question consultants on the nature of their trip and about which client they were seeing. He asked her to record all the details for later reconciliation with the returned dockets.

He bet Viviana would be the first to object. Within the hour she, a regular user of taxis, bounced into his office. Fortunately, the door was open, otherwise she would have gone straight through the panels.

'Who does that Janice think she is?' she demanded. 'She's asking me all sorts of questions about where I'm going and who I'm seeing. I don't report to her. She's only a secretary.'

Viviana was once a secretary herself in this office. She had sought promotion from a previous manager and was the only consultant without a tertiary qualification. She was conscious of her status and that she received the respect due to her.

'We've had to tighten security, I'm afraid.'

'How am I going to service my clients if I can't have access to them?'

He ignored her lack of logic.

'Easy! I'm sure they'll manage.'

Having made her protest, a frustrated Viviana bounced out of his office, with the same mannerism she used when avoiding him at Sunday's breakfast. Janice could have been more diplomatic. She was a straight shooter, abrasive sometimes, and there was a continuing simmering tension between her and the girls of the office staff. Felix inherited her from the previous manager, Horsey, who hired her because of her direct manner. He believed the office girls had become slack and too emotional and someone was needed to straighten them out. From the first day, war had simmered between Janice and the other girls and occasionally boiled over into tears and outbursts. Viviana had remained aloof but now found herself embroiled, having to negotiate with Janice.

It occurred to him that some people in the office might think him brave for standing up to Viviana, known for her anti-management sentiments. She belonged to that group of employees who believe their manager is an idiot. Their contempt allows them to continue working day after day – a novel thought that dissolved into a yawn just as Yvonne, who oversaw the test room, approached his open office door and told him there was no water in the kitchen or toilets. Water supply was out of his control but, as more staff informed him of its absence, he needed to do something. He rang the manager of the building.

'The water had to be turned off because of work being done on the mains outside the building.'

'When will it be turned on?'

'Later today.'

'A pity we weren't told earlier. We could have planned.'

He didn't like these petty unpredictable and avoidable irritants. Geoff Pepperstone, who had been so absorbed in his work that he was unaware of the water crisis, detoured into his office on a trip back from the men's, with the old news that the toilets wouldn't flush. He surprised gentle Geoff with his reaction.

'God. I really *am* responsible for turds in the toilet.'

'Nick Featherby wants to talk to you,' said Janice later that day.

'Fine, tell him to come in.'

'He's a lovely man,' said Janice. 'Everyone likes him.'

'Particularly the girls. I've seen him do some flirting.'

'He's harmless.'

They both laughed as Janice left to deliver the message. The water was restored, the turds were on their way to the sewers and no one else complained about having to ask Janice for cab vouchers. Nick was the training consultant and had been successful running the training division as a one-man band. Felix liked Nick, not only because he had done an excellent job, but he had an outgoing manner, was the girls' darling, got on well with the clients and was able not only to run the training programmes but to get the business as well.

'You're a bit formal, aren't you, Nick, asking for an interview? Everyone else just walks in.' Nick was an uncomplicated young man with no agendas or axes to grind.

'I wanted to make it formal, Felix. Business has been quiet in the training area,' he said. 'I come from the west, you know, and I'd like to go back. There's a demand for training over there, though, and I was wondering if there was an opportunity to transfer to the Perth office.'

'You're right, Nick. Training has been slow.'

Nick had been kept occupied by interstate work. Felix had loaned Nick's services to other states, including Western

Australia, where there had been strong demand from the mining companies.

'I'd be sorry to lose you. I'll raise the matter at the next management meeting.'

'I'm pleased Nick came to me,' he explained later to a curious Janice. 'He's been underemployed and going through the motions of appearing busy. It wouldn't be long before Peter pointed his bony figure at the reduced income from training.'

'I think he wants to go back to the west because his old girlfriend is still on the scene. The one he left to come to Sydney.'

'Have you ever met her?'

'No, but he's talked about her.'

Andrew rang. Felix was apprehensive about taking Andrew's calls, preferring to call him back with some notion of what he wanted. That way he had time to develop counter arguments if his idea was hair-brained.

'I'm going to try out the PR consultant, Jon Christie, and see how effective he is. I've organised for a media release to go out nationally tomorrow morning.'

'What about?'

'We should give our vocational guidance service a boost. I'm going to say that the schools offer poor career guidance to their pupils and that they leave school without any idea of what they should do.'

'But I thought schools did a reasonable job.'

'That is not the point. We need to say something controversial that's going to attract the media's attention.'

'Whether we believe it or not? Whether it's true or not?'

'It's just a hook to get the media interested.' Andrew was

impatient; Felix could be dim-witted sometimes. 'Can't you see the point? The idea is to get them involved, get some cover and we can follow up with our own advertising. This will be a national programme.'

Felix was not dim-witted about Andrew's impatience. 'You're asking me to do it. And when you're asking me to do it, you're telling me to do it. Right?'

'Exactly. I want Sydney's cooperation.'

Andrew had pulled rank. Felix was uneasy as he replaced the phone, annoyed with himself for not taking a strong enough stand. He would have to speak to the media about an issue that was barely credible and that he believed was untrue. Another joy of being manager!

The following morning, Jon Christie rang.

'I've just issued a media release to all the newsrooms and chiefs of staff in Melbourne, Sydney and Brisbane.'

'What does it say?' an apprehensive Felix asked.

'That the schools have failed their students by not providing adequate career guidance.'

'Who's the author?'

'For Melbourne, it's Andrew. It's you in Sydney and Sam for Brisbane.'

His heart jumped and his stomach stirred. He doubly regretted failing to take a stand against Andrew.

'You should expect some response later this morning.'

The first response came within the hour.

'This is the Triple M newsroom,' the caller said. 'We received your news release, and we would like to interview you. Your telephone call will be recorded. Is that okay?'

'Yes.' Underneath it was anything but okay. Fear competed with anxiety to swamp out his confidence.

'Would you mind waiting a moment until Danny Crute is ready?'

'Sure.' Secretly, he hoped the lady would press the wrong button and cut him off.

Danny Crute was a popular radio announcer and news reader. Although Felix waited no more than two minutes, the time stretched into eternity. His anxiety was getting out of control by the time he heard the familiar smooth voice of Danny Crute.

'Are the schools doing enough for their students in the way of career guidance? I have on line one man who believes they are not. Felix Schmidt who has had many years' experience in guiding young people into worthwhile careers says that the schools are not providing enough direct guidance.' Danny's voice grew in volume as the telephone line was switched on

'Good morning, Felix.'

'Hello, Danny,' he replied, trying to sound relaxed and confident, ultra-conscious that he was either on air or that his voice was being recorded.

'Would you tell our listeners why you believe the schools are not doing enough? At the school where my kids go, they have a library full of information about jobs.'

He had to be quick on his feet.

'That may be right,' he said, 'but the kids don't know what they should be looking at. They might have plenty of information, but they get lost because if you don't know what you want to do, you don't know where to look. All the children should receive testing on their abilities, interests and temperament and that will tell them the type of careers they're suited to. That way they can narrow down their search and save a lot of time and energy. A wrong career choice can result in years of frustration and unhappiness.'

'Does your organisation provide that type of service?'

'Certainly! We have tested thousands of young people and put them on the right path to a career that's suited to them.'

'There you are, listeners.'

Felix was conscious of a lowered volume. Danny Crute had finished his interview, switched Felix off, left him suspended in the void and had returned to his audience. Felix was satisfied he had managed to spew out the company patter, but he read into Danny Crute's comment the radio station's awareness that they had been conned into promoting the company's business. Free airtime. He felt all the more hypocritical.

Shortly after, a breathless Viviana rushed into his office.

'I just heard you on the radio.' She was quite excited. 'I was just driving into the building, and I heard you being interviewed, and I thought, *Wow, that's Felix.*'

'How did it come across?' he asked.

'I didn't take it all in. It came on so suddenly. Something about career guidance. You sounded so convincing. I'm impressed.'

That's not how he felt. Viviana was usually his best (or worst?) critic. This was a rare event, one of the few occasions that she had praised him.

'Thank you very much. At least one listener heard me.'

One of the girls had a Walkman and listened to the news broadcasts of that radio station for the remainder of the day, but his voice was heard no more.

'Something more newsworthy must have come up and pushed you off the airways,' Janice said as if to console him.

He was pleased that no one else was hearing his lies. He asked Janine to screen his calls, but shortly after lunch she interrupted him.

'Kel Pringle's on the phone.'

His stomach took a tumble. Kel Pringle was one of Sydney's talkback radio hosts, a shock jock notorious for his cutting tongue and ability to crucify his interviewee, particularly politicians. Listeners loved his style and ratings were high. Felix knew that he broadcast in the mornings so he would have been off the air at this stage.

'Kel Pringle here. I got your press release this morning, but it came too late to include in the programme.'

'That's disappointing,' he lied. His relief eased the tension in the muscles on his neck.

'It would have been an interesting story and we could have had quite a talk,' Kel Pringle continued. 'Tell your PR people they should get their press release in early.'

'*What about tomorrow?*' he should have said, but he was silent, happy to escape the clutches of Kel's inquisition.

The working day was almost over and, there were no more calls from the media. He was on the point of congratulating himself for having escaped when Janice came through.

'It's the ABC.'

'This is the ABC newsroom.' The caller sounded a young research assistant.

'We have this press release from you that the schools are not doing their job in offering career guidance for their students. Do you have any research?'

The company patter did not provide for this question. 'But so many parents tell us how unhappy they are.'

'I see. Are you a company that provides career guidance services?'

'Yes, our company has tested thousands of young people and put them on a path that's suited to them.'

'I see. And do you have any research on your effectiveness?'

'We have many satisfied clients.'

'I see. Thank you.'

She hung up. He felt classic female passive aggression pulsing down the line. He guessed he would not be featured on the ABC news that night.

There were no further calls from the media. Andrew rang at the end of the week.

How did the PR campaign go?'

'No good,' Felix replied, trying to sound disappointed. 'There were no inquiries regarding career guidance services this week, so I reckon, as far as Sydney is concerned, the PR programme has been a dismal failure and the fees for your PR consultant wasted money.'

'It's a different story in Melbourne and Brisbane.' Andrew was bursting with enthusiasm to tell his story. '*The Herald* sent out a journalist and a photographer. The story is on today's front page. I'll send you up a copy.'

'There couldn't have been any other news. Just joking! That's impressive.' Underneath he was anything but impressed. He had to feign enthusiasm. Face to face, his smile would have given him away.

'What about Brisbane?' He tried to sound interested.

'Sam wouldn't have anything to do with it.'

'Why was that?'

'Something to do with morals and principles. I couldn't make it out.'

Felix knew exactly what had bugged Sam. Except that Sam had the balls to voice his protest. Andrew continued.

'David Hardcastle disagreed with Sam and decided to do something when he took calls from Channel 7 and Channel 9.' David was one of the Brisbane consultants. 'He finished appearing on the current affairs programme of both. Positive results in Melbourne and Brisbane and a little bit in Sydney. That's what I call a success.'

'Let's see if we get inquiries about career guidance.'

Felix could be just as convincing as any if he believed in what he was saying, otherwise he was doing a con job.

He hoped Andrew didn't get any other crazy ideas about PR.

Chapter 13

Andrew had no more crazy ideas about PR because other problems distracted him. The company's results took a dive and August figures were well below budget throughout the country. Pharoah's famine was on the way. Difficult for Peter to point the finger at any state at the monthly managers' meeting; he pointed at everyone.

'The company won't last long if these results persist,' said Peter.

'What did Rob and I do in the early days when the figures were down?'

Sid had flown out of his retirement bearing a tropical tan from the warm north to chair the meeting in a bitterly cold Melbourne. Life on his avocado farm was doing him no harm; he smoked one cigarette and one only during the meeting. In contrast, Rob, still amid the turmoil, lit one Camel from the other. Sid told his usual stories. They'd heard them before. Some were like glasses of wine from good old bottles in the cellar. They were rich in colour, wisdom, and worth savouring. Others were of indifferent vintage.

Sid didn't wait for a reply to his rhetorical question. 'We'd get out and visit clients and drum up business. Didn't we, Rob.' Between puffs, a head-nodding Rob agreed. 'That's what you blokes have got to do. You've got to be proactive. If the business doesn't come to you, you've got to go out and get it. Get off your arses and get out there among the clients.'

'Of course, we do that,' protested Sam. 'But the country's

going through a credit squeeze, thanks to our federal government.'

'The clients aren't hiring anyone,' Ron added. 'They're getting rid of their people.'

'Rob and I struck a credit squeeze just after we started, and we got through that. There were only two of us then. How many in the company now?'

Sid hadn't mentioned that overheads were low then. They survived their bleak times by only paying their office staff and not taking any drawings for themselves. In these modern times, the families were not prepared to finance the company anymore and had been regularly withdrawing surplus funds.

Everyone around the table knew the company had to rely on its own earnings. Easy enough in the good times, the situation was changing with the prospect of bad times looming. In contrast to the early days, current fixed overheads were massive with a staff approaching one hundred and offices in five states. Two men in a small boat can be quite versatile and flexible and change direction easily. One hundred people in a large ship are more cumbersome and, although changes can occur, they are slower to manoeuvre. There was only one way to lighten the load – to reduce costs and throw a few people overboard.

'Any more business?' Sid asked.

'Yes,' answered Felix. 'I have a request from Nick. As you know, he is our training consultant. He has done an exceptional job. Lately, he has been doing work in the other states. His hometown is Perth. He is interested in a transfer back to the west.'

'It was great, Felix, that you made Nick available for other parts of the company,' said Andrew. 'But that's dried up now. Do you have enough work for Nick?'

'Afraid not. He is underemployed at the moment and if requests from other states have dried up, he'd be twiddling his thumbs.'

'What has Ron got to say about that?' asked Andrew.

'I'd love to have Nick,' replied Ron. 'He's a lovely fellow. But it would be hard to cover his costs. When conditions get tough, training is the first to get the axe. I have had two cancellations this month already.'

'Looks like we don't have a job for Nick,' said Andrew turning to Felix.

Felix was left speechless. His attempts to save good-hearted Nick had floundered. He could have been angry with Ron but accepted he was a realist. He had to be a realist, too.

'Does anyone have anything else to say?' asked Sid.

No comment. Their silence echoed around the room, pregnant with meaning that shouted the company was facing a grim future.

'We've had it good for so long. It's easy to be a manager in good times. You can afford to carry some fat. But when times get rough, you have to make tough decisions. You have to look at your staff and weed out those who aren't performing.'

'Easy for you Sid.' Sam was the spokesman. 'You'll be disappearing back into the wilderness among the avocado trees, leaving the dirty work to the rest of us.'

'You're the managers.'

Felix found relief in leaving the smoke-filled room and breathing in fresh air. Even the cold Melbourne winter was welcome, just to get away from The Champions. A couple of beers on the plane back to Sydney did not relax him. He did not want to think of the unpleasant task ahead, but Sid's phrase about making tough decisions would not be dismissed.

Back in Sydney, he procrastinated. The sword was still suspended. He had anticipated that Nick might want to know the outcome of the management meeting discussion and had expected him to ask to see him. But Nick had concentrated on keeping himself busy. Felix was grateful that he hadn't approached him. The fateful meeting was delayed.

Andrew rang.

'Have you spoken to Nick yet?'

'No.'

'Has he got any work on?'

'No.'

'Or any prospects?'

'No.'

'You'll have to let him go.'

'Could we employ him elsewhere?' This time he had to put up a fight.

'He's got no other skills. He's never done recruitment and you've already more than enough consultants in that area.'

This was truer than Andrew realised. At one time, he'd discussed with Nick broadening his skills and getting some experience in recruitment, but Nick had told him he was not interested. He wanted to further his career in training.

Silly Nick, Felix thought. If he had agreed to that career management suggestion, they would not be having this meeting. He had no difficulty in sacking Natalie, for she had been dishonest and had made him look slack. But Nick was a good man, a decent bloke who had performed well.

With a heavy heart as if he'd been ordered to carry out an innocent's execution, he called Nick into his office. In he came, bright and breezy, an expectant smile broadening his features.

'I've been winding up things here so I can get over to Perth quickly,' he said.

'Nick, there's no point in pussyfooting around. I'm afraid there's no job for you in Perth. We don't have a job for you here, either.'

Nick's smile vanished. Stunned, a raucous voice protested in his mind, but he said nothing and stared at his boss who filled the silence with babble about the company needing to cut down on costs. The major costs were in salaries and the only way to reduce salaries was to reduce the people. The words poured out of his mouth like vomit. Nick wasn't sure what he was saying. He was digesting the bad news and a feeling he'd been taken to with a whip. The stream dried up and Felix sat back waiting for a reaction. Nick was waiting for him to finish. He was shaken.

'I understand what you're saying,' he said eventually. 'The last thing I expected. It's like you've belted me in the guts.'

Felix winced inwardly.

'I'll organise with Melbourne to give you three months' salary retrenchment. Hopefully, you'll find yourself a job in the meantime.'

Conventional company wisdom dictated that Nick should leave immediately. That had been the practice in other partings. But they had been for incompetence. Dismissals had been carried out in anger. He could remember the passion with which Sid had terminated earlier consultants for non-performance as if he had to generate some heat to justify his intentions. People were turned out immediately, keys removed, accompanied to the door in case they took precious client files or tried in retribution to sabotage the company on the way. But here he was terminating Nick, a good performer, in cold blood, the first retrenchment in the company's history.

'You can take your time to leave, Nick, to get yourself organised.'

Nick thought for a moment.

'I'll leave on Friday,' he replied. The day was Tuesday. 'Would my money be ready by then?'

'I'll make sure it is.'

With a bad taste in his mouth, he rang Andrew to let him know the deed had been done.

'Three months is too generous. We won't be able to afford that if we let anyone else go. One month's enough.'

'I've already committed the company.' Felix was annoyed that his concern for Nick was questioned. He wanted to do justice and show respect for Nick, caught up in a situation not of his making. Andrew did not override his decision. As Branch Manager he had more power than he realised. Peter was equally critical when he rang to ensure Nick's money would be ready.

'You've set a precedent which will come back to haunt you.'

Peter knew that others would have to be thrown overboard.

The news of Nick's departure spread through the office like a wildfire, affecting everyone with a fear for their own job.

'I want to reassure everyone,' Felix wrote in a memo, 'that if we can work hard at getting in business, we can avert any downturn.' His reassurances sounded hollow to himself and everyone else. The economy of the country was beyond their control. If the government had raised interest rates to curb inflation, curtailed investment, created a credit squeeze and sent business confidence diving, what could they do against such an enormous tide? Like every other business in the country, they would be caught up in the tsunami and left floundering. The puny efforts of David were no match against the force of this Goliath.

In memo after memo, he encouraged – no, implored – his consultants to get out into the market, to visit all their clients and anyone who was a potential client. He asked them to keep a record of all their contacts, either phone calls or visits, so that he could produce statistics at the next management meeting to prove Sydney had not been sitting on its arse, wringing its hands like misery guts, waiting for doom to overcome it. No! They were doing all that they could to prepare for the coming siege, arming the catapults and boiling the oil in anticipation of the enemies' onslaughts. He got lost in his maze of metaphors.

Despite all this desperate frenzy, there was little immediate result. No consultant returned to the office, jubilant, ready to dance on the desktop, chanting the theme song, *We Are the Champions*, with an armful of recruitment assignments. Instead, they returned with variations of the same dreary message: 'Mate, we'd give you the business if we had it. But we haven't got it. We can't recruit. In fact, we will have to cut back our own staff.'

'Sometimes, you have to wait for your marketing to produce results.' Felix tried to reassure his disappointed consultants. But it could be too late. The citadel may have been overrun; the sword may have already fallen; the boat might have been emptied of more bodies to save it from floundering before their prospecting produced some gold. He was running out of metaphors.

In the meantime, a sympathetic office farewelled Nick at the Great Northern Hotel. Nick was a popular member of staff. Everyone moved the short distance at the close of business on Friday. Felix was wondering whether he should attend, as his own hand had swung the sword that cut Nick off from the company. He wanted to farewell Nick, too. Nick did not spend his last days bad-mouthing the company. He had accepted his fate and made no further attempt to bargain. Three months' salary softened the blow. Felix decided to go even though he would feel uncomfortable. Besides, not to go would be a worse outcome as it would make him appear heartless. So, feeling like a murderer attending a party for his victim, he made his way a little later than the others. The party was in full swing, and he felt as if he had walked in on a wake, except that the dear departed was not lying in a coffin but was standing by the bar, wearing a fixed grin, his tall, slim body swaying like a reed in the water and held vertical by the solid wooden bar. He took a moment to drink in the unambiguously inebriated Nick. With a mixture of emotions, he approached Nick. He wanted to express his sorrow at doing what he had done, but instead, over the din of conversation he asked:

'How are you getting home, Nick?'

'I'll get a cab.' Nick took a sip of his beer, licked the foaming residue off his lips, leaned forward, grinned even more fixedly, took Felix's hand and grasped it firmly. He had to shout to make himself heard.

'I want to tell you, Felix. I couldn't have been sacked by a nicer bloke.'

Nick's comment made him wince. He did not accept himself as a 'nice bloke'. It would have been more bearable if the alcohol had released pent-up anger, and Nick had called him a 'bastard'. He felt powerless against Nick's benign acceptance of his lot; he was turning the other cheek. Surrounded by the laughter, shouting and drinking of his staff, who were relaxing from the strain of the last few days, he felt isolated. He wanted to involve himself in the forced gaiety, to get pissed with Nick and the rest of them, to curse the government for its incompetence, to blame the company for insufficient prudent planning for hard times, Peter for his turning the company into an accounting exercise, the families for milking the company of funds, etc. But he couldn't hide behind Andrew and say it was his decision. He was the company. He was management. As a prisoner of his ambitions, he had aspired to this role, but management was not what it was cracked up to be. He was not enjoying the job. What the role forced him to do was not what he wanted. He wanted to be a 'nice bloke', to be sociable and friendly, like back in the days when he was one of the boys. But now, he had to be the 'bastard' and not get too involved because he might have to inflict more painful decisions on people whom he liked and cared for, such as lining them up against the wall for rounds of job cuts, wave after wave, and, because the cuts had been too savage, make those who survive do all the work of the people he'd just fired. He could no longer be the 'nice bloke'. He loathed himself for what the job had forced him to do. He had climbed the ladder to nowhere.

'I wish you well, Nick.' He shook his hand firmly, then turned and left. His head was spinning as he walked out of the Great Northern, and he felt moisture rising in his eyes. He could not let his staff see him with tears. He could not surrender to his anxiety. He had to set an example of resolve for the coming battles, but he was fearful he could weaken and go down under this pressure and be destroyed. As he walked back to the office along the highway, thunderous with peak-hour traffic, he was feeling worthless and struggled to muster a tiny grain of self-respect. The traffic noise did nothing to clear his brains.

Glad it was the weekend, he passed the evening watching the football and, to add to the misery, his team was slaughtered. He needed a few drinks to deaden his wretchedness. As he shuffled off to bed, he thanked God he wasn't in the army. If he were ordered to shoot some poor bastard, he'd probably refuse and they'd stick him in front of the firing squad, too.

Chapter 14

Felix woke up Saturday morning feeling mediocre, but his head was clear enough to look around. How can you live somewhere and not notice your surroundings? He viewed the place as if for the first time. His eyes saw the paint peeling off the ceiling and his ears heard his neighbours in loud conversation through the thin walls. His nostrils detected the odours of cooking and dust that were once part of the background. His memory recalled the smell following a storm that reminded him of mushrooms. In this part of Sydney, he could have had harbour views except the windows faced the walls of the adjacent building. If that was not enough, the windows had the benefit of facing south and never saw the sun. Because he had been so involved with ambition, with work and its dramas, he had not thought about his home. His unit was part of the grey background of a life not worth the bother. Now the defects he had endured for far too long stood out with startling intensity like the proverbial prick on a skinny dog. The three-storey building that housed his unit was one of the blocks constructed in the thirties. Built of red bricks rounded at the corners, it was crying out, almost screaming, for tender loving care in the form of refurbishment, or else waiting for a hungry developer to flatten it and start again.

It was time for renewal. He once regarded his dwelling with indifference, as if where he lived did not matter. The catharsis of sacking Nick cleared his mind, the shades fell away from his eyes and the plugs dropped out of his ears. He disliked this unit. He had to do something. He got up late but early enough to walk up the hill to busy Military Road to catch the real estate agent, Otto, before he found useful things to do.

'Your lease is up, Felix. Do you want to renew?'

'No. I need a change. Something more modern, with a better outlook, even a view.'

'You might be in luck,' Otto replied, looking up his lists. 'Here's one in Neutral Bay. A new building. A tad more expensive than what you've been paying. Do you want to look?'

'Why not?'

As soon as they arrived at the address, it was not difficult to see why the rental was in another class. The unit Otto showed him was at the end of the seventh floor, jutting out from the building like the prow of a ship, windows facing north and a balcony overlooking the harbour. The light feel of the unit was warm and inviting, such a contrast to the dull, heavy atmosphere of his current abode. The lift was a bonus, removing the burden of carrying everything, yes everything, up flights of stairs.

The bad news was it was expensive, but the good news, he could afford it. It was time to spend a little money on himself. He was earning an excellent salary. For how long, he did not know, but for now, it would be nice to come home to a happy place to relax after the turmoil of work.

'I'll take it.'

'You've made a particularly good decision,' was Otto's predictable reply, happy to see these units move so quickly, another profitable Saturday arvo. 'These units won't last long. There's a lady moving into the unit next door today. This is the last on this floor. All the units on the other floors are taken. Most of the purchasers intend to live in them, not too many for lease.'

As they walked along the corridor, they met the lady in question. Her resemblance to Pascaline struck Felix – same height, same slim build, same dark hair and complexion, except that her hair was shorter. She was carrying two shopping bags, evidence of a visit to the supermarket. She put them down to get to her key. The agent stopped.

'Let me help you, Caroline,' said the agent as he took her bags. 'How are you settling in?'

'Fine, Otto. I'm stocking up the pantry,' replied Caroline. She found her key, opened the door and stood on her threshold, ready to chat.

'Caroline, meet your neighbour, Felix. He's just taken up the lease next door.'

'Pleased to meet you.' They exchanged greetings and shook hands. You would call it a formal meeting, not too gushy but at the same time, warm with the possibility of further developments. She would be a pleasant neighbour to ask for a cup of sugar.

What a contrast! He did not even know his present neighbours, though he could hear a lot of their living. They might nod to each other on the stairs but never any real communication.

Saturday night he stayed inside, thinking about his new home. In his mind's eye, he planned the layout of the floor. He imagined the furnishings. He would toss out the crap surrounding him and buy something stylish. It would be a place he could really call home and invite people to visit. It would reflect his success. Indeed, although he did not feel it at the time, to the outsider, he had a successful career.

Apart from his house hunting, Felix did precious little that weekend. He spent the time reading the newspapers, both the Saturday and Sunday editions, hundreds of pages and containing an encyclopaedia of information. He usually gave the paper no more than a cursory look, delving no further than the business pages and the job advertisements to see how the company's job ads were placed and what the opposition were up to. As well as the general news, he read every section, even the entertainment pages. He found himself reading film reviews, something he had not bothered with for years. He could not remember the last time he went to a movie. In their Melbourne days, Pascaline saw many films, in French, usually on her own. She would ask him to come, but something always cropped up. She used to tell him the story outline and he would listen with half of his mind, the other half dwelling on the latest company drama. Once she realised he was not listening, she gave up, and when he did ask about the film (which was rare) she'd reply with few words.

One review took his attention. *The Last Days of Chez Nous* dealt with a relationship on the rocks. Its story resembled his own, except that the husband was French and the wife Australian. He was interested in comparing this floundering relationship with his. The reviewer suggested its distribution would be limited to the art-house theatres. He checked the film guide and found it was featured at Walker Street Cinema, not far at all, close enough to walk if you had an hour to spare. What better way to while away a Sunday?

He chose the late afternoon session as he did not want a

late night. The cinema was small and less than half full. The film followed the emotional life of Beth and focused on the interpersonal life of the people who lived in her house, an inner-city Sydney terrace. These included JP, Beth's French husband, Vicki, Beth's younger sister, just returned from overseas, Annie, Beth's daughter from another marriage, and Tim, a young boarder. JP has an affair with Vicki. Beth ends her previously close friendship with Vicki, and the film ends with JP and Vicki moving out. The film emphasises the fragile and changing nature of relationships, how people relate, how they can be both cruel and kind. What was obscure in his understanding of his relationship was so clear on the screen. It made him realise how fragile his own relationship really was when he thought it was solid. It made him realise how cruel he was with his neglect and indifference to Pascaline's needs. He was cruel in failing to give her his time. The omission was so simple, but the outcome was profound.

He left the cinema in a reflective mood, prepared for a guilty walk home in the cool night. He glanced at the faces of the emerging patrons. One girl looked like Caroline. He was about to let her go but as she moved to pass, he realised it *was* Caroline, and she was on her own.

'Caroline!'

She turned towards him, expressionless. She did not recognise him.

'It's Felix, soon to be your neighbour. We met yesterday.'

'Of course! Sorry, Felix. I was deep in thought about the film.'

'There was a lot to think about.'

The last time he thought about Caroline he was keen to

know her better. An opportunity even Blind Freddie would not miss was presenting itself. No need to guess what came next.

'It's not late. Have you got time for a cup of coffee? We could chat about the film.'

He was no film connoisseur, but he was sure they would find something to talk about. He should shut up and let her talk. He waited for her answer. She took her time.

'Yes, Felix. I've got time.'

In far less time than it took to be seated in a bar and buy the girl next to you a drink, they were opposite each other in a quiet little coffee shop.

'How are you settling into your new unit?'

'Fine. Everything's in a mess, but I'll get there. I just felt like unwinding and getting out of the place for a break. I thought I'd see a film.'

'Do you get to the movies regularly, Caroline?'

'Yes, I'm a film buff. I find them a good way to relax. What about yourself?'

'I haven't been to the movies for ages. I can't remember the last time.'

'That's interesting. It's not a film that would appeal to everyone. It's a women's film. Men like action. Why choose *The Last Days of Chez Nous*?'

'I read the review in the paper. It sounded like my own situation.'

'You've got me curious now. How so?'

'In the film the husband was French. My girlfriend was French. Their marriage went on the rocks, and so did our relationship.'

'I'm sorry to hear that. Where's she now?'

'Back in France. There were differences in our situation. JP mentioned that the two languages, French and English, were a barrier. He couldn't even pronounce Beth's name properly. The French say *t* for *th*. The two languages made no difference to us. We were fluent in both, and we'd slip from one to another.'

'Did you live in France for a while?'

'Yes. I was walking in France and then went to Spain to follow the old pilgrimage route, the Camino, to Santiago. I met her one extra-sweltering hot day and somehow, we stuck to each other.'

'I'd love to do the Camino one day.'

'She came back to Australia with me, and we lived in Melbourne. She decided to go back to France, and since then I've worked in Perth and here in Sydney. The company sent me.' He had been talking too much. 'What about yourself? How did you find the film?'

'I liked it. I like the arty films and this one's set in Sydney.'

'Yes, there were plenty of scenes with the Harbour Bridge in the background.'

'I liked the way it went into the relationships between all the characters. I liked the way it dealt with everyday things, but it was subtle and at a deeper level. I liked the way it focused on the darker side of relationships.'

They finished their coffee.

'Well, I'd better be getting home. I've a busy day tomorrow, and you have, too, I'm sure. Thank you for the coffee, Felix. When are you moving in?'

'In the next couple of weeks. My lease is up on my current place,'

'When you settle in, I'll have you in for a welcoming cup of coffee.'

'I'll look forward to that.'

Talking to Caroline reminded him of Pascaline, he reflected on his walk back home along the darkened street. Would he ever get Pascaline back? The letters that she continued to write confused him. She was telling him that she was able to find a satisfactory life without him, but they gave him hope that someday they might be able to talk. Hope was preventing him from committing himself to another relationship. The absence of a commitment had left him a *hollow man, headpiece filled with straw.* The Champions had anesthetised him to his deep personal issues. He had lost sight of who he truly was. The freedom that he had given himself over this weekend had reignited his intense feelings of loss. He was grieving for Pascaline and blamed himself for losing her. She used to say he was once in love with her, but the company became his lover. Even if he were in love with the company, the company was not in love with him, forcing him to make harsh decisions about good people.

As he climbed the Cremorne hill to his unit, the company's dire situation emerged from its temporary hiding place and resumed its place at the top of his thoughts. The young chap walking down the hill on the opposite side of the street heard his sigh and looked across.

Chapter 15

As he lay in bed that night, Felix tried not to think of Monday morning, but of the pleasant weekend. Deciding to move was a definite respite, but he needed more. Sacking Nick took more out of him than was healthy. If he were to survive the coming months, he needed to calm his agitated spirit. Physical activity was one way. Pascaline believed if you wanted to finish the long haul, you needed to look after yourself. She once quoted an old French proverb: *Qui veux voyager loin garder sa monture* (He who wishes to travel far spares his mount). Two options. Option One: he could join the stream of early morning joggers flowing through the streets, but from their strained faces, none enjoyed themselves. Poor beggars. It wasn't hard to see the art of jogging added to the strain they were trying to relieve. They were heart attacks waiting to happen. That was all he needed, a cardiac arrest to do a proper job of stuffing up his life. Second option: he had admired the local swimming pool but had never plunged into its waters. Never a better time. A bonus would be going to bed early. That would cut down on the grog.

No time like the present. So, Monday morning he rose early and headed for the pool. Surprised how many people rose from their beds to take in an early morning swim, he would have preferred the freedom of a lane to himself as he was a slow swimmer. He hoped to travel the length of the pool leisurely, as opposed to others whose frenzied grim pace had them surging through water as agitated as themselves, fleeing demons their psyches were trying to escape. An equally slow swimmer sharing his lane presented no problems in maintaining a spaced distance between them. But the nervy ones swam head down, blind to what lay ahead, ran him down, entangled his legs and upset the rhythm of them both. Although slow in swimming, he was fast in learning that 6.30 am would give him the best chance of avoiding other's demons. By that time, the early arrivals had completed their frantic dash and were already in the change rooms, shaving naked before the mirrors, showering and donning their business suits in preparation for the onslaughts of their hectic days, no more relaxed than when they arrived.

Another group arrived about 7 am, older, retired, or late starters, missing the pressure of a full day's work to whip them into distraction. He swam for half an hour and did not mind sharing with one of the early arriving 7-amers, but he always enjoyed the luxury of a lane to himself. For thirty minutes he could forget the day ahead, concentrate on his breathing, the side-to-side rhythm of his head and the steady stroke of his arms and legs, lulled into tranquillity by the body's regular movement, his mind as blank as the empty tiled pool floor.

He resolved to take to the water most mornings. He would look forward to his swim and would always be disappointed when the pool clock mounted high on the wall told him it was time to leave. His morning swim would prepare him for the daily turmoil. He would keep this time for himself. He did not want to follow other managers. He suspected Andrew was drinking. He was putting on weight. Sam was experiencing similar stress in Brisbane. He was a non-drinker but the gossip stream that flowed from office to office told him, apart from his prayers, he regularly took to Valium. Felix had taken the same drug once, but all it did was produce an uncomfortable 'cataclysmic reaction'. He had tried pot once but being stoned had no appeal. His brain was addled enough without adding to the muddle. He would stick to physical activity. If nothing else, he had the best chance of maintaining his health and reducing his grog intake.

The company continued to struggle. The next two months saw low figures throughout the country. Cash reserves were vanishing. Peter delayed paying all invoices and, just to add heat to already spicy days, Felix had an added challenge of countering a string of angry phone calls from creditors seeking their money.

'A cheque's in the mail,' he would lie and then ring Peter pleading for payment. Peter took no action, and the creditors rang again. After three or four calls and threats of legal action, Peter paid. In the meantime, Felix had to endure the creditor's anger using his limited diplomatic skills.

He complained to Andrew.

'Cash is extremely tight,' he said. 'If we want to pay salaries, we must hold the money. Peter's doing an excellent job of juggling. Look at your own costs and see what you can save.'

He revisited the Sydney office costs. Salaries and rent were the major items by a long shot. There were sundry items, ranging from fresh flowers at reception, to courier costs. None of them was significant although the total mounted up. There never was a time when a vase of flowers at reception did not provide an attractive entrance for visitors. They were supplied twice a week from the florist on the ground floor and there were no strong objections when he cancelled the order. It had been the practice to send all reports by courier, which ensured clients received them the same day. He issued a memo to staff indicating the need for cost savings and mentioned couriers. Reports should be sent by post in future. Clients would not be troubled greatly if they received them the following day. Viviana rushed into his office and delivered a blistering lecture on how he was lowering the quality of client service to save just a few dollars. Clients should receive their reports as quickly as possible. If clients felt they were getting good service, they would repeat their business.

'I believe I should send my reports by courier if I consider it appropriate,' she announced as she flounced out of his office.

Felix did not argue. Viviana had a point. She was one consultant who was genuinely busy, whose clients had not deserted her.

At the following management meeting, Peter pointed out how limited the cash reserves were. No one hinted that, had the families been less enthusiastic about the company's profit, there would be enough cushion against these troubled times. Even if the families could be persuaded to reinvest the funds they had withdrawn, they could not because the money had been committed, spent or lost. At this stage, there was no point in opening the families' closets and exposing their skeletons to the light of day.

'The padding's very thin for the bumpy ride ahead,' said Andrew. Limited income meant little cash flow. Andrew estimated the downturn would last for another two months and if they could get through, they would be safe, like crossing a turbulent river to get to the dry land on the other side. When asked for the evidence for his hunch, he replied it was his gut feeling. So, based on nothing more than his stomach's reaction, he had arranged to borrow enough money against the company's keyman insurance to cover costs for the next two months. His optimism was taking a severe beating and he urged everyone not to wait for the economy to turn around but to work hard at bringing in the business. Sid followed with vintage stories of the old days.

By now, everyone realised the company was in a crisis, and their hold on their jobs tenuous. Marketing activities were renewed with frenzy. They could have written a marketing treatise of hundreds of pages covering the range of their business-seeking efforts and strategies, both tried-and-true and novel, a best seller, on the syllabus of dozens of sales courses and management schools, internationally distributed and reprints negotiated at double the price. A couple of lines is sufficient to say simply that the seeds of their efforts, which would have germinated vigorously and flourished in better times, fell on stony terrain. The borrowed money vanished in the rent and consultants' salaries, like hard-fought-for worms into the mouths of relentless hungry chicks, with barely a trickle of new business to match.

'Our fixed costs are killing us,' said Andrew at the next management meeting. 'We've got to reduce costs. We've got to cull staff. That's the only way. We'll have to cut our salary bill by a third.' He had no reasoned basis for the figure, just the same gut feeling that if they did something – anything – conditions would improve. Felix left the meeting with heavy heart. On the plane home, he drank in silence a can or two of VB and ignored the passenger seated next to him. He was a jolly sales type, keen to pass the time in chatting. By now the company had scrapped first-class travel. He was squeezed into the back of economy.

He brooded over the task ahead. He had to translate reducing the salary bill into flesh and blood. Real people would have to be 'let go'. He hated that euphemism – tossed overboard, booted, sacked, dumped, axed, canned, given the heave-ho, turfed, released. He hated the word 'culled', as if he were reducing a flock of sheep or a mob of wild horses. Who could it be? He would have to move quickly because, if his counterparts in the other offices acted promptly, word would reach the Sydney office with the speed of light. He would have to separate out his feelings for his fellow consultants. He would like to get rid of Viviana. She could be charming if she wished. She was intelligent and she knew it, did not suffer fools gladly and had little time for anyone who did not benefit her. But she was a performer and was one of the few in the office who was still bringing in business, lucky that her clients had not suffered yet from the credit squeeze.

Betty annoyed him sometimes. She was one of the stenographers. She was older than everyone else, in her late fifties. Of Indian origin, she smelt sometimes of her cooking. She spoke with a precise accent. She was rigid and fastidious, pedantically correct. But her work was neat, and she made few, if any, mistakes. Both her age and ethnic background ensured that she did not fit into the office, and she was disliked. He had already protected her from dismissal. At one time, she annoyed his predecessor, Horsey, who wanted Felix to get rid of her. But he had refused, saying there were no grounds. There were still no grounds, apart from insufficient work to keep all the stenographers busy.

He thought of Bill Brundy, Mick Clark and Lydia Purdy. The three had been recruited to man a Parramatta office. At one time, Horsey had persuaded an expansionary-minded Andrew that Sydney was large enough to accommodate another office. Accordingly, an office was established out west and staffed by the three to concentrate on recruitment. At the time, Felix thought the idea was crazy, nothing more than empire building. Arguments about being closer to the clients held no water. One office was sufficient to service the Sydney market. How to divide up the clients when most of them were in the west and already held allegiances with existing consultants who were territorially jealous would be a major challenge. When Andrew found himself involved in settling geographical disputes as to which office managed which work, he cooled on his expansionary ideas.

The Tweed River was a natural barrier to separate New South Wales from Queensland but there was no geographical line to divide the Sydney market. There were enough disputes already between the two states without creating further intrastate feuds. So, when Horsey resigned and Felix took over, Andrew was happy to accept his recommendation that Parramatta be closed and the staff brought back to St Leonard's. Apart from the saving in rental costs, work could easily be overseen by the one office and there was surplus office space to accommodate them in the two floors the company leased. They had been lavish in their office fittings, which they brought with him – huge desks and padded executive chairs better suited for the captains of industry than for recruitment consultants. The three, plus their furniture squeezed in, never fitted into the office and tended to remain apart even socially.

The office never fully accepted these interpolators as most agreed that a Parramatta office was never a clever idea in the first place. The three, fed-up with the vacillations of management, never quite fitted in because they were resentful of their forced move, cut off in their prime just as they were ready to sign on 'new' clients who were already clients of the St Leonard office. Felix felt no loyalty to these three. They should never have been recruited and they made no effort to assimilate themselves into the St Leonards office.

A further complication resulted from Horsey's breaching the company's car policy. He had arranged for the three to lease company vehicles on employment instead of waiting for a probation period, causing further resentment among the St Leonards consultants. Felix did not thank Horsey for this extravagant legacy and for leaving him with a bad case of indigestion.

He looked over the three of them as they came under his charge. Given the right circumstances he might have recruited Lydia Purdy, but he was not sure of Mick Clarke or Bill Grundy. Mick certainly had a quick brain but was young; his male brain was still developing and slow to form those parts that inhibit impulsive risk-taking behaviour. Being older, Bill's brain had developed a higher level of functioning, but he deliberated far too much and was always slow to reach a decision. Horsey could see the talents that each could bring to the company and had recruited them as a pair, as a foil one for the other. Bill was to be the influence that applied the brakes and guided Mick into considered action. As he found them here and now, Felix would have recruited neither. He regretted the idea of retrenching them. They had accepted their jobs in good faith and were victims of erratic management. Decisions made were not always the right ones. His task was to put things right although he did not have a clue what was right, the same as everyone else blundering their way through unfamiliar territory.

By the time the plane had landed, Felix had decided who he should retrench, and during his swim the following morning as he was trawling the lanes, he firmed that he should act that day. Betty, Bill, Mick, and Lydia were outsiders, none of them popular like Nick, so he hoped their departure would be less unacceptable to the rest of the staff. Not that any retrenchment was popular, for it would surely enflame the collective anxiety.

'I ran into Nick at a pub last night,' Janice mentioned as she handed him the mail.

The mention of his name brought on a stab of regret.

'What's he doing? I thought he might have gone west. Has he found himself a job?'

'No. I met his girlfriend.'

'I thought she was in the west.'

'She is, but he's brought her over for a holiday. I think they're spending their time lying on the beach.'

'How is he?'

'Good. I got the impression he won't go job-seeking until his money runs out.'

Felix had not done him a favour. He should have given Nick one month's retrenchment pay, he reflected, as he reached for the phone to call Andrew.

'Okay,' said Andrew when he told him the list. 'Don't be so generous this time. A month's pay is all we can afford. When are you going to talk to them?'

'I'll talk to them today.'

He spent the remainder of the day working himself up, trying to summon the courage. He spent too much time gazing out of his sixth-floor office looking down on the old cemetery opposite, with many graves from colonial times. By now, all family and friends would be under the ground themselves and no one visited these graves apart from the occasional office worker sitting in the sun on a slab with her lunch. No one had been interred for years. Now overgrown and wild with rank weeds, the air of neglect and isolation fitted his current mood. He was alone and could expect support from no quarter. Nick was mild mannered and unprepared. His reaction was quiet and restrained. But these people were expecting something to happen. He could expect them, particularly Mick, to be aggressive. The staff knew the parlous financial state of the company and that the sword was likely to fall on someone, sometime soon. He was aware of the apprehension among staff since Nick's departure. Whenever he called someone into his office, body language revealed anxiety and quickened pulses, as if expecting unwelcome news. A sigh of relief replaced the tension as soon as he stated the reason for seeing them. He could not speak to anyone those days without raising their blood pressure.

He tried to think of euphemisms, nice or pleasant ways of passing on the unwelcome news but always ended with telling the harsh truth. He imagined speaking to Betty.

'Betty, I feel terrible about what I'm about to say. But I'm afraid I must let you go.'

'Let go? What does that mean?'

'It means you're being fired.'

In his own mind, he ran through his speech. Beginning

with comments on the company's fairness and integrity, he would move on to the decline in business and the efforts taken so far to avoid cutting staff by reducing costs in other areas. Everyone had tried to gain more business. The time had come when, if the company were to survive, fixed costs such as wages will have to be reduced. People will have to go, and his victim was one of them.

'We will give you a payout to help tide you over and what assistance we can to help you get another job.'

Feeling like a coward, he spoke to Betty first. She might have been the easiest. He tried to be perfunctory and blood-less, but his body mirrored the conflict that lay beneath as he tried to suppress his compassion to do the job. He hated what he had to do and loathed himself for the pain he was about to inflict on this old woman. Pascaline would have called him *un bourreau*, which meant executioner or hangman. Betty's brown face reflected anxiety as she waited for him to speak. She sat stiffly, like a frightened animal ready for danger, cornered and waiting for the adversary's attack.

'The company's going through tough times.' The vomit spewed out of his mouth. He felt sick. He was about to give a detailed account of the firm's decline, as rehearsed, but Betty's frown of concentration made him decide to be merciful and go for a quick kill.

'We have to cut back on staff and you're one of them.'

'But I wasn't the last to be employed,' she protested. Betty was always firm on rules and principles. They gave security and order to her life. 'Last on, first off, I thought was the way firms are supposed to go when they lay off staff. That is what they did in India.'

'We don't necessarily do it that way here, Betty.'

'Why not? It is because I am the oldest? It is because I am Indian? Because of the colour of my skin?' She spoke loudly, struggling for survival, gurgling as she slipped underwater.

'Of course not!' He restrained the urge to speak just as loudly, but he knew he was in trouble.

'I did not think this firm was racist. I thought this firm was fair and treated everyone equally.' Her voice rang with contempt.

'We are! We do!' He remonstrated, then realised, just in time, he was being forced down paths he did not wish to tread. Betty burst into tears. The aggression of protest had been too much. This was the last thing he needed. His heart melted. He allowed Betty to weep and although he was bursting with more justifications, he said nothing and waited, full of self-loathing for what he was doing. He knew not to drive the conversation as he didn't know how it needed to go.

'I thought my work was satisfactory.'

'It is, Betty. It's because of the downturn that we must let you go.' He found himself using that term he so detested.

'How am I going to get another job at my age?' she lamented. 'I have my mortgage to pay. I have to support my old mother back in India and my daughter at university.' He knew nothing of Betty's circumstances and chastised himself for his ignorance.

'I'll make sure you have an excellent reference, explaining you're leaving because of lack of work, certainly not because of your performance. We'll give you a month's pay to help you to tide over things until you get another job.' As a stenographer, she was entitled to one week's wage, but he was obeying Andrew's directive to the letter.

Betty gained her composure. A firmness replaced her anger and despair and crept over her face as she steeled herself for a bleak future.

'You can stay until the end of the week to help you sort out things.'

He was trying to add dignity to the business of tipping bodies overboard. He was prepared to run the risk of sabotage.

'I will leave this afternoon, thank you. My work is up to date.'

'That's okay.'

Betty left his office with resolve oozing out of every pore. A tough lady, she was used to coping with adversity. He had done nothing to lighten her load.

Betty's interview drained him. The last thing he wanted now was to speak to the other three. Couldn't he leave it for another day? Too messy! The news of Betty's departure would have whipped through the office. He had to go on, in his role as *un bourreau*, not much better than a serial murderer, compelled to commit further heinous crime. He wished he were somewhere else, anywhere, away from this Sydney suburban office, up in the mountains, on a tropical beach, say, under a cloudless sky, gazing at the bottom of the sea through clear blue water, but the waters he had to stare through were muddy and troubled. He could not see past what he was about to do, actions supposed to be a better outcome for the company. Just then, he could not see it.

He wanted to give the process dignity and had planned to speak to each of them individually, but he could not bear the thought of going through the ordeal four times in one afternoon. He could send them a memo, but that would be the coward's way of not facing up to what he had to do. He thought of more euphemisms to soften the truth – 'downscale, downsize, release, reshuffle, separate, unassign, workforce imbalance correction', and even 'career alternatives, freeing up their future, early retirement opportunities'. They made him heave. They were the language of evasion, hypocrisy and deceit.

He called for the three together. At least he would not have to cope with racist accusations. The three were white, fair and blonde, all Caucasians.

'Now what?' said Bill Brundy, as the three sat down, grim-faced, expectant, knowing what was about to happen. Their anger was bubbling barely below the surface, but the stream was seeping through the cracks.

'The company's going through tough times,' he started. He paused, deciding as with Betty to get to the point, but matters were taken out of his hands.

'Just cut out the crap,' intervened Mick Clark, 'and tell us if we've got a job or not.'

Mick's manner was aggressive, menacing and demanding.

'I'm afraid not. The company's gone through tough times, and ...' He started his speech again but did not get far.

'What a fucking rat-shit mob this is!' Mick exploded and was yelling loud enough to be heard through the closed door. 'You took us on full of promises, all fucking crap, and you've broken every one of them.'

Mick had identified Felix with the company. He wanted to say he had nothing to do with the decision to employ him, but he had to accept the accusation for, as much as he wanted to shed the identity, tear it to shreds, burn and bury it, he was management.

'It's not you personally, Felix.' Bill was more conciliatory. 'But we've had a raw deal. We were employed for Parramatta. Horsey was full of promises and the money we could make. Then the office gets closed before we could even make a go of it, and we've tried to fit in here where we were not wanted.'

'It's been so dreadful.' Lydia took a handkerchief out of her pocket and wiped her eyes. 'I felt like a leper. No one would talk to me.'

Felix was getting into trouble again, into deep shit up to the neck.

'I'm sure you can appreciate the problems the company has had. The time wasn't right to be opening more offices. I'm sure you can understand that.'

'Don't be so fuckin' patronising,' Mick exploded. 'We left good jobs to come here, enticed by false bloody promises! It was all crap, bullshit!'

Mick may have needed anger management training, but Felix knew just how correct he was. He was not going down the twin paths of either defending or blaming Horsey. Felix had made a mistake. He should have taken them on one at a time, not three in one go. They were only reinforcing one another and gaining support for their anger from each other, rage building on rage.

'Okay,' said Bill. 'What's done is done. What about the payout?'

'You can use the company cars until you leave. You'll get a month's pay plus your leave.'

'Nick got three months.' Having spent his rage, Mick was quieter but still protesting. No secrets in this office!

'He was the first, I'm afraid. He was on his own. Staff are

being retrenched all around the company. The company cannot afford any more.'

'Stuff the company,' said Mick. He began his reply with an *f*, thought better of it and changed his curse. 'We've got to live. We've got to find ourselves other jobs.'

'I want to make things as easy for you as I can,' Felix replied. 'You can hang on to the cars for a week or so after you leave.'

'It's great,' said Mick. 'Sorry! Services no longer required! Throw the bastards on the scrap heap.'

'I'm sure you'll find something soon.'

'Anywhere would be better than this place. Listen, mate, I've kept my nose clean around here and haven't said anything, but this would have to be the worst place I ever worked in. Management changes its mind every five minutes, the staff are snotty-nosed snobs and you're just a weakie, piss-poor manager.'

Felix felt his anger rising. He was ready to defend himself in case Mick leaped over the desk and dealt him a king hit. As a kid, he engaged in plenty of school-yard scraps as a redhead and son of the schoolteacher. At one time he learned boxing. He knew how to defend himself against a thump. He was tempted to change his mind and to tell them to leave the premises immediately and 'fuck off'. Retaliation would have been a gross misuse of power. With considerable effort, he remained calm, fair and respectful on the surface.

'Okay, there's no point in talking any further.'

There was nothing to be gained from prolonging the interview and from being the butt of their anger. Three grim and dissatisfied people left the office, each reacting differently to the anguish of their retrenchment – Mick in an impotent rage, Lynne weeping quietly, and Bill, quiet, philosophical and resourceful, as if accepting the situation and already working on plan B. After they left, he had to calm down. The deed was done; blood was on his hands; his heart was thumping. He had taken a battering. If he had taken a blood pressure reading, he'd be off the scale. He had tried to respect the person behind the retrenchment. He felt weak, piss-poor. There was truth in Mick's blast about his competence as a manger. Felix did not feel competent as he looked out the window and gazed down at his cemetery.

'This part of the job disgusts me,' he said to Andrew when he rang to inform him of his action and to organise the payouts. He was not seeking support and found none.

'When you're in management, you have to make tough decisions,' Andrew replied. 'Otherwise, you shouldn't be in it. You're not cracking up, are you?'

'No.' He accepted Andrew's reprimand. To himself he said, 'Felix you must toughen up, ignore the cries of your inner spirit crying out to be compassionate. Felix, you must be impervious to the pain you are creating and show no mercy.'

'When the going gets tough, the tough get going,' said Andrew, plagiarising one of his father's clichés. 'Hopefully, we've taken sufficient action, but there may be more. We may have to face another wave of retrenchment,' said Andrew with uncharacteristic pessimism.

'God, I hope not.' He did not mean to say that, somehow it burst out. 'I don't think I could stand it.'

'You might just have to, Felix,' warned Andrew. 'You've got to get your hands dirty sometimes.'

In his way, Andrew was trying to be supportive, wiping

blood from the sword for further action. It did not work. Blood was still on his hands.

In better days, Andrew had introduced a generous car policy. Each of the consultants selected a model in the GMH, Ford or Toyota ranges according to their status in the company, state managers selecting from the top models and consultants from the basic. A car maintenance and leasing company maintained the vehicles. When a consultant left, the vehicle remained for the next consultant. He found himself with three additional company vehicles in the basement. Bill and Lydia left their cars behind on the day they departed, but Mick accepted the offer of keeping the vehicle until he could find a replacement, returning it four weeks later, in a state of neglect and dry of oil and water. His way of retaliation? Felix would not have minded too much if Mick had driven it so recklessly that he wrote it off. One less vehicle to worry about. He took to driving these cars two days at a time, just to keep them in condition, until management decided what to do with them. How much easier it would have been if the departing consultant had taken over the car and the lease! Another example of Andrew's optimism! Even he admitted it was a grand idea but a crazy policy.

Chapter 16

Once upon a time, Felix Schmidt lived in a fairy-tale land of loving his job and working with passion for The Champions. Nowadays, he cared little for the onerous tasks the company forced on him. The stress had him close to floundering. He needed to do more about his mental health before he fell apart. What a relief it was each evening to return to his apartment. Although a lift was available, he didn't mind climbing the stairs, as if the clambering were a transition from one life to another. He was leading two lives. His new home was a refuge offering respite from the daily struggle. For the first few days he did no more than admire the light and the view, but as he attuned to his new surrounds, he turned his mind to what might lead him back to a fuller life. He needed to steer away from the insistent demand of The Champions. He needed to remind himself of Pascaline's proverb, to take care of himself. He needed to find the time for physical activity for both its immediate and long-term benefits. Regular exercise held the promise of an improvement in quality of life, which was average at the moment, in fact, dismal.

He was reclaiming old ground. In addition to his morning swim, he took up exercise in the evening. Not that it mattered much, but for the records, in the good old days before the company took him over, he was a gym junkie. Sneaking off to gym several times a week to lift weights, run the treadmill, take spin classes and listen to his personal trainer's relationship problems took up time he should have spent in working out more strategies for further company expansion. But eventually, a bad dose of the guilts about devoting precious time to matters other than the company's problems got the better of him and made it too easy to quit.

The gym was two streets away. The first part of his session he spent in the exercise room, open to all to see and envy the sweating addicts, pitting their strength against the weights, eyes and muscles bulging, veins purple with the strain. The air smelt of competition. They had failed to leave behind their workplace struggle to excel. Then he joined other maniacs in the spin class, conducted in a dimly lit corner room. He appreciated the darkness and the privacy. He pedalled in the dark, getting nowhere fast, trying to tune out the shrill voice of the instructor and the thumping music. The mindless routine did not prevent the company crisis intruding into his thoughts. One time, he imagined that it was the sharp voices of Andrew and Peter that he was fleeing. In this dark humid atmosphere delusion was possible. Then it dawned on him that the instructor's piercing, 'Faster, faster, faster' was directed at him. He had stopped pedalling and was staring into the emptiness of the mirrored wall, as if he had arrived and was figuring out where to now. How long he had stopped, he did not know but, judging by Danni's shrill instructions, it could have been a while.

'Felix, Felix, Felix,' she shrieked. 'Crank it up!'

He apologised to her after class. Danni's body was so well defined and polished she could have been carved out of wood.

'You seem distracted, Felix. Your mind's not on the job.'

'I'm afraid I've got a lot on my mind. My company's experiencing difficulties and I must juggle to keep the balls in the air. I come here to get away from it all, but it keeps chasing me.'

* * *

He was relying on fast foods and takeaways. Time to return to cooking his own meals. He pulled out the recipe books, watched cooking shows on TV and read the recipes on the back of packages. Not that he tried new dishes, but he felt hopeful that one of these days he might have the time and leisure to focus on healthy food. In the meantime, he enjoyed cooking simple meals such as grills and salads, usually accompanied by a glass or two of red. He tried to control his alcohol intake as he had more than enough problems to deal with, without adding an addiction.

It would be nice to invite someone to dinner, he pondered and thought of his neighbour. He had not spoken to Caroline since he moved in, not even in the lift. She worked on a different schedule. Occasionally, he heard her door shut and that was the only sign of her presence. Sound proofing was good at this address, so different to his former building where through its thin walls, he shared life with his neighbours. For some reason he could not identify, he was reluctant to contact her. Where would a dinner invitation lead to? Into a relationship? A one-night stand was okay for the occasional lady he met in a bar but awkward for a neighbour. He had resolved never to develop a sexual relationship with his work colleagues, so perhaps the rule should be the same for neighbours. Besides, he pined for Pascaline and hoped that one day he might see her again. He thought of her before he fell asleep – the words she said, her delightful accent, the things they laughed at and the silent moments they shared.

Down the road from the gym was a bookshop. At one time

he was an avid reader and would never pass a bookshop without entering and buying. The bargain tables outside on the footpath were always a trap. He carted these books with him as he moved around the country. He could not get rid of them because they were precious. Every book that he had read had left something of its essence within him and contributed to his development. Many of them sat unread on his bookshelf. He added a few more. One of these days, it would be great to be an author himself. In a fanciful moment he thought he should write a book on the rise and fall of The Champions. He had delicious fantasies imagining how he would describe the various characters who strutted The Champions' stage, of the lawsuits that might follow and defending himself against accusations of libel.

Sadly, his efforts to detach himself were fitful because the problems of the company were never far from the surface of his chattering mind. He had found a place of light but was in danger of slipping back into the dark hole, as if he had lit a candle of hope, the flame of which flickered in the cold winds. As he tried to read at night in bed, he struggled to concentrate on the printed word and saw instead the consultants he had 'let go' and the looming horror of having to get rid of more. He was already an arsehole without adding to his self-loathing. His efforts to put his life into two boxes and not allowing one to seep into the other were not working well. If he were not to fall apart at the seams, he would have to drag himself out of the mire and have another go at involving himself in the book and identifying with its main characters.

Chapter 17

Like a gloomy rain cloud, an air of resignation settled on the office. A trickle of work flowed in as a delayed outcome of the intense marketing of the previous months. Optimist Andrew believed the sun had blundered through and the company was in the first stages of a recovery. But the clouds closed, the trickle of work disappeared like a river in sand and the limited income generated failed to cover costs. Once again, Felix urged his consultants to renew their marketing. They held brain-storming sessions to generate innovative ideas, and, once again, a marketing text of hundreds of pages could have been written on their creative efforts. Suffice to say in less than a line that their efforts came to nothing. The ground was just as stony. The politicians explained, 'This is a recession that had to happen'. Business confidence, ephemeral at the best of times, dissipated like a fog in the glare of the harsh morning sun. Investors refused to lay out their funds while mums and dads hid their money under mattresses and stayed away from the shops.

It took no more than his two ears to hear his people cry and one heart to feel their pain. The office's collective nerves were under siege, from battering rams shaped like headaches, fatigue, bickering and blame laying. Sick leave took a jump and the error rate in reports increased. Melbourne head office was always a source of derision and there was more than the usual amount of paranoia regarding the 'real' reason behind its decisions. The last thing Felix needed was his staff fighting each other and having to settle petty disputes. They should have been fighting the enemy; worrying about rude or irate people within the office distracted consultants from the task of gaining more business.

'Things are getting no better,' said Andrew at the following management meeting. 'We'll have to look at our costs again.'

'If we cut back on staff again, we won't have enough resources to cope when the economy recovers,' Felix, along with the other state managers, argued, taking a leaf from the same optimistic book as Andrew. But Andrew and Peter persisted. Rob said nothing. Even Sid, who usually was able to draw on his cellar of fine vintage bottles to produce a glass of wisdom in an old story, was silent. Both looked sad, as if witnessing the demise of a life's work.

This time will be burdensome, he mused in the plane back to Sydney. Last time, the choice, difficult as it was, was obvious. Further retrenchments will be like snipping the threads out of a tapestry. A tapestry could be a matted tangle of knots and rough ends fighting each other, but the intertwining threads can combine to build the colours and shapes that create beauty to the human eye. Once you start removing threads, you destroy the harmony and symmetry and end up with a tangled mess. He wanted to keep the remaining staff intact. They had been recruited with promises of bright prospects, grateful to be given an opportunity. Those who were already working in the office when he arrived in Sydney, accepted him as part of the team. He appreciated collaborating with them, shared in the joys of obtaining assignments and in the disappointment of losing them. He enjoyed their company socially. They congratulated him when he was elevated to branch manager. Now he was going to repay their acceptance with brushing them off like a piece of lint. He would then have to work at creating harmony and symmetry out of the tangled mess, regaining the trust of the survivors and rebuilding their confidence.

When the going gets tough, the tough get going. The cliché overran his mind like a mantra and during his early morning swims he found his arms and legs moving in rhythm. *When the going gets tough, the tough get going,* they repeated. The words spilled out and floated on the water until the entire surface was covered with platitude. They should have comforted and given him resolve. Instead, they threatened to drag him down and drown him. He watched his shadow, projected by strong overhead lights on the pool floor, moving below him in loyal unison with his movements. He enjoyed chasing himself one length of the pool and being chased the other, but today his shadow had its own mind, its own tangents and was taking another direction. *Can you believe that?* it seemed to ask. *The trouble is, you're not tough.* He felt himself in turmoil, as if he were approaching a whirlpool and would soon be gyrating out of control, caught up in the rush of events. He tried to shake off his self-doubt, but it clung persistently like an unwelcome parasite sucking away his strength.

He was not tough, he had to admit. The prospect of management was elevated as an inducement to the young and ambitious. He had always aspired and fought for the role, but, like millions of others, he had been sucked in, seduced by false prophets on the gains of climbing the ladder. Now he had the taste (or rather, distaste) of power, he knew management was not what it was cracked up to be. If this was management, he did not like it. He did not want to be in it. Another part of him, another voice, replied, *Mate, you are in this shit right up to your neck. You're the one who must make the decisions. Right now, it's your responsibility. You must go through with it.*

He would have to wield again the sword before he could forever lay it down, walk this road and call it a day. He would have to flounder in this messy sea before he reached dry land. He would have to crawl down this dark tunnel before he could see light.

Whatever decisions he made would be expedient, but he needed to base them on principles. As this brief was to cut costs by reducing the salary bill, he could remove the higher paid consultants. But they were the most experienced and skilled. In the eventual recovery when economic conditions turned favourable and companies began to recruit, their services would be in high demand. Those consultants who were currently a financial burden would become an invaluable resource again. The younger, less experienced consultants were on lower salaries but so much effort had been put into their training. Such a shame to throw that effort away. Retrenching the younger consultants was the way to go.

Felix looked over his people. The Sydney branch of The Champions was divided into three sections, each with a sub manager. Geoff Pepperstone oversaw Assessment Services. Under him were two younger consultants, Bob Goodfellow and Garry Ryder. Robin Hawkwell headed Recruitment. Viviana Farley, Allan Cross and Gavin Wade were his consultants. Secretarial Services was housed in a separate office in the city. They ran themselves under the leadership of Shirley Watts. Secretarial Services offered recruitment of secretarial staff as well as temporaries. Secretarial Services was one of Andrew's babies. He served part of his apprenticeship in the Melbourne division. Because it had been so successful in Melbourne, he saw no reason it should not do well in Sydney. He sent Shirley from Melbourne to establish the service. Felix was never quite sure whether Shirley reported to him or not. She was a tough, level-headed campaigner not to be messed with. A grey area on the organisation chart, she reported theoretically to the Sydney branch manager but was far more loyal to Andrew and bypassed Felix to discuss every detail with him. Felix did not mind. He was not into empire building. He had enough to worry about in the St Leonards office. Besides, he did not know much about Secretarial Services and was not sure if he could help Shirley should she seek his advice. Andrew's hunch paid off. Temporaries had been busy and helped Shirley to ride the rough waves. Felix left Shirley alone but shared the burden with the other sub managers.

First, he called in Geoff. He entered Felix's office grim-faced as if he were expecting his own head to roll. Any invitation to talk was regarded as unwelcome news.

'Geoff, we must cut down on staff. We will have to let one of your people go.' He found himself using that hated term. 'I want to hang on to you as you're the most experienced. What about Bob or Garry?'

Geoff sighed with relief that his own job was not involved. He settled back in his chair.

'Don't ask me,' replied Geoff. 'You're the manager.'

'Okay, which one could you do without?'

'Bob's more experienced. Garry is still learning but he's coming on extra well. A bloody shame if he goes.'

'Of course.' Geoff had given the answer he expected. 'We better call Garry in now and let him know.'

Geoff and Garry worked on the floor below, but Garry was outside his office within a minute. He had anticipated being called. He entered with a half-smile on his young face. Like Nick, the first to go, he was popular around the office. He found Geoff and Felix grim-faced. He allowed Felix to regurgitate the spiel about the company going through hard times, etc.

'I was expecting it,' said Garry as soon as Felix had reached the punch line. 'I was one of the last to be employed. Last on, first off!'

Felix was relieved at his resigned acceptance. No argument or flashes of anger, unlike Betty and Mick.

'I'm sorry to have to do this.'

'I know you've got a real tough job.'

He was grateful for this sympathy from one of his victims. The news that Felix had given popular Garry the heave-ho flashed through the office in two minutes flat. He was about to call in Robin the submanager in charge of Recruitment, but Robin approached him.

'I've just been to see a client with Allan Cross to present a short list,' Robin began. 'Allan did not do at all well. There were six candidates to discuss, and he got them mixed up. He was confused and so was the client. I don't think he's going to make the grade. I've been concerned about him from the start.'

Robin had made his decision. There were two other consultants in selection, Viviana and Gavin. He would have willingly let Viviana go, but she was the best performer.

'Okay, we'd better call him and discuss his future.'

Allen's body language gave his mood away. He hung his

head; his body was slack, and he looked everywhere except at Felix.

'I don't think this style of work is suited to you,' he said, as the three of them settled down.

Allen said nothing. The only sign he had heard was a slight shrug of the shoulders.

'This is a tough and demanding game. If you fall behind, it's hard to pick yourself up.'

Silence. Allen looked out of the window.

'I'm sure there are many jobs that would suit your talents better.'

For the first time, Allen looked directly at him, but his expression was flat, and his eyes were glazed as if the lights had gone out. Felix did not like his response. Others put up a fight and gave an indication of their fear for security and sense of betrayal. But Allen? He pressed on.

'You can stay a few days to organise yourself. I'll contact Melbourne to arrange your payout.'

'I'll go now.' Allen spoke for the first time.

'Is that okay?' Felix asked Robin.

'Yes, I can take over any work in progress?' There was precious little. 'I'll help Allen tidy up and see him off. I'll order a taxi to get him home.'

'I don't like his reaction,' he said to Robin after he had taken his keys and seen Allen to his taxi. 'He didn't ask any questions. Didn't even ask about his payout.'

'He never asked about anything much,' replied Robin. 'He was difficult to teach the job to. I never knew whether he understood or not. Whenever I asked him if he had any queries, he said no.'

'I hope he doesn't do anything silly.'

'What? Like bad-mouth the company?'

'No. Like doing himself harm. You hear stories of people jumping off The Gap after losing their job.'

'He was seeing someone.'

'Seeing someone?'

'I'm not sure. I didn't want to pry into his private life.' Robin's answer did not reassure. Felix was annoyed that Robin hadn't mentioned earlier Allan's poor performance but decided there was little point in raising it.

'A manager should know something of their staff's mental health. Sounds like Allen was just hanging on to his adjustment and we've just sent him off into the great unknown.'

'But he wasn't performing,' protested Robin.

'I'm having a go at myself, not you. Of course, he wasn't performing. He had to go. The company can't afford performers today, let alone non-performers. I would have liked him to bite back, that's all. He knew he wasn't performing and was glad to get out of the place. Let's hope so.'

He was not so sure. He took both Garry and Allen home with him that night, albeit for different reasons. He did not need to worry about Garry. He was a good young guy, likeable and well regarded. He had an infectious bubbling enthusiasm. The girls regarded him as a 'sweetie'. Garry had a resilience that would enable him to dust himself down and set about the business of finding a job or getting on with life. In fact, he spent the evening in a bar with mates who, too, had lost their job. He tossed Felix's words of dismissal around for all to hear and let them glide downwards like an ageing seagull all the way down to the bottom of his schooner. They were planning to take a few days off and hang out on a beach on the south coast until their retrenchment money ran out.

Allen was different. He was fragile. Everything Felix saw about him had him concerned. He had added to his wretchedness. He had given him a blow in the guts when he was already on the way down. Did he have the resilience to recover? What support did he have to help him through?

He did not have to wait long to find out. The following morning shortly after nine, Janice, who monitored his calls, spoke to him.

'Allen's wife is on the line. Do you want to talk to her?'

He did not, but he said 'Okay.'

'Hello, Mr Schmidt, this is Tanya Cross here, Allen's wife.'

He was preparing himself to cop an angry spray and ready to repeat the tired old story about the company hitting hard times, etc., but she continued.

'I want to thank you for forcing Allen to leave the company.'

'Really?' The last thing he expected.

'He was unhappy right from the start. I could see it was affecting his health. He suffers from depression, but he was getting better. I kept telling him he should leave, but he kept saying that he would be letting the company down. The decision's been taken out of his hands.'

'Tell me, has Allen ever tried to take his life.' He had to ask that question.

'Goodness, what a question to ask? Allen has been down at times and has been seeing a psychiatrist, but he's never talked to me about suicide.'

'I'm glad to hear that. What will he do now?'

'He's often talked about going back on the land. His father

runs a farm on the Manilla Road out of Tamworth. He'd welcomed back Allen any time. We'll take time out and visit his dad for a talk.'

'What about yourself, Tanya?'

'I'm a country girl myself. I wouldn't mind going back to the bush. I grew up in Tamworth, too.'

'Thank Christ!' he confided to Janice when she inquired how the phone call went. 'Allen's got a plan. I haven't cast him off completely adrift.'

'Boss, you're too hard on yourself.'

'Perhaps, you're right.'

He felt a strange envy for Allen. He had found his escape from this rat race of a life by escaping to the farm, back to his origins. Felix grew up in the Victorian bush, moving from place to place with a schoolteacher parent. He had fond memories of the countryside, and, if he had followed his father's profession, he might have been teaching in country schools, too. He had been enticed to the city after his university studies and overseas trip where he met Pascaline. He enjoyed getting out of the city for a break, but in recent years he had been so involved in The Champions that he did not have time and energy for anything else. Pascaline had told him more than once that he had surrendered his interests, himself and his love for her to the company.

After the departure of Garry and Allen, he did not have to add two more company cars to the fleet already in the basement as they were still in their probationary period, although Garry would have been eligible within days. What he did find was an excess of office space. The company had leased all the sixth floor and most of the fifth. Even with the full complement of staff, they had spare offices. They had been used for candidate waiting, individual testing and client consulting, but were earmarked for future consultants – a hangover from expansionary days. He counted the staff who were left and decided everyone could squeeze into the sixth floor. An architectural practice occupied the third and fourth floors and part of the fifth. The occasional conversation about business with the partners in the lift or the car park indicated their firm was expanding. They had squeezed in more staff and contracts on the horizon promised that they would need more.

'We've spare offices,' he mentioned to Andrew in one of their frequent telephone conversations. 'We could take the long-term view, hang on to them and fill them again when times improve, or we could take the short-term view and try to get rid of them. I know the architects are expanding. We might get them to take over the lease on the fifth floor.'

'We better take the short-term view.'

'Can you get Peter to ring me with the lease details?' All leasing arrangements were managed by head office.

'We've still got two years to go with the lease, but we could sublease for the time being. Don't let them beat you down too much,' said Peter when he rang with the details.

Felix girded himself for the haggling. He hated bargaining at any time, but at least if he saved money through reducing the rent, he might spare another consultant.

'We've got reduced requirements for office space,' he said to the principal architect, a serious man with large-lensed glasses and bald head. 'We could all move into the sixth floor and pass over to you all of the fifth.'

'I noticed there doesn't seem to be as many of you these days,' the architect replied. 'We could be interested, as we've got jobs coming up and could need more staff. Right now, we would not have the space. I was thinking about leasing space down the road, but additional space in this building could be handy.'

Felix was pleased. They were getting off to an excellent start.

'How much would you sublease it for?'

He told him the amount per square metre the company was paying and would expect a similar figure.

'I see,' said the architect as we walked around the area in question, empty offices filled with furniture, desks, chairs and bookcases. 'You've partitioned the area into offices. We would be more interested in open space. We might have to remove these partitions.'

He was tempted to offer to pay for the cost of the removal but said nothing. He repeated the amount they were currently paying.

'Very well.'

Felix was elated. The architect was a poorer negotiator than he was.

'How did you manage that without him beating you down?' asked Peter when he rang him.

'I just stuck to the figure.'

'You should have added ten per cent and made some money.'

The last thing he expected from Peter was praise, but his initial reaction indicated he was pleased with the negotiations.

Next followed the consolidation. He organised Janice to obtain quotes from removalists. None of them were cheap.

'God! You would think we were moving to the other side of the world.'

Hoping no one would ask questions about insurance, he decided, as they were only moving one floor, they had enough able-bodied men and women on staff to do the job themselves. Friday afternoons were usually quiet, so he asked everyone to bring in old clothing for manual work. The money saved went on a party, making it a festive occasion. He arranged a luncheon before the work and drinks to follow. There was much grunting and puffing as desk after desk was manoeuvred into the lift and carried the one floor then out into the foyer and into the respective rooms. The surplus of furniture was piled in two rooms at the end. Despite their clumsiness, they moved everything without damage to themselves or the items.

The party followed. The grog flowed and the laughter was loud and raucous.

'If the worst came to the worst, we could get ourselves jobs as removalists.'

'We could start a business on the side, charge top rates as the most educated removalists ever and make as much money.'

'We could wear our suits to make the point.'

'You wouldn't get much for them,' said Andrew when Felix asked him what he should do with all the extra desks and chairs. 'Keep the lot for when we expand again.'

Andrew was always the optimist.

Chapter 18

On the national level, the newspapers told their story of gloom: unemployment numbers had soared, business confidence was plunging, bankruptcies were on the rise. On the company level, The Champions failed to prosper. Morale spiralled ever downwards. Consultants kept on calling and visiting their clients who would have given them work, but their own organisations had imposed stringent limits on staffing. There was no recruitment work on offer.

Only so much blood can be squeezed from a stone and when there's none in the first place, your efforts do more damage to yourself. Felix wished he could share this thought with someone, anyone, but he kept it to himself as he saw his job as creating rather than destroying consultants' confidence. Many clients themselves felt their own positions under threat. In fact, some clients had already lost their jobs and visited The Champions looking for work. Felix made sure he gave these ex-clients his time. When they were in a position, they had helped the company. Now they were needing help themselves, if not the prospect of an actual job, at least emotional support. The way Viviana treated her former clients saddened him. She had used all her charm when they had something to offer her, but she was not interested when they could give her nothing but a request for help.

'I'm far too busy talking to people who might have work for me to be dealing with those who can't,' she replied when he suggested that she give a certain former client a little of her time.

'He might have an opportunity to give you work in the future,' Felix argued. But she was more concerned with the moment and did not hear.

'I've come up with an idea that might save the company,' said Andrew during a phone call regarding the agenda for the next management meeting. 'No details now,' he replied when pressed. 'Not until Peter and I have worked it all out.'

Another of Andrew's impractical ideas! An intense curiosity for the details obsessed Felix. He ran over the possibilities. Surely not more retrenchments! There would be no one left at this rate. No. If Andrew had that in mind, he would have said so and not clothed his new idea in mystery. He spoke to Ron from Perth during the week and spent a minute on company gossip to see what he knew, but he knew nothing. Neither did Kelvin from Melbourne. If anyone would know, it should be Kelvin, so close to head office. Andrew was doing an excellent job of keeping his new idea under wraps. He tried to be optimistic. Andrew had hair-brain ideas but occasionally came up with a good one.

Apart from a change in economic conditions or a massive injection of cash, Felix was sure nothing could save The Champions. The government had acted to restrain an economy on the boil and, as usual, such action had the effect of overreaction, loss of business and investor confidence. Sick businesses were going bankrupt, healthy ones were shelving plans for expansion or investment in new plant or products. Everyone was in a defensive mood, waiting for something to happen that might offer a sign of worse or better things to come.

On the day of the management meeting, he was on tenterhooks with apprehension and expectation. He tried to be hopeful, but optimism was losing the race.

'Basically, our company is sound,' Andrew began by way of preamble. 'We are leaders in our field. We have well-trained and resolute staff. Our systems and management controls are working well. We will go leaps and bounds ahead as soon as this downturn is over.'

The management team listened in silence.

'We need to ensure that our managers and good consultants stay around to reap their rewards in the future,' Andrew continued. 'At the same time, we need to ensure that we have sufficient cash to maintain the company and to meet our fixed costs until a steady income stream returns.'

A collective frown spread itself across the faces of the team. The air was dense with scepticism. The unspoken question was 'how?'

'I can see you are all puzzled,' Andrew replied. 'What I'm proposing is that we offer selected consultants a share in the company. That way, consultants will have a stake in their own future, and this will be a strong motivation to work harder. As the company grows, the value of each consultant's share will increase and leave a tidy sum for their retirement. In the meantime, the consultants' investment in the company will give us extra working capital.'

Everyone was bursting with questions, but Sam got in first.

'It's sounds like you're not talking peanuts. You're talking thousands. Where are people going to get that sort of money?'

'That's true,' replied Andrew. 'People have mortgages and other commitments. But we've thought of a way to finance.'

He waved his hand at Peter, Sid and Rob, three wise men who had said nothing at this stage. Their facial expressions indicated that they knew what was coming and had been involved in the development of Andrew's plan.

'Our plan is to revamp the company superannuation scheme. There's a lot of money tied up in that. As you know, members of the scheme contribute a proportion of their salary and the company contributes a similar amount on their behalf. To date, the insurance company has been investing the funds on the scheme's behalf, but Sid and Rob, as the trustees, could decide where the money gets invested. The obvious place is in company shares. There's a lot of money lying there allocated to consultants who have left. Each current contributor would get back their allocation and contributions plus a share of what those who have left were allocated. It will add up to quite a sizable sum. The longer someone's been in the company, the more they're entitled to.'

Silence reigned while the present company digested the plan. Then everyone had a question, but again Sam was the first cab off the rank.

'What you're saying is that the company will give us our share in the super fund, then we give it all back to buy our share.'

'Exactly.'

'What if we don't want to give it back? What if we want to invest it elsewhere?'

'This is a great offer,' said Peter. 'Like Andrew said, you'd be investing in your own future.'

'Anyone who knocked back the offer would be saying their future's not with the company,' added Andrew quietly.

'Sounds like an offer we can't refuse,' said Sam.

Felix was too busy absorbing the information to comment. He was less than happy with what he had heard. Apart from the founders, he was the longest serving staff member and had built up a substantial equity in the super fund. He would receive the largest payout. He did not view the company as a sound investment. Despite Andrew's optimism, he saw the company as being in a precarious situation, with good prospects of going down the gurgler if the economy did not pick up shortly. He would prefer to keep his money and run.

'Don't put it that way, Sam,' said Andrew. 'What it means is that the consultants will own the business they're working in. They'll be working for themselves. I want all of you managers to go back and explain the scheme to staff. We're still working on the details and drawing up agreements.'

'How much is the company worth?' asked Ralph, quiet at most meetings but succinct when he did speak. 'How do you work that out? What I mean is what will each consultant get for what they pay?'

'Like I said, Peter and I will work out all those details and get back to you. I'll visit each of the offices over the next two weeks and answer questions. In the meantime, I want you all to sell the idea to your consultants.'

Back in the plane to Sydney, Felix pondered as he sipped his beer. Had Andrew gone off half-cocked before he had worked out all the details? Once they had worked them out, there was bound to be a devil or two in the fine print. How does one value a company? Good question! How does one counter temptations to inflate the price to the maximum? Another good question. There was no tangible stock to speak of. Profit for the last three years was often one criterion used to value a company. But the last three years had been ridiculously easy. Making money had been a pushover. It would be a while, if ever, until such good times returned. What if you disagreed with the valuation of the company? Could you get another valuation? Could you get more than one?

The more he thought about it, the less he liked Andrew's plan. He saw a vast gap between owning one's own business and owning a share of the business you worked in. In your own business you have control and could make all the decisions. In a larger enterprise, one had to share the control and be lucky if you made an input of any significance. If he felt that way (and he was management) how would a typical consultant feel?

At this stage, he had some control over his destiny; he could walk out any time. Under Andrew's scheme, golden chains would lock him in. Until when? Until retirement? Did he want that? He had aspired to being in management, but the experience fell far short of the dream. Owning your own business was supposed to impart a sense of freedom and control, but, instead of freedom, Andrew's idea would entrap him in his own ambition. Instead of shedding light on life, darkness would enclose him in a prison-like vice.

How was he to sell Andrew's plan to the consultants? When he was passionate about an idea, he had no difficulty infecting others with his enthusiasm, but when he was not committed ...?

Back in the office, he called an after-hours meeting to explain the proposal. There weren't many consultants left, only five, Robin, Viviana, Gavin, Geoff and Bob. He invited Shirley from the city office to attend but did not expect to see her. She continued to think she reported directly to Andrew.

He had gathered the core from which the Sydney branch of The Champions would one day regrow and flourish.

The grapevine had been busy and, as usual, had added its own twist.

'What's this I hear that if you want to keep your job, you have to buy shares in the company? In other words, you've got to pay to keep your job,' Viviana asked as soon as he opened the meeting. Every ear strained to hear the answer. Every mouth was silent. The only competition was the sound of home-bound peak traffic below on the Pacific Highway.

'That's not quite right,' he replied. He endeavoured to explain objectively the intent behind Andrew's plan. His audience listened intently, as much to what he was saying as the way he expressed it. Felix was no poker player. He spoke in a flat monotone in contrast to his usual enthusiasm. He tried to conceal his ambivalence, but his doubts struggled within like a restless child in harness and were difficult to suppress.

'Do the families see the writing on the wall and is this their way of getting all their money out before the company goes down the chute and all us consultants will go down with it?' Robin made himself the spokesperson for their suspicions.

'I'm sure that's not their idea. I've known Sid and Rob for many years. They are honourable men. They are sincere in making an offer that will keep the company afloat.' But he was not sure himself and the question he hoped no one would ask arose.

'What do you think, Felix?' asked Geoff.

He sat on the fence.

'It's up to each of us to decide what is best for ourselves. Andrew will be here in a week or so and will have all the details worked out. I'm sure you will have plenty of questions for him. In the meantime, I'm available.'

Felix expected consultants would want to talk to him over the next few days and to air their concerns and expectations. After all, they were expected to make a major career as well as financial decision. Not that he could add more to what he had already outlined, but he wanted to help Andrew as much as possible by being a willing listener and allaying any fears and suspicions before paranoia got out of hand and wrecked the scheme before it left the ground.

He was surprised and uneasy that no one sought time to see him. He was surprised when no one raised the topic with him informally. This was not like his consultants. They were ready to challenge and question every decision, particularly those made by Melbourne. Something was up.

During this time, he kept up his practice of a swim in the mornings and a visit to the gym most evenings, his strategy for survival, for keeping fit and sane. Danni, his gym instructor, organised fun runs on Saturday mornings along various parts of the harbour. On Friday evening, she spoke to him.

'Felix, you haven't been to any of our fun runs. You should come tomorrow. We're going to Centennial Park.'

Why not? he thought. He hadn't visited the park since his arrival in Sydney. It would be a good diversion to keep his mind off the company. Saturday morning saw him running with about a dozen other gym members on a beautiful early summer day. He enjoyed pounding along the paths in the park and the socialising that followed. At the gym he was so intent on exercise that he didn't get to know his fellow sufferers, but here in the park he met them over coffee at the kiosk. They were like him, getting respite from high-stress jobs, but they didn't discuss their work. Instead, they talked about sport, the just-completed football season and the cricket season that was getting under way. The parlous state of the economy was not mentioned. They were like Felix, overseeing major crises, trying to keep enterprises going, coping with broken relationships and attending the gym because they were seeking balance in their lives. They seemed happy but they had their moments when they questioned whether they could go on. No matter how confident they looked, they had times when they felt unsure and insecure. No matter how strong they appeared, they had days when they felt like they were falling apart.

He continued in a relaxed mode over the weekend. He read most of Saturday afternoon, an unheard-of indulgence just a couple months previously. He was regaining his passion for literature. He looked at the book he was currently reading and flipped through the pages. Thousands of people would read this book but in each person's mind the characters would look different and the settings would change, but they were all reading the same words. It was unique to each one of them. He found that amazing. He wondered if Pascaline still enjoyed her reading.

Sunday was another beautiful day. He gave the car a run into the Blue Mountains to get out of the stuffy city and had lunch in the warm sun at Katoomba overlooking the Three Sisters. He felt a pang of loss for Pascaline. She enjoyed the countryside, particularly the mountains. If only he could be the sun to light up her life. What a fool he was to allow the company to supplant her.

On Monday morning, Geoff asked to speak to him.

'The consultants had a meeting over the weekend.'

Felix said nothing.

'At my place,' Geoff replied to his unasked question.

'At your place?'

Felix didn't like the sound of it. Why was he not asked? Wasn't he in the same boat as everyone? Why did they prefer to have a clandestine meeting without him?

'What's going on, Geoff?'

He cleared his throat as if he was about to deliver well-rehearsed points.

'The team asked me to be spokesperson. Because we'll get a share in the business, we'll have more say about what's going on.' He presented his reply as a statement rather than a question.

Felix noted the word 'team', one that hadn't been used much of late in a company that placed so much emphasis on individual effort and reward.

'I'd like to think that would happen,' he replied with a sigh. 'But everyone will continue to work as consultants and the managers will continue to manage and make decisions. The only say I reckon you'd get would be at some kind of annual general meeting of shareholders.'

'We reckon we'd want a lot more say that that.' He paused. 'We want to be a team all with a share in the business and a say on how it should be run.'

Felix was more uneasy.

'What are you trying to tell me, Geoff?'

'Some of us wouldn't be happy with you as manager.'

'Who's us?'

'Viviana is one.'

'That doesn't surprise me. Viviana wouldn't be happy with anyone as boss. She bad mouthed Horsey heaps.'

'She could be hard to work with,' said Geoff. 'She always wants her own way. If she doesn't get it, she uses the tears.' He could hear the frustration.

'Why are you telling me this, Geoff?'

'I don't want you to get hurt, Felix.'

He had recruited Geoff. He had grown restless, like him, with his job in the Public Service. He rescued him from boredom. When he became state manager, he stepped up into his job.

'Thanks for your concern, Geoff, but I'm not sure I want to be in it.'

'Why is that? Are you not telling us everything?'

'As the longest-serving consultant, I am due to get a sizable sum from my share of the superannuation fund. I'd like to keep my super and decide how I should invest it.'

He didn't add that he thought The Champions was a bad investment with the possibility of losing both money and job should the company go belly up. He still had his responsibility to Andrew to sell the idea.

'Sure, you've been here far longer than any of us. We won't get that much. We don't have that much to lose.'

'By the sounds of it, consultants are prepared to give it a go. I'm pleased with that.'

'I don't think we'll have much choice,' said Geoff, 'if we want to keep our jobs.'

'You really are making it sound like an offer the consultants can't refuse.'

'Yeah, let me give you a piece of advice.' Geoff frowned and became serious. 'The owners are only disbanding the super fund so that they can get their hands on the money. They'll think of ways to keep yours if you're not going to give it back to them. For Christ's sake, you better get yourself a lawyer.'

'I don't think Sid and Rob are like that. I worked with them for years. They're decent blokes. They'd keep their word.'

'I hope you're right. There's a lot of money involved. Better get yourself a lawyer. You're bloody naïve if you don't.'

'Have you got yourself a lawyer?'

'Yes, Robin has a friend who came to our meeting and gave us a bit to think about.'

'You're getting yourself organised.'

'Yes, just in case the owners get up to anything tricky.'

He couldn't help his sigh. The level of paranoia within the office had risen in proportion to the difficulties the company had found itself in. Managing the office was difficult enough as it was. It would be a nightmare under the new regime with the consultants fighting him and possibly each other for their say.

'I appreciate you telling me this, Geoff. Thank you.'

Felix's ears were burning. He wouldn't be human if he did not say he was hurt by the consultants' actions. He had fought for their welfare and here they were, as soon as they had sensed a taste of power, however illusionary it might be, tossing him out. He had the same cast-off feeling as when Pascaline dismissed him – discarded like a worn-out sock by people he thought he could have trusted.

The last days of Felix! For so long, his identity, sense of self-worth had been intertwined in his progress within The Champions. The company had seen him develop from an interesting young man into a middle-aged bore who had no other interests than the company, who had no other topic of conversation than business, who had foregone close friendships for the treacherous acquaintance of colleagues. He had become addicted to work. He had foregone so many interests and pleasures. Worst of all, he had lost his beautiful French girl. And what did he have? A big salary, certainly, but never any time to spend the money. Disillusion! A bitter taste! A sense of regret that he had spent a large slice of his life chasing nothing. He had pedalled in the dark and got nowhere. He had climbed the ladder into a void. What had he achieved? Where was he heading? His youth had well and truly passed.

'Look out, Old Age! Here I come!'

PART THREE

DAYS OF RECOVERY

Chapter 19

The Sydney office waited. Although it had been only five days, it seemed like an eternity. The air was dense with tension and suspicion hung low over every interaction like a thick, dark cloud of smoke from a smouldering bushfire.

Felix spent hours looking out his window at the cemetery below, his eyes wandering along the unkempt rows. He felt a deep sense of disappointment, firstly, that his career with The Champions was wrecked and no more than floating flotsam. These were surely the last days of Felix. He had reached a void on his road to nowhere. He wondered how much disappointment lay buried in those graves below. Away from the office, he tried to focus on his early morning swimming and his gym visits, but as he swam his lengths and did his spin classes, images of the company distracted his efforts, and brought down on his head the wrath of his instructor Danni. 'Get with it, Felix.'

He still had his job of managing the Sydney office of The Champions, to encourage the consultants to seek more business. They had gone stale from their lack of success. His heart had gone out of the job. He had gone stale, too, waiting for Andrew's visit to force matters to a conclusion. No one wanted to talk to him about their future. They, too, were waiting for Andrew. That he had lost their confidence was the most hurtful part. He wondered if he ever had it.

Andrew was on the phone daily, trying to gauge the

reaction of the consultants. Felix had little to offer. He had no intention of warning Andrew that the consultants had held a 'secret' meeting. He suspected Viviana was doing her best to undermine him, quietly chatting about her misgivings and was already on the phone to Andrew.

As he indulged in his favourite occupation of window gazing, he mulled over Geoff's suggestion. Back in Melbourne he had worked with Sid and Rob. He regarded them as honourable men who would do the right thing legally and, more important, morally. On the other hand, the survival of their life's work was at stake. Would self-interest intervene? He had already seen self-interest at work with the Sydney consultants and he felt infected by their paranoia. They knew Sid and Rob only as distant bosses in another city and were sceptical.

'Felix, you're naïve,' Geoff admonished him. 'You're relying too much on your memories of the early days when the founders were struggling to establish themselves, before the good times arrived and they realised they could make money and plenty of it.'

One of the company's clients was a firm of corporate lawyers. The partner in charge of recruitment used the company's psychological services to assess candidates for their junior positions. He met Phillip about a year previously when he visited his office in the city after his initial inquiry. He should talk to Phillip. Legal fees were hefty. He thought The Champions' fees were high enough, but the law profession left recruitment consultants for dead. He could not imagine taking legal action against The Champions. If he won, he could see his super payout disappearing in fees. However, Phillip's firm advertised a free initial consultation. Discussing the matter might help him see things more clearly. His thoughts, like noisy squabbling birds, would fly out of sight and leave him some peace.

He rang for an appointment and with misgivings visited Phillip's chambers in the city. Feeling out of his comfort zone, his anxiety competed with a touch of disloyalty to Sid and Rob who had treated him so well over the years. He was doing something behind their backs, revealing confidential information to an outsider. After accepting a cup of tea, he ran through the story that led him into Phillip's office. Phillip listened. His smooth, urbane manner, which would have made the housemasters of his old school proud, encouraged people to reveal their secrets.

'After years in the company,' Felix began, 'I've grown weary. It's time for a change, to do something else.'

'Like go into business for yourself?' Phillip asked.

'I don't know. The pressing question. Could they refuse to pass over my share? My experience of the founders is that they are honourable men, but, if I refused to buy any shares, they could hold back the money. In any event, I'd have to leave, because knocking back the shares gives them an unambiguous signal that I don't see my future in the company.'

'That sounds clear enough.'

I'm talking to you as a precautionary measure. If the founders accept that I want to run with my money, there would be no worries. I'd resign, no doubt I would be wished well, and off I'd go. But, if there were objections, I might have to have legal representation.'

Phillip said little. He did not offer advice as his firm had offered a free consultation to which he did not need to add any value.

The afternoon's chat left Phillip with hopes of hefty fees to meet his budget, but it helped Felix to sort through the threads of the scenarios he could be facing. That night, his mind was clearer. One thing was becoming insistent. It was time to quit the company. The decision gave him relief; a burden had been lifted. He had been carrying a contradiction for so long, a sense that his skills did not fit the management role. That discomfort would endure should he remain in management. He would continue to battle. He was not even sure who or what the enemy was; perhaps it was himself.

He switched off the television and sat in the darkened silence, the distant noise of North Sydney traffic in the streets below, the glow of the city's lights warding off total blackness. He was hoping to relax but soon grew restless. He sensed the presence of a silver lining, and out of his heart sprang a yearning for Pascaline. He felt guilty that he had not written for a while. He had not told her his new address. Who knows, she may have written to his old address and her letter had been lost, discarded by its current residents. He should fill the vacuum and start a letter. He switched on the lights, found paper and pen and wrote:

Dear Pascaline,

I am afraid I have not written to you for a long time. I seemed to have been busy with work. You know what that means. I have difficulty fitting in anything else. I hope things are going well for you and that you are happy. I have changed my address. I have moved not far away to a newer building. It is much nicer. It is on the sixth floor, is much lighter and has a pleasant view. I am sure you would like it. I feel my mood lifting every time I come home. My main news is that I have decided to leave the company. I am sure you would be pleased to hear that. You always said that the company consumed me and there was nothing left for anything else, including you. I can see now that was my mistake. The company has not been in love with me. My love has been unrequited. I will leave with a good deal of money, and I will not need to work for a while. I would like to take a break and do some travelling. Could I come to France, to Chambéry, and visit you and your mother? I would love to see you again. But I am respectful. I would not visit if you do not want me. I would not want to distress you. Please give Ghislaine my regards.

He reread the letter, which he had written in English. Pascaline would have no difficulty in reading it. On second thoughts, he thought that he should rewrite this letter in her maternal tongue. She might be more comfortable with his request to visit her, as if he were prepared to accept her terms. If he wrote in English, it might sound pompous to her as if he wanted to meet her on his terms. He wanted to make it as easy as possible for her to say 'Yes. Please come! *Oui. S'il te plaît. Viens!*' He took down another sheet and began to translate:

Ma chère Pascaline. Je regrette de ne pas t'avoir écrit ... A Ghislaine mes salutations.

He found an envelope and as he wrote the address, he felt as if he were embarking on the first step of a new life. There would be a thousand steps before he could say he had reached contentment, but he had broken through a stalemate and was on the way. He went to bed late but slept soundly and woke to a fine day, as if the dark clouds were breaking up and revealing the sunlight.

Chapter 20

The day of Andrew's visit arrived. Felix woke early and looked out the window towards North Sydney, stirring to a fine cloudless morning. Below, the streets were filling with traffic, and he joined it for the short drive to the pool. He swam his lengths and focused on his shadow on the bottom of the pool without thinking too much of the day's events. By now, he recognised the regulars and engaged in small talk in the dressing room. Back home for a breakfast of toast and tea, he dressed into his suit and arrived at the office by nine. None of these distances were long. In fact, his home, the gym, the pool and the office were all within walking distance, no more than two or three kilometres, although it had never occurred to him to walk. Now, he realised on what might be his last days with The Champions that he had missed another opportunity for exercise. It amazed him that he had missed what seemed so obvious.

He looked out to the cemetery opposite and wondered what else was out there that he had failed to notice. The sky was blue, but clouds were in the distance, and he wondered if by day's end the weather would turn, storm clouds would gather and rain would descend, an ominous sign of the day's events. He made too much of the weather. How often do the good people of Sydney go to work in a fine morning and come home in storms and rain? The weather seemed normal for the time of year. The sun reflected off the blue glass cladding of the building on the other corner. Traffic flowed densely in both directions along the highway. An ambulance siren suggested that an accident victim was on the way to the nearby hospital.

He could feel his abdomen rising in his chest, so he tried to ground himself in the present moment. He focused on his breath, relaxed his body and said quietly: 'I am here, sitting at my desk, and I am going to breathe in through my nose and out through my mouth, slowly.' This he repeated for a minute until Janice walked in with the mail.

'You okay, boss?' she asked in her Welsh accent, unaccustomed to seeing him trying to relax.

'I'm okay. Just taking a breather before the big meeting.'

She smiled as she placed a list of appointments on his desk. Andrew would speak to him first and then to the consultants in a group and later talk to each consultant in turn. He would be present at the group meeting and sit in on the individual interviews. He asked everyone to remain in the office for the day, a change from the routine of late when he encouraged consultants to get out into the market as much as possible. Janice knew these arrangements; in fact, they had organised them together and given the consultants their time. Viviana, as usual, was the only one to present difficulties.

'I'm waiting,' she told him, 'for an important phone call from a client. I may have to visit his premises.'

Felix suspected there would be no such call. She was only making the point that she was still bringing in work, lucky enough to have clients such as corporate undertakers whose businesses were expanding in face of the economic downturn. One of her clients was a national debt collection agency, another was an accounting firm that specialised in insolvencies.

'Andrew just rang from the airport,' Janice mentioned. 'His plane was delayed, and he'll be late.'

'Just let everyone know we may have to be flexible with our timings.'

Felix was annoyed at more delay. He wanted their meeting over as quickly as possible. He tried to relax and went through the motions of sitting behind his desk, breathing through his nose and out through the mouth. What was he worried about? He tried to convince himself, not very successfully. Let the day unfold.

He did not have to wait long. Andrew arrived shortly after. Janice showed him into his office while Carol on reception brought in a tea tray, complete with carrot cakes she had made at her cooking class the previous evening.

'The taxi had a good run from the airport,' was Andrew's comment as he helped himself to a cake. 'Right, let's get down to business. I've got a busy day.'

'No worries.' Felix was pleased that they were not going to dally in small talk. Andrew sat in the visitor's chair and looked at him intently as if he had given him a lot of thought. Felix's acceptance of his proposal would be an important influence on the others. Andrew looked tired. His skin was sallow, and he had put on weight around his neck. He had not looked after himself.

'You're going to do very well out of this payout, Felix. Peter has worked out a formula to determine what each consultant should receive based on how long they've worked for the company. He's added in what those consultants who've left would have received and added that to the total, which will be divided among those still here in proportion to their length of service. You've been here the longest.'

Felix listened and sort-of understood what he was saying. Indeed, he was the oldest hand. He had visions of Andrew, still at school, who came into the office during school holidays, the only one of Sid's boys who took an interest in the company. When he started work, he had the job of mentoring him. Now, he was the boss and had his future in his hands.

'What you receive will enable you to buy a substantial number of shares. The return on those shares will be significant once the economy gets going and business starts to flourish.'

The traffic on the highway below continued to rumble, indifferent to the major decisions six floors above. In Andrew's view, once the company shares were distributed to the consultants and the economy recovered, everyone would move into fantasyland and live happily ever after. Felix listened but was not motivated. In fact, the opposite. He was more resolute that he would not participate. If he had been more astute, he would have bargained. First, he would make sure he fully understood the logic behind Peter's reasoning and then suggest other methods to his benefit to ensure that his share doubled. Then there was the issue of what the company was worth and how it was valued. The usual formula was based on the last three years' profit. Those were three excellent years. What about adding the current year's profit, which would be bugger all, and, in fact, in minus territory. By how much do losses subtract from a company's worth?

There was no point in biding time. He could engage in all manner of negotiation, milking as much as he could out of the deal, playing it hard until he had squeezed out the last dollar. If he were aiming for more money to buy a bigger share, he could justify his actions. But it struck him as immoral if, at the last minute, just as he was about to sign the piece of paper, he dropped the pen and told them he was never going to sign anyway. He was no poker player and by now, Andrew had read his body language and had guessed he was less than enthusiastic.

'I'm afraid, Andrew, I'm not keen on the idea of buying into the company. I know it's an offer I can't refuse. I know it sounds like I don't see my future in the company. Looks like it's time that I left. There's a time for everything and it looks like my time with The Champions has come to an end.'

Andrew was silent. He reached for another cake, took a sip of his tea and looked out the window. He was avoiding eye contact. Down below the traffic continued to rumble. A series of motor horns suggested drivers were getting frustrated.

'I felt you weren't coming on board, Felix. You're missing a fantastic opportunity.' His manner was flat with none of his usual enticing enthusiasm and conviction, as if he had accepted Felix's decision and there was nothing he could say to dissuade him.

'That means you're resigning?'

'Yes.'

'We'll miss you.'

'That could be a compliment.'

'What are you going to do? Are you going to retire?'

Andrew was concerned that he would join the opposition or set up his own business and go about stealing the clients as others had done, as Sid and Rob had done back in the past when they established the company.

'Assuming I'm able to take my share, I'll take a break and travel overseas. I'm fluent in French, and I'll spend time in France.'

'Don't worry, Felix. You'll get your share once Peter sorts out the details.'

Andrew knew that Pascaline had returned to her native land. Felix would not be a threat on the other side of the world. Felix was relieved to hear he would receive his share of the super fund regardless of how he planned to use it.

'Will you stay in France?'

'Not sure. That will depend.'

He was not ready to divulge his thoughts about trying to contact Pascaline and win her back because he had not worked that out himself. Many things had to occur before he could see Pascaline. Whether she would accept him back was another matter. She might want him to remain in her homeland. Living in France might not be a bad idea but living in Australia was better.

'Okay. I want to talk to the others now. Do you want to sit in, Felix?'

'That was the plan, Andrew. Wasn't it? We'd both do a selling job of getting the consultants to agree. But if I'm not coming on board, I'd better stay out of it.'

'We don't have to tell them that, just now. You could still join and help explain.'

'I don't really think that's a good idea. I wouldn't have my heart in it. I'm not good at hiding my feelings. The smart ones would pick up the vibes. Some have already asked me what I thought. I might be a negative presence. I think you should tell them straight off. You've not only got the job of selling your idea, but you'll also have to gain their trust.'

'What do you mean?' Andrew stood up, walked to the window, looked down at the cemetery and turned to face him.

'There's a lot of suspicion, paranoia, in fact. They don't know you, Sid and Rob as well as I do. I've worked with you and know you are honourable men. You're not going to shunt morals to one side. But they don't know that. They've only seen you from a distance. They'll have questions. They want to know how the company is valued and what a share will be worth. They want to know how their share of the super fund will be worked out. They'll want to reduce their uncertainty as much as possible. If they find out later that I'm not joining, they'll be asking why. What does Felix know that they haven't been told? I think they should know from the start that I won't be coming on board. I don't need to tell them that I think it's a bad investment. I could say that after so many years it's time to do something different. I think they'll accept the idea that there's a season for everything, like in the Bible, and my season is over.'

Andrew listened without interruption. Felix was expecting him to defend his scheme, but he was silent and let him continue.

'Also, apart from explaining the scheme, you need to tell them that owning a part of the company does not necessarily mean they'll have a say in management. I think some have an idea of a committee running the company.'

'Okay,' Andrew said at last. 'I'll talk to the consultants and then I see them separately. I'll get you to come in too. This will be an information session and an opportunity to ask questions.'

'I promise I won't sabotage you in any way. Owning a share of the company is an attractive idea. People like the idea of owning their own business, and this is getting close.'

The more he talked about it, the clearer his mind became.

When the lines of management were uncomplicated, managing his consultants was difficult enough. They were vocal already, unlikely to hold back if they didn't like an idea, but he envisaged a nightmare trying to manage them when they thought they had a stronger voice. He would be likely to get a vote of no confidence, moved by his *bête-noir*, Viviana. No thank you! He would take his money and run in a free world, armed with a nice financial buffer between him and the poorhouse.

'Okay, let's get the consultants together,' said Andrew, rising from his chair. At other times, Felix would have arranged for Janice to gather them but this time he walked around the office and spoke in turn to Geoff, Bob, Robin, Gavin and Viviana, asking them to assemble in ten minutes. Everyone was at their desks as they had been asked to keep the day free. Everyone was early, waiting for the word from Andrew.

'This is an opportunity for you to own the business that you're working in. You'd be working for yourself.' Andrew started well. He had a sales job to perform. 'This is also an opportunity to secure your future, to ensure the viability of the company you're working for.' No one interjected yet. No one went off half-cocked, to use Sid's phrase. They were waiting for the details. Then came the questions, the same questions that Felix had raised.

Eventually, Geoff asked the question.

'What do you think, Felix?'

'I'm like everyone else. Like you, I have to evaluate the company's offer and see how it works out for me.' He tried to be as non-committal as possible.

Andrew would have loved him to back his idea with words

like 'Fantastic', 'Brilliant' and a range of other superlatives. Instead, he continued with the truth.

'I'll be straight with everyone. I've been thinking for a while that it's time to move on. I've been with the company a long time. I'm getting stale and I'd like to do something else. The company's scheme has prompted me to decide, so I'll be handing in my resignation.'

'Okay,' said Andrew. 'I'll talk to everyone in turn. People might want to ask their own questions.'

For the remainder of the day, each consultant had their run. Felix did not sit in. Instead, he returned to his office, and not long after, Janice entered. Although the offer was made to consultants and not to office staff, she was nevertheless interested as were all the women. Their future was tied up in this too. She knew the details of the offer as she was part of the conduit pipe between Melbourne head office and Sydney branch office.

'How's it going, boss?'

He should be straight with her. He saw no point in keeping her in the dark.

'I'm not sure that I want to participate. I decided to leave the company.'

'This comes as a surprise.'

'I think it's time.'

'Who's going to take over your job?'

'I've no idea.'

'I hope it's not Viviana.'

Little love was lost between the two ladies. Viviana resented taking any directions from Janice, even though she was passing on instructions. Viviana had not forgotten nor forgiven him for ensuring that Janice maintained strict control over the cab charge vouchers. Janice had followed his directions faithfully. She could be forthright in ensuring there was no fudging, not that Viviana was likely to use the vouchers other than for company business, but having to be accountable was the irritant that troubled her.

'I wouldn't think it likely.'

It was unlikely but it was possible. It was his guess that whoever became manager would fall out of her favour, just as he and Horsey did.

In the meantime, Andrew conducted his personal interviews. Felix debated whether to write a letter of resignation and give it to Andrew to take back to Melbourne but decided against it. He would see how things played out. Andrew had planned to fly to Brisbane the following day, so he had booked a room in a city hotel. Instead of rushing off to catch a plane, he had time to join everyone for drinks.

'Everyone wants to come on board,' was his comment when he checked with Felix in his office before joining the others. 'Everyone except you.' Rather than accusing, his manner was matter of fact as if he were tallying the results for the day. By now, Felix had become weary of explaining his case, so he let it pass.

'What happens now?'

'I'll talk to Brisbane tomorrow and slip over to Adelaide. I'll sort things out with Perth over the phone. Everyone in Melbourne wants to be involved. Once we've talked to everyone, I'll sit down with Peter and we'll work out what everyone is entitled to.'

'Okay, let's join the others.'

At first, there wasn't much gaiety about this gathering. People were absorbing the afternoon's information. There was a period of silence, but after two drinks, their tongues relaxed and the conversation flowed. Everyone knew that he was not going to accept Andrew's offer, an offer that one did not refuse. In a quieter corner, Geoff showed his concern.

'They haven't forced you out, have they?' He maintained a sense of loyalty even though he was the messenger that conveyed the consultants' disquiet.

'No, it's my own decision. I've thought hard about it. It's time that I moved on. I've been with the company long enough. It's time for a change.'

'What will you do?'

'Not sure. I'd like to travel. I spent time in France when I was younger, and I'd like to go back.'

None of the Sydney consultants had known Pascaline. A decision to visit France depended on whether Pascaline was ready to receive him. He was waiting for a reply to his last letter, so until he heard from her, he had no plan. He was not interested in going to France if Pascaline was no longer part of his story.

Even Viviana sought his ear, saying she was sorry that he was leaving. He thought she would have been pleased to see him out of the way – an obstacle in the way of her ambition. He had given up the fight and was content for her to get on with it. He was surprised she spoke to him, assuming he was no longer of any use to her.

In the meantime, Andrew was holding forth. Consultants listened as this was a rare occasion to meet him socially over drinks. He told them that this was a time for celebration. After a dark night, the company was moving through a new dawn. Felix was surprised to hear him using such imagery. He had always regarded Andrew as pragmatic rather than poetic. Sid, he thought, was the bard in the family. He was half expecting him to invite everyone back to his hotel and make a night of it, but Andrew added that the moment when all was signed would be the time for rejoicing. Felix was pleased Andrew did not want to make a night of it. He was tired and after an emotional day was keen to seek solitude in his nest in North Sydney. Andrew ordered a taxi and when he left so did the rest. By now, the blue sky of the day had clouded over, and a fierce storm battered the traffic. He had no time to think about the day, concentrating on getting home without mishap, driving slowly and avoiding those other drivers intent on ignoring road conditions. His main thought: the storm was a portent of troubled times to come. By the time he drove into the basement of his building, the storm had subsided as quickly as it arrived, and the clouds had cleared away. His interpretation: The Oracle was forecasting calmer times in his private life and troubled times back at The Champions, not the other way around.

Felix settled in for the evening with mixed feelings. He was not up to any more challenges for the day. He had had enough. He did not want to visit the gym and face the harangues of instructor Danni. He sat before the mindless television watching nothing, content he had made a decision but at the same time saddened that the last words of a significant chapter in his life had been written. His time with The Champions was not without anguish but he had golden moments. He meandered through the early days when they really were a team, supporting each other and rejoicing in their triumphs, dancing on the desktops before the arrival of Peter who transmuted flesh and blood consultants into money machines and converted the company into an accounting exercise.

That night as he settled down to sleep, he wondered about his future.

A lot had to be done before he could go travelling. His last thoughts were of Pascaline. He wished he could wake up with her beside him, hear her gentle breathing, feel the warmth of her body and the touch of her fingers on his skin. Would they ever make love again?

Chapter 21

Pascaline's letter arrived two days later, sooner than expected. In the past her correspondence had been infrequent, and he had been equally casual in getting around to a reply. He was expecting he might have to wait months while she deliberated over whether to re-admit him into her life. The day it arrived he didn't check the mailbox when he returned home. He left shortly after for the gym and did his workout under Danni's watchful gaze. He was more relaxed and in no hurry to return home and dallied for a beer at the nearby pub with Alec, who he'd met on the fun run. They were kindred spirits. Alec was working his passage through a broken relationship. Felix told him about Pascaline and was hoping she'd reply to his letter. Back in the foyer, he couldn't remember if he'd checked the mailbox. He opened it anyway. His heart leapt when he recognised her handwriting and the French postmark among the junk mail. As he hurried up to his apartment, something shifted in his chest and once inside, he tore open the envelope and settled in his couch to read.

This time she had written in English:

Dear Felix,

I am happy that you have decided to leave the company. You know how distressed I was because they were between us. They were like a lover to you. You gave them all your thoughts and energy and had no time left for me. I know now that your life will be more balanced. It is a long way for you to come to France. If you want to visit me, that is all right. I will not chase you away. I told Maman that you wanted to see me, and she said I should let you come.

He jumped up from the couch with a shout of joy. Her letter was a passport to freedom. Thank you! Thank you! Thank you! He imagined his gratitude travelling through the cosmos to the other side of the world to Chambéry, to the house of Pascaline and Ghislaine. In his mind's eye, he saw himself greeting her, folding his arms around her in a soft vice, feeling the warmth of her body, hearing the gentle cadence of her voice and delighting in her accent. He sat down again and reread the letter, noting every word and reading in between the lines. She was right to chastise him for his addiction to The Champions. He had no intention to be less attached to her, but he had only a limited amount of energy and The Champions had consumed all of it. Now that the ball and chain had been removed, she would have his full unfettered attention. The entire day through, he could keep Pascaline on his mind. He would find her image just as sweet, clear and gentle as the sunlight through the leaves while he travelled the road leading back to her. He wanted her. He wanted her for the times he was scared, sad or happy, when they could hold hands throughout the best and worst. Would she allow him to revive their love? Writing in English was a positive sign. Just as he reached out to her in French, she was replying in English, as if she were removing the language barrier. Not that it mattered. They were bilingual, but using each other's maternal language seemed to level out the bumps.

Ghislaine was keen to see him. If he were to win back Pascaline, he might have an ally in her mother. What did Ghislaine see in him? He answered his own question with hopeful conjecture. She had fond memories of the time with him. He remembered her gratitude, even though he took her daughter to the other side of the world. He remembered his promise to take care of Pascaline. He had not done a decent job. Perhaps, Pascaline hadn't been happy since she arrived back. Perhaps, Ghislaine was keen to see him return to the scene because his arrival might restore her daughter's spirits. Would she be happy to say goodbye again to her daughter? Hang on! He was getting way ahead of himself. In the meantime, he still had to extract himself from The Champions. He wanted to walk out of the door and wipe The Champions' dust off his feet but there was still tidying up that would delay travel arrangements. He replied to Pascaline, this time with a Sydney postcard. He thanked her with the message:

Je te ferai connaître mes détails de vol dès que je les aurai fait. (I will let you know my flight details as soon as I have made them.)

He wanted to write over and over on the card that he loved her (*Que je t'aime, Que je t'aime, Que je t'aime ...*). She might remember the time when together they watched a touring Johnny Hallyday sing with such intense passion that his face glistened with sweat. At the time the *artiste* used the phrase *Un chanson d'amour* (song of love), but that might have been too ardent and frighten her off. If he were to win her back, he would have to hasten slowly. The French language is tricky, sometimes, particularly when it comes to expressing emotions. He thought about an ending that was neutral and, in the end, wrote: *Mes felicitations a toi et Ghislaine.* At least, he was using the familiar forms – *toi* rather than *vous.* He sang softly over and over, *Que je t'aime,* as he stuffed the card into the envelope. He felt as if he were arranging to go home. Everything about Pascaline felt like home – her eyes, her hands, her hair, her heartbeat.

For the next two weeks he made the daily run into The Champions. He had disengaged himself emotionally and directed his heart in another direction. He had to remove himself physically, but not before a time of grieving. He grieved for the company, not as it was then but for the heady old days when The Champions was on the threshold. They were only a handful – Sid, Rob, Owen, Aaron, Felix and Tim. Poor Tim. Not for a while had he thought of that fatal flight to Mount Hedley that he wanted to be on. They were a team, in it together and for each other, sharing their triumphs and disappointments, like a football team with its bag of wins and losses. Sid was their coach, egging them on to greater effort, their successes an intermittent reinforcement that bound them more tightly to each other.

The priority was to negotiate with Andrew and Peter his termination package. Infected by the paranoia of the Sydney consultants (they were no longer *his* consultants), he could not help but feel that arrangements would not be smooth. He needed reassurance.

'I trust nothing will go wrong at the last moment,' he said to Peter during one of their phone calls.

'Don't worry, Felix. You'll get your money. I'll make sure none of the Champion family renege at the last moment.'

He almost felt Peter could have been on his side and that he had been too harsh in his judgment. He was doing his job of protecting the families' interests, but he had an idea of what was fair and just. Felix believed that Sid, Rob and Andrew were decent people, but he was not sure about Sid's other sons. Up to then Leon and Hugh hadn't been involved. They hadn't displayed the slightest interest in the company's management – its profits, yes.

The consultants' paranoia surrounded him.

'Don't think it's all settled until your cheque's in the bank and cleared,' was Geoff's comment.

'I'm afraid, Geoff,' he admonished him, 'your premise that the family's going to screw you at the last minute is not a clever way to start negotiations.'

'You've been here far longer than any of us. Your payout will be huge. You need to look after yourself. You're too bloody naïve. You're too trusting.'

'It's better to be trusting rather than suspicious all the time. I assure you, Geoff, The Champions are honourable people, and they would be fair in valuing the company and in apportioning the shares to the consultants.'

He didn't change Geoff's view. He didn't expect to. Felix was still the manager and his role up to the time he left was to support his employers, not to sabotage their plans. Besides, he wanted to burn no bridges. He had happy memories; he had been given opportunities. He had received benefits and experience. Whether he would ever draw on that experience, he had no idea. Whether he would work in staff recruitment again, he had no idea. He saw no further than the next challenge – to visit France, see Pascaline and decide whether they had a life together.

His mood oscillated during those last days. In the mornings he felt expansive, lightheaded in the relief that the burdens of management would soon pass, and he would be on the path to freedom. But on the other hand, his work was different, the particles in the air had been rearranged. At one time, the air was dense with fear and anxiety, but he was happy it would not be long before he would be breathing air of a different form. The air the consultants breathed was toxic. Uncertainty about their future and that of the company hovered like brooding demons. Their messy ill-defined paranoia hung over them. Fearful that they might be taken down in their negotiations, they had defined The Champions as the enemy and were building walls around themselves, manning the ramparts against their fantasies. Felix's demons had evaporated. He was content as he went about the routines of the morning's work. Then in the vacant lull after lunch, he would be seized with restlessness, wanting to race out of the office in a headlong rush to the lift and down into the building foyer out onto the Pacific Highway and join the traffic back to his apartment. He had to restrain himself to remain in the office until the normal hour of closing.

Once he was home, he shed his restlessness, his expansive lightheaded mood returned, and he relaxed. On the evenings he didn't go to the gym, he cooked himself a nice dinner, in practise for Pascaline. The old saying, the way to a man's heart is through the stomach, applies to the female as well. Experiment with cooking, and if it turns out well, keep it in mind as a treat for Pascaline. One night, he tried pork chops with apple sauce. He heated olive oil in a frying pan and over a high heat cooked some sage until it was crisp. He transferred the sage to a plate, turned the heat down and added a pork chop, which he cooked for about four minutes on each side. He put the chop aside. Then he added butter to the pan and once melted, added a sliced pink lady apple. They were a favourite of Pascaline for he had seen her eating and relishing them. Then he added brown sugar and cider, which he brought to the boil. After that, he added cream and Dijon mustard and mixed the lot. He returned the pork chop to the pan, in the meantime steaming some beans. Finally, he placed the pork chop on a warm plate and spooned over the sauce and apple, topping off with the sage and the beans on the side. The first time, the dish was too sweet; he had mixed in too much sugar. Next time, he used a sprinkling. The improvement was significant. That recipe was one for the list.

At another time, he tried Parmesan-crumbed lamb cutlets with a tomato, caper and green olive salsa. For the cutlets he combined breadcrumbs, Parmesan and thyme, and after dusting the cutlets with flour and dipping them into whisked eggs, he coated them with breadcrumb. For the salsa, he combined cherry tomatoes, green olives, shallots, red wine vinegar, capers, anchovies, lemon zest, parsley and olive oil. The crumbed cutlets were a success, but the salsa was a flop; the anchovy was far too strong, and he could taste nothing else. He tried the salsa again, this time without the anchovies. The blend of favours was more subtle but not particularly exciting. He kept the cutlets but crossed the salsa off the list.

On the evenings he attended the gym, he joined the

sweating addicts in the exercise room, far more relaxed than his companions whose eyes and muscles continued to bulge, their veins purpled with the strain. They had not left their competitive workplaces behind. Soon he would not be one of them. He joined the spin class and in the dark humidity pedalled furiously to the thumping music and the shrill voice of Danni. This time, he did not drift back to the day's problem, nor lose himself in reverie. Instead, he listened to Danni and was obedient to her commands to speed up or slow down and take a drink. He stared at the image in the mirrored wall and saw a far more relaxed Felix. His body was showing the benefits of exercise and the relief from stress. He would be in great shape for his anticipated meeting with Pascaline. His self-loathing at inflicting so much pain on others had passed. He was liking himself again. He wasn't such a bad bloke. The only person who decided his worth was him. It didn't come from his position in the company, his bank balance or some-one's view of his worth. It came from deep inside, just being him. He had forgiven himself and was proud of who he was.

What a piece of work is a man, how noble in reason, how infinite in faculties, in form and moving how express and admirable, in action how like an angel, in apprehension how like a god! The beauty of the world, the paragon of animals.

A few months earlier, his self-worth was soaked in melancholia and cynicism. He was an arsehole and would have heard only the remainder of Hamlet's speech:

And yet, to me, what is this quintessence of dust? Man delights not me – nor woman either.

His world view had been jaundiced. He could think of nothing else but the company; but now he was leaving it behind, he was free to like himself, explore, wonder and to be open to what was ahead.

He continued with his reading. His mind did not chatter, and he was able to concentrate on the printed word without drifting off the page to the company's problems. Now if he were quizzed on the chapter's content, he would have no trouble. Previously, he would read to the bottom of a page and not have a clue. Now, he could identify with the characters and their struggles. The more he was involved, the longer he read into the night. At one time, he tried to put his life into two boxes, separating work and home. Now he didn't need to. He was coming together again, integrating into one whole.

One time, he visited the second-hand bookshop near the gym, browsed through the poetry section and found the complete poems and plays of TS Eliot in one volume. The book sent him travelling, back to his school days when TS Eliot was one of the poets they studied. His poems were obscure, but *The Hollow Men* was a favourite, to recite for its sound rather than its meaning. Even as a schoolboy, he loved the metre, the cadence of the lines and the flow of the words, each one perfectly chosen.

Chapter 22

Last day with The Champions.

Felix Schmidt rose early and jogged down the hill to the pool. The sky was blue and cloudless, a bright start to a new future. A warm humid day was looming and by the time he'd arrived at the pool, the sweat was streaming down his face. The refreshing plunge into the water was a joy. He emerged cleansed, in body and in spirit; his mind was clear, rinsed, and ready. On the way back, the traffic noise and polluting smog were building up, and, if there were no wind, it would remain, a health hazard for those who chose to stay on the streets. How had he managed to live with this din and stagnation for so long? Thankfully, soon he would be leaving the toxic air. On the way to the office, he looked around at the landmarks, buildings, traffic lights, shops, hospital – all familiar, but he was seeing them for the last time. Traffic was slow, stationary at times, so he tried checking if there was anything he had missed, but he was conversant with every feature. He had walked the route recently. You observe more detail when passing by foot. You are in touch. In a vehicle you are in a capsule, remote from the world, intent on your destination, not your surroundings.

Inside the office of The Champions, he gazed out of the window at the familiar cemetery below as he had done every day. He had always observed from aloft. He had never walked along the rows of graves, intrigued by the inscriptions, and wondered about the stories they could tell. He never would.

They were expecting Andrew, armed with the details of each consultant's payout, the amount they would receive from the super fund and the number of company shares they were allotted. In his case, he was anticipating a cheque for his super payment and other entitlements. He wasn't sure about the car that he had just parked in the basement. A company car, he expected to leave it in the basement along with the other cars that former consultants had left. Andrew was due to talk to him first, then the other consultants. Two farewells had been organised, a morning tea with the girls and drinks at the end of the day with the consultants. Having dealt with Sydney, Andrew was booked to fly to Brisbane later in the evening.

'Good morning, boss. Last day!' Janice's greeting was familiar, always bright and cheerful. He never tired of her Welsh accent.

'Morning, Janice. Yes, Janice. Last day. Thank you very much for being a good secretary.'

'A pleasure, boss. You were always a good boss. I've enjoyed working with you. You never put me down. You treated me as an equal.'

'Thank you, Janice. That's nice. I tried to be fair with everyone. I don't think I like being a manager. The job came with a poisoned chalice. I've had to do things I hated, that went against my grain. Climbing up the ladder isn't what it's cracked up to be.'

'Yes, I understand, having to do those awful retrenchments. I could see how it took a lot out of you. Do you have any plans once you leave?

'I'm going to book a flight to France and have a holiday.'

'That would be lovely. I had a holiday there once, before I came out to Australia. Have you been there before?'

'Yes, I travelled after I finished my studies. I can speak French. I met some lovely people.'

'You might meet them again.'

'Yes, I hope so.'

He had never mentioned Pascaline to Janice. Nor did he mention that the purpose of the trip to France was to win her back.

'After today, I won't be your boss anymore. Have you worked out what you'll do?'

'It depends on who the next manager will be – whether I'll get on with them. I got on well with you and with Horsey. Do you know who the new manager will be?'

'No, Janice. That'll be one of Andrew's jobs today, to appoint someone. I suspect it would be either Geoff or Robin.'

'There's a rumour among the girls that it might be Viviana. I don't think I could work with her.'

Felix could not think of anyone less suitable. Yet it was possible. She had been a consistent performer, which would put her in Andrew's good books. She always managed to look her best with him.

'I don't think that will happen. Still, you never know. I'll write you a reference today in case you need it. One of the last jobs I'll do as manager.'

'Thanks, boss.'

'It's the least I can do.'

Andrew rang from the airport to say his plane had just landed and he would be late. He gave Felix enough time to handwrite the reference on company letterhead and place it in an envelope, which he handed to Janice as she ushered Andrew into his office. His young face was showing the strain. For a moment, Felix felt sorry for him. Poor bastard! He had a tough job, keeping the company afloat, meeting the expectations of people with different agendas. That feeling was replaced by a sense of relief. He only had six hours to endure before he would be free. He was leaving Andrew to work out things as best he could. Whether the company flourished or floundered would be of no significance to Felix. Not right. He still had an emotional attachment. For Andrew, saving The Champions was of vital importance. He was working to save his inheritance. Even if he were fed up and wanted to quit, relax on a golden summer beach and spend his day surfing, he couldn't. The family fortunes depended on him.

'Well, Felix. Your last day with The Champions. Our longest serving consultant. How do you feel about that?'

He was not expecting Andrew to lead with an inquiry about his mental health. He usually got straight to the point, straight to the jugular, no beating around. Was he leading up to something, softening the target before moving in?

'My emotions are mixed, Andrew. It's sad because I have memories, particularly the early days. But then, it's time to move.'

'You've seen the company come a long way. You wouldn't want to reconsider things, would you?' Andrew leaned forward as to say something in confidence. 'Once this recession's over, the company will go leaps and bounds ahead. With your share of the super fund, you'll be able to purchase a substantial number of shares. Your future's assured.' Andrew was always the optimist.

'I've made up my mind. Time to go.'

'I was discussing with Rob whether it was the moment to raise your salary and Kelvin's. Both Melbourne and Sydney have borne the brunt, have had to do the cost cutting. You've both had to release people. It's been tough work. Not for the faint-hearted. You've been up to the job. The smaller states didn't have much fat to shed. You'd get a small raise now and another in two months. That will help you in the short term until the tide turns and you start to see a return. A small reward for loyalty.'

'I did what I had to do.'

He was pleased Andrew acknowledged the emotional toll retrenchments can take. Kelvin had retrenched consultants from the Melbourne office. He didn't know the numbers and didn't want to know. Felix hadn't compared notes on his mental health. Kelvin subscribed to the platitude, 'When the going gets tough, the tough get going'. Kelvin thought he was tough. Felix was not, although he was pleased with Andrew's compliment. The most painful aspect of the debacle was the Sydney consultants' apparent rejection of his leadership – not exactly a palace revolution, but not what he would have expected from his colleagues. If he were in politics, yes. No loyalty there.

'Thanks for the offer, Andrew, but no thanks. It's time to go.'

'I didn't think you'd change your mind,' Andrew replied. With a sigh he leaned down to his briefcase and drew out an envelope and passed it across. 'You'll find two cheques. One's drawn on the super fund, the other's on the company account. That's all your entitlements.'

He opened the envelope, trying hard to conceal the tremble in his hands. Inside lay the grounds for his future – two cheques and a handwritten letter from Rob wishing him well. The total of the cheques was substantial. He blinked twice.

'What are your plans, Felix?'

'I'm going to France as soon as I get a flight. Not sure what I'll do when I come back. Not sure if I'll come back. Depends on what happens.'

Andrew knew about Pascaline.

'I left my car in the basement. I'll leave the keys with Janice.'

'Don't bother, Felix. Take the car with you and use it until you go overseas.'

'Thanks. It will be handy for running around. I'll look after it.'

'I'm sure you will. You're the sort of bloke that would.'

Another compliment. Ironic to think, now that he was leaving, that Andrew regarded him as a man of integrity who could be tough if the going got tough. Andrew left to talk to the other consultants. No cheques for them. Just an indication of the number of shares their super fund distribution could buy. They had questions to ask. What was the value of the company? How was it valued? What was the value of a share? How was the value determined? Could further shares be purchased from one's own savings or from borrowing? Felix hoped the Champion family remained transparent. He hoped that the consultants would not be disillusioned.

He had morning tea with the girls, now down to four, Janice, his secretary, Carol on reception and Christine and Helen in the typing pool. At one time, there were twice as many. Carol made a cake, trying another recipe from her cooking class. This time, she had baked a variety of banana cake. He was pressed to have two slices. Janice made a short speech thanking him for being a good boss and gave him a card, which all four girls had signed.

Back in his office, Robin was waiting. He surprised Felix by closing the door behind him.

'What's up?'

'I've just had my talk with Andrew.' Although he had lived in Australia most of his life, he retained his Canadian accent. He spoke in a whisper. He did not want anyone else to hear. If they were in the spy game, he would have been scanning Felix's office for bugs.

'He told me the amount I would receive from the super fund and how many shares in the company that would buy. He mentioned you were not taking up the offer. He tried to get you to change your mind, but you wouldn't. He offered me your job. He offered me branch manager.'

'Do you accept?'

'No.'

'Why not?'

'Because I'm resigning, too.'

'What?'

'I'm uneasy about this company's future. It doesn't take much to figure out that The Champions are heading for the rocks. God knows how long this recession is going to last and when business confidence gets back to normal. The families are reluctant to inject more money. Don't blame them. Good money after bad. Who knows? They might be looking around for a buyer. Andrew comes here like a snake-oil salesman promoting a scheme to save the company. The idea of scrapping the super fund is bad in the first place. Trying to get the consultant to buy shares is a risky investment. It will tie you to the company.'

In one of the longest conversations Felix had with him, Robin released his pent-up feelings. Not one to socialise, he never talked much about his private life. A non-drinker, he seldom joined after-hour drinks. Here he was, letting it out on this last day. Before today he had not spoken about Andrew's scheme. Geoff had done the talking. Robin had been silent and only now, found a voice.

'I can only say I share the same thoughts, Robin. I've had the same misgivings. That's why I decided to leave. I'm looking forward to my trip to France.'

'I'd like to have another talk when you get back.'

'That's assuming I come back. I quite like France. I might stay. What do you want to talk about Robin?'

Felix wasn't sure if Robin knew of Pascaline. Perhaps, he'd heard on the grapevine that Felix's girlfriend left him because he was too committed to the company. It always amazed how information got around.

'I'm thinking about what I might do,' Robin continued. 'I've always wanted to run my own business, ever since I left school. I haven't worked out any details. I'd like to have my own recruitment company. Perhaps, we could go into it together. Our skills and experience could complement each other.'

'What? Set up in opposition? I hadn't given any thought about what I might do after I return.'

Despite their experience in Adelaide The Champions had never developed a policy of insisting that departing consultants not go into opposition. Whether they could enforce it or not was another matter.

'I'm not sure if I want to be in the same sort of business. I'd like to do something different. Not sure what.'

'Think about it while you're overseas. We could have a talk when you get back.'

'Sure thing. Good luck.'

Robin left Felix pondering his invitation. He wasn't sure he wanted to repeat the Champion brothers' story, starting as a two-man show and focussing on nothing else except building a business. He wanted to be a well-rounded person again. He felt a loyalty, perhaps misguided, to Sid and Rob for everything they had done for him. Besides, he didn't know enough about Robin.

Geoff dropped by.

'I've spoken to Andrew. He told me what I will receive and the number of shares that entitles me to. Nowhere near the amount of money you'll receive. I've been here five minutes compared to you.'

'Does that mean you'll be joining the scheme?'

'Yeah. Don't know how it'll go. I can only give it a go. He offered me your job. He's offered me the management job.'

'And you've accepted?'

'Yes. I thought Robin would get the job.'

He didn't know yet that not only had Robin knocked back the job but that he was resigning. Felix didn't tell him. Either Robin himself or the grapevine would let him know. Geoff smiled broadly. He mostly wore a frown rather than a grin. He had caught the virus. He had begun to climb the corporate ladder, the one that Felix found led to nowhere.

'Congratulations.'

'Thanks. And you? You happy with what you're getting?'

'Very happy. Andrew has even given me the cheques.'

'Well, don't crack open the champagne until the cheques are in the bank and have been cleared.' This time a laugh accompanied his advice as if to justify his decision to act contrary to his suspicions. Receiving a promotion and a salary rise helped him work his way through his misgiving.

Felix was still the manager, so Andrew dropped in. Except for Felix's resignation, he was pleased with his day's work. He was sorry Felix was leaving. He had memories of Felix being his first mentor when he joined the company. His father, Sid, insisted he undergo an apprenticeship and learn all the ropes. Felix found Andrew an enthusiastic learner; he used to joke and call him 'my labrador pup'.

'I've talked to everyone. Everything settled. Geoff, Viviana, Gavin and Bob want to stay. They're interested in buying more shares. Robin decided not to stay. You're leaving, too. I offered the management job to Geoff and Viviana will step up into Robin's job and run Recruitment. Bob will step up into Geoff's job and run Assessment. I wasn't planning on Robin leaving. That leaves Sydney office thin on the ground. I told Geoff to recruit two more consultants, one in Recruitment, one in Assessment. The company will have the funds for expansion and by the time the new consultants are trained and up and running, the economy will be back in business.'

Andrew's second name was optimist. Felix hoped his planning worked out for everyone's sakes. He hoped, too, the politics of the office would settle down, that Viviana would be content with her elevation and not work on undermining Geoff. He felt a touch of pride in Andrew. He was working hard to get things right. Felix was the old schoolteacher proud of his pupil's achievement. At the same time, he was annoyed. If he could have foretold Andrew wanted to recruit so quickly, he could have argued to avoid at least two retrenchments.

'Have we got time for a drink with everyone before I head off to Brisbane?'

'I'm sure we have.'

On the cusp of departure, his last action as manager was to ask Janice to summon the consultants into his office. Over the next five minutes, they came, not many these days. He played around with imagery. They were survivors of a rough voyage and had only just found safe refuge on a dry landing. Bedraggled, wet and almost exhausted, they were originally ten in number, but the storm increased in ferocity and the captain had to lighten the load and tossed five overboard. The storm showed no signs of abating, but the commodore developed a strategy to cope and claimed the sun was close to emerging and dispelling the dark clouds, the difference being that two, including the captain, would not be joining them. That left four, insufficient to handle the boat. He appointed one the new captain and ordered him to find two more crew members. In the meantime, he suggested the former captain breach one of the barrels of rum rolling around in the bottom of the boat by way of celebration. Commodore Andrew, or, as Pascaline used to call him, the *Dauphin*, was pleased with his plan to save the company. He was confident he could salvage the Sydney office through the remaining consultants. Felix was leaving that day, but Andrew had asked Robin to remain a week, giving him time to hand over to Viviana. She was her charming best in Andrew's presence. He congratulated the survivors for taking advantage of a fantastic opportunity. The company was entering a new era, etc., etc., etc. In the meantime, Robin and Felix chatted, small talk nonsense – about Australia's prospect in the coming test series, the early bushfires, which could pose a problem this summer and the possibility of disrupted holiday plans. Robin gave no mention of their earlier chat, except to whisper, out of Andrew's hearing, 'Keep in touch.'

Thus ended his career with the company. *This is the way The Champions end. Not with a bang but a whimper.* With mixed feelings, he walked out of the office for the last time. He climbed into his car and began the short trip home. His mind shifted into automatic as, instead of concentrating on the traffic, he reflected on his story. The best part lay back in the early days, a thousand light years from the present traffic chaos. There began his infatuation with success. The Champions gave him meaning as well as money. He was clocked on twenty-four hours. He was immersed in a world where his intimate relationship with Pascaline became peripheral. Success was almost better than sex, well, almost, because nothing was better than sex with Pascaline. The trade-off was the loss of her love. Ever since her departure to France he had suffered a yearning for her presence, sometimes dulled by the chaos of the present moment, but never absent. How long had she been gone? He had to think. Since his time in Perth and in Sydney. A car horn reminded him he was in the midst of the peak-hour rush and had upset someone.

Ambition is a virus, he repeated like a mantra as he waited for the lift. Once it infects, it is hard to cure. He aspired to management, but he was an imposter and, although he carried out what was required of his role as Sydney manager, he was never comfortable, never sure of his identity. He was not tough.

He was just a fragile, vulnerable, sometimes faint-hearted, complex human with contradictory motives, suffering under the strain of masquerading, of being what he was not. He was pleased to open the door to the safety of his home.

275

Chapter 23

Felix waited for the cheques to be cleared. Once the money was in the bank, he could get on with his life, but first, he needed to sit himself down for a good talk.

'Get over yourself, Felix Schmidt. Cease justifying your sense of failure, your shame at quitting. Untangle the web of emotions. Shake The Champions' dust off your feet. Get them behind and look ahead, with hope, to a life that will include Pascaline. Addiction to work reduced you as a person. Now's the time for renewal, to restore yourself, to resume your old interests, to take care of your body and mind.'

He stayed longer at the pool and prolonged his gym visits. With no pressure to get anywhere, he did not bother to watch the clock as he continued with his laps. He spent more time browsing the book shops, discovering treasures and adding to the pile of books on his bedside table. One afternoon, he checked the Lonely-Hearts section and found a book (*Matchmaker*) offering seven steps to winning a girl back. He flipped through the chapters and found one was devoted to each step, with plenty of case studies, photos and lots of advice on approach. It quoted surveys that suggested that twenty-one per cent of men pine to get back with an old flame while up to twenty-five per cent lust after her. He found two similar books. One offered twelve steps (*Living Flowers*) and the third capped them off by offering twenty-one steps and seventy love quotes (*Love Antics*). All three were full of tips. He approached the bookseller holding the Seven, Twelve and Twenty-one books.

'Do these three sell well?' he asked.

The bookseller took the books, studied the covers and replied, 'Yes. There's quite a market of men who have fouled up their relationships.'

'Fair enough.'

'Do you want to buy them?'

'No, thanks.'

The bookseller put them back on the shelves.

Back home he meditated. He was fearful he was not ready to meet Pascaline. If he were to win her back, he had to be clearer about what sort of person he was drawing her back to. In his neediness, he was fearful of leaning too heavily on her, of expecting far too much from her. Their relationship had provided the deepest, richest experience. It baffled him how he sacrificed their happiness and let The Champions tear them apart. Would he once more allow himself the pleasure of loving and being loved in return? He did not want a superficial, shallow substitute. He did not want to change Pascaline to suit his needs. Before he could accept her as she was, he had to be happy with who he was.

The Champions' money was tucked away and financial security assured. He could grab the first flight to Paris and take the train to Chambéry. He was busting to see Pascaline again, to admire her dark hair and complexion, to receive her gentle kiss of greeting and to notice if the intervening years had aged or changed her and whether she observed any changes in him. He needed more time. Before boarding the plane, he should undertake a further inner journey of self-discovery and spend time with himself. The first step was to quit the confines of the big city. With summer's heat looming, he thought of the small towns by the beach, but then the mountains came to mind. The last few days they spent together were in the Snowy Mountains, an apt place to start searching for the authentic Felix, to discover his essence in the solitude of those rolling hills, high plains and lakes.

He ran for the last time with his gym mates. They had developed a blokey camaraderie and he enjoyed their company – no expectations or agendas. They ran along paths skirting the Parramatta River and finished at a coffee house by the waters. Over their steaming mugs, he told people this was his last run, he had resigned from his job, was taking an indefinite holiday in France and was not planning to live in Sydney again.

'I bet there's a woman involved,' Alec joked. He knew, of course, because Felix had told him he had written to Pascaline and was expecting her reply.

The others agreed. There had to be. How right they were. He didn't think it was so obvious because he hadn't talked about her in the group, only to Alec. He was sad saying goodbye. Felix liked these blokes. They had their own issues, which they concealed beneath the mask of their bonhomie. They wished him well with a hint of envy because he had decided to quit his hell. Perhaps they wanted to quit theirs. On his last night at the gym, he invited Danni, his instructor for a drink at the nearby pub, his thank you for her role in his recovery. He always admired her body; it showed years of physical activity and reminded him of ironman competitions. Over a cocktail, she talked about her family. She spoke softly, not in her loud raucous gym voice, but gently. She had a daughter in the army of whom she was immensely proud. She showed him a photo of a young woman in uniform and slouch hat. Her son had two children whom she longed to see more often. He, too, was in the army but was stationed north in tropical Townsville. She showed him a photo of them, too. Without asking directly, she hinted that the reasons Felix was visiting France were romantic.

'France is a country for lovers.'

'They do a lot more in France than make love,' Felix replied. He thought of suggesting another cocktail, but decided one was enough.

'Thank you, Felix, for inviting me to a drink. None of my clients has ever asked me.' He wondered if she had a husband or partner. She didn't speak of anyone. He didn't inquire.

His neighbour, Caroline, was the only person he knew in the block. Such is the impersonal big city. He had greeted her when they met in the lift or in the passageway but had no conversation of significance. He knocked on her door. She was slow to open but smiled when she recognised him.

'I'm leaving, Caroline,' he began. 'You'll be getting a new neighbour. Otto says he'd have no trouble getting a new tenant.'

'I'm sorry to see you go, Felix. You have been a good neighbour.'

'We never got to know each other so I thought it would be nice if we went to a picture show together and had coffee afterward, a good way to say goodbye because that was the way we met.' He felt comfortable inviting her out because it wasn't a date, sort of, with no chance of further development.

'This is a pleasant surprise. I would love that.'

She selected a film at the Walker Street art-house cinema. He called by on his last evening and they walked the short distance down the hill. The film was nothing extraordinary, an Italian historical romance that he thought was melodramatic. They had coffee at the same coffee shop as their first meeting; the same waiter served them. He mentioned that he was travelling south to the Snowy Mountains for a few days of solitude before departing for France.

'I need some time with myself before embarking on a significance challenge.'

'I think there's a lady involved.' Caroline said. Once again, his motives to a casual observer were obvious. He had already told her about Pascaline. He needed to air his concerns.

'What could I do to remove any obstacles in the way of her having me back?'

'Nothing. Just be yourself,' was her answer. 'Don't try to be anything else. She will see through it.'

'I suppose that's what I'm trying to do. Trying to get back to the person I was. Pascaline used to call me *un bourreau de travail*, a workaholic.'

As they walked back to their units, he felt a surge of affection for Caroline. Gratitude for listening to him was the main component with, he had to confess to himself, an underlying tinge of sexual interest. What was she like in bed? In other circumstances, she could have been someone to get to know intimately. He said goodbye and thanked her at her doorstep. An awkward moment. He was not sure what he would have done if she had invited him in. He might have interpreted her action as a signal she wanted to play, and he might have been in the mood. He was pleased she didn't. He would have had to make a choice and hope afterwards that no difficult consequences would complicate his plans, to say nothing of a bad dose of the guilts for somehow betraying Pascaline. In bed that night, however, he did wonder about Caroline's foreplay repertoire, whether she went in for one-night stands, imagining them rolling around together naked, giggling like naughty children. But he made love with himself instead. No complications that way.

The next day he drove the company car south to the mountains. His destination was the town where they had their last romp together. He had developed an affection for this portal to the ski fields. He liked its history. Originally settled in the 1840s, it was a picturesque village established on the Snowy River as the main crossing for cattle travelling between the Monaro region in New South Wales and Gippsland in Victoria. He imagined the Snowy River flowing through a broad grassy valley, its banks lined with willows and poplars. In 1860 a gold rush at Crackenback brought wealth to the settlement, and churches, shops, a hotel and a bridge followed. In 1959 the residents began preparing for the relocation of their town to allow Lake Jindabyne to fill as part of the Snowy Hydro Scheme. Eight years later the waters rose, by which time everyone had moved.

When they visited previously, the pioneering heritage had disappeared under the water, and a new town catered for the snowfields and offered a variety of accommodation, shops, restaurants and nightlife. He recalled the thrill of rounding a bend and feeling he was about to drive into the water as the lake appeared with the township on the opposite shore. He slowed down to avoid two kangaroos trapped by the hillside. He followed the road as it crossed the dam wall into the town. He stayed in the same caravan park on the edge of the lake in a similar cabin to their previous trip. The weather was warm enough for swimming although the water was cold. Not long before it was snow on the mountains. He spent several days walking the main range, Blue Lake and Mount Kosciuszko, the top of Australia. He admired the snow drifts along the way.

For much of the time, he was not conscious of meditating, of asking himself who he was or where he was going. He just stayed with the moment and focused on what he was doing, whether it was putting one foot in front of the other, basking in the sun by the lake, choosing a meal from the menu of one of the restaurants, reading one of the many books he had brought with him, or just immersing himself in this glorious part of the world. At other times, he thought of nothing but Pascaline. He heard her voice in the breeze whistling in the high peaks. He turned to see her face and the warmth of the wind caressed him. He felt her touch in the sun filling the sky. He closed his eyes and imagined her embrace. One afternoon, the weather turned, and he sat in his cabin watching the falling rain. Its splatter uttered her name and he saw her eyes in the windowpane. He pictured holding her close to his heart and he felt complete. He daydreamed about her presence and their conversation, committing themselves to honesty and active compassion for each other, accepting each other as they were on both their good and bad days and welcoming each other's changing emotions with open arms. His dream reflected the hope that, should they decide to make a go of it, their relationship would be genuine and authentic.

He meandered around the town. In the park by the lake, the Australian Polish community had erected a huge statue of Count Paul Strzelecki who explored the wilderness of the Snowy Mountains and named Australia's highest mountain after the Polish leader and patriot Tadeusz Kosciuszko. He recalled Ghislaine mentioning that her family immigrated to France from Poland after the Napoleonic Wars. On the far side of the lake, where tiny East Jindabyne had grown directly above the site of the old township , he followed the roads disappearing into the water to continue as submerged roads in Old Jindabyne. In the shopping centre, he found a bookshop run by a lively lady named Sharon who told him the town ran a readers and writers festival to which well-known authors came. Pascaline, he hoped, had happy memories of their visit in the last days of their '*chez nous*'. As a reminder and as a gift, he bought a beautiful book of photographs of mountains and snow gums dripping with snow and of kangaroos and wild horses, part of the Snowy heritage. He could not pass by a lovingly illustrated book of the poem/bush ballad *The Man from Snowy River*. Directed at children, it was a joy to browse as it captured the spirit of a poem known to every Australian child.

There was movement at the station, for the word had passed around ...

Chapter 24

He had passed through Gare de Lyon before. A classic Parisian landmark, the third busiest station in France was such a chaotic place. Thousands of passengers took up every available seat, the remainder perched on suitcases or backpacks, every head craned to the boards watching the train information flashing across the huge screen. The food and drink stalls below were in constant demand. The passengers rushed, like a mice plague, in search of their train once their number was announced, while thousands of travellers arrived, anxious to quit the station as quickly as possible. The air was dense with the roar of announcements and anxious conversations, while the slow-pacing soldiers with weapons at the ready strolled in threes through the crowds, their darting eyes constantly on the alert and everyone keeping their respectful distance.

Felix, too, kept his distance. He was not worried about the veterans; they had years of experience dealing with emergencies and had learned how to react to danger with prudence. The unblooded young ones with pimples concerned him. They were yet to learn. He did not want any sudden movements to be confused with those of a terrorist, so he took his time. He walked with steady gait, aiming to draw zero attention to himself. He sat on his backpack until he found a seat and kept out of harm's way while waiting for his train to Chambéry, time enough to observe his fellow travellers. He was surprised how much stuff people brought with them on a trip.

Some were dragging two large suitcases. Although they had the benefit of wheels on flat surfaces, getting onto the train was the challenge – a gap and steps to negotiate and lifting heavy cases onto racks. How did the elderly manage? It was different to air travel where staff handle luggage and bundle it into a baggage hold. He had his old backpack on his back and a small daypack on his front. He looked pregnant but had the distinct advantage of free hands and was able to move with relative agility, ready to catch an elderly person suffering a heart attack. He joined the surging herd when the platform was announced and found his window seat on the second tier, but not before helping two ladies to get their hernia-inducing bags on the racks, followed by '*Merci beaucoup, Monsieur*' and his '*Je vous en prie.*'

Over the next four hours the French countryside flashed by at incredible speed, a kaleidoscope of open farm country, forests, bridges, tunnels, towns, villages and mountains, each passing under a bridge accompanied by a great thump of air that threatened to knock the train carriage off the rails. Just days previously, he was tidying up in North Sydney, depositing belongings in storage, returning the company car and farewelling his former colleagues. He was expecting wintry weather but imagined he could buy the latest fashions in winter dress. He had already noticed he needed a heavy jacket. He had flown about 16,958 kilometres from Sydney to Paris and was travelling the extra 454 kilometres from Paris Gare de Lyon to Chambéry-Challes-les-Eaux.

Not sure what to expect to find at journey's end, he was happy to be speaking French and surrounded by French-speaking people. He had not spoken the lingo since Pascaline departed. He wished he had spent time brushing up his skills because he would be immersed in important communication, but then he reflected he would soon remember vocabulary and think in French. They would be bilingual because he assumed Pascaline had not forgotten her English. Then he wondered about what other assumptions he had made about Pascaline. Many times, he had pondered on why she left him. He placed the blame squarely on himself. He had become too absorbed with his work. Now that the competition had been removed, was she ready for renewal? She had made sacrifices for him; she left her family, friends and country. She had crossed barriers of space and culture for him. He was the only person she knew and could seek support from in the strange new culture called Australia. She needed him. He had promised her mother Ghislaine that he would look after her. At first, he did. They were in the first flush of their life and love together and his job with Social Welfare did not absorb him in the same way. He gave her the full attention and support that she needed, but once he joined The Champions her support system changed. Without her family and friends, she fell into a vacuum. She was not isolated completely. She had her contacts with Alliance Française where she met Jean-Claude. She did not fight to get Felix back. They had no arguments, no scenes, just a resigned acceptance until she could no longer handle being second fiddle. Like a French chevalier on his white charger, Jean-Claude rescued her and filled the vacuum that Felix left. He promised to return her to a familiar world – her family, her culture, her former support systems, her comfort zone. He caught her at her most vulnerable. Their relationship did not last. He wondered why.

Such thoughts rumbled around in one half of his mind while the other half watched the French countryside rocketing by. That latter half absorbed the French ambience, and he began to think in French, remembering vocabulary for the items in the kaleidoscope. He was feeling comfortable in his adjustment. Not that it was new. He was returning to familiar territory. The other passengers slept, chatted, read, played cards, ate snacks, drank, stretched legs, checked bags to see if they were still there and, like him, gazed at the constantly changing landscape. Some looked as if the trip were new and a source of wonder, others looked bored with the repetition. Each one to his taste. *Chacun á son goût.*

With one ear he listened to the clickety clack of the wheels below; with the other he heard his ruminations to date. He had done what he could to set himself up for success. He had read the books with the buzz words – 'Authenticity is a prerequisite to deep, meaningful romance.' That did not help much because he just wanted Pascaline back, to find the deep, meaningful romance that they once had. Whether Pascaline wanted it back, too, was the crux of his concern, his angst. He liked to think he was not the same person that she left. He had done his self-analysis and wasn't that thrilled with what he'd found. He didn't like himself for failing to support Pascaline when she needed him. It didn't matter whether she was a needy person or not. His neglect made her fragile and, thereby, needy, vulnerable to the first Jo Blow who came along bearing promises of sweet charity. He did not like himself for allowing ambition to muddy his judgement, have him aspiring to management and climbing a ladder that really led to empty lofts, harbouring pain, disenchantment and self-disgust. He hated himself for having to make decisions that hurt people. He wanted to let Pascaline know he was free of that encumbrance and never again wanting to seek management or corporate life. He was on the road towards forgiving himself. He did not want to write off his corporate experience as valueless but, in experiencing life as it happened to him, he would have liked to believe he had grown spiritually and in humility. He did not want to be better or more deserving than others. He did not want to exaggerate his importance. He had taken a plunge into vulnerability. He had dropped his guard and was exposing his soft underbelly, which, in other domains, was a sure road to death or injury. Softness is weakness. He was exposing himself to risk. He did not want to set conditions on giving himself to Pascaline, but, at the same time, he believed that he deserved to have all his personal needs met while considering himself worthy of happiness. His heart needed to be cherished, his soul was a temple and his eyes deserved to shine, not cry.

As France whizzed by, Felix's stream of consciousness led him to wonder how he found Pascaline. Once upon a time they soaked each other's souls in love. The fact that she had accepted his request to visit gave him hope of a positive and welcoming reception. Would he see any changes? Had she done any self-analysis? He did not expect her to indulge in the same degree of introspection. She was more practical and matter of fact. He expected she would have been pragmatic, assessing her personal needs and considering whether his presence fitted into her quest for happiness.

As the TGV approached Chambéry, he was conscious of a journey back in time – not to a place, even though a travel writer would have told him that walking through the streets of the old town was a step back into another era. He was thinking about a journey back into his own life, to a former version of himself, to the person he was when he visited Chambéry in the last days of his backpacking.

The man sitting next to him had been reading, totally immersed in his book. He seemed to have reached the last page. He closed the book, stirred in his seat, placed the book on his lap and leaned back as if savouring the last few words. Apart from the ladies who he helped with their bags, he had spoken to no one. This was an opportunity to cease his self-reflection before he tripped himself up going around in circles and reach out in conversation, a chance to brush up his rusty French.

'Avez-vous apprécié votre livre?' (Did you enjoy your book?)

He seemed friendly enough but looked at Felix closely as if deciding whether he was worth the effort. He must have reckoned he was okay.

'Mais, oui! C'était un thriller et m'a impliqué jusqu'à la fin.' (Yes! It was a thriller and involved me until the end.)

'C'est une diction en anglais, que l'on connait un bon livre lorsqu'on tourne le denier page et on a l'impression d'avoir perdu un ami.' (It's a saying in English that you know a good book when you turn the last page and feel as if you've lost a friend.)

'C'est vrai.' (That's true.) He laughed, then looked at Felix closely again. *'Votre accent? C'est déroutant. Vous avez l'air d'être allemande, mais vous ne l'êtes pas.'* (Your accent? It's puzzling. You sound as if you're German, but you're not.)

'Non.' It was his turn to laugh. *Je suis Australien.'*

'Australien? Australie. C'est loin. (It's a long way). *Pourquoi êtes-vous venu en Europe quand c'est l'hiver? Les étrangers visitent en été, sauf s'ils aiment skier. Le ski vous intéresse?'*

(Why have you come to Europe in winter? Foreigners visit in summer except if they like skiing. Are you interested in skiing?)

'Je rends visite à des amis, mais je pourrais faire du ski. Je n'y ai pas pensé.' (I'm visiting friends. I could ski. I haven't thought about it.)

'Des millions de personnes passent par Chambéry chaque hiver pour se rendre aux pistes de ski.' (Millions pass through Chambéry every winter on their way to the ski runs.)

'Je n'avais visité que Chambéry en été. Je ne l'avais pas lié avec les sports de neige avant.' (I've only visited Chambéry in summer. I hadn't linked it with snow sports before.)

'Ha! Vous devez rendre visite à une dame. Sinon, pourquoi aller si loin? Quand on pose les yeux sur une dame, on ne voit rien d'autre.' (You must be visiting a lady. Otherwise, why come so far? When you set your eyes on a lady, you see nothing else.)

Felix smiled. To everyone, even to this Frenchman who he had met a minute ago, it was obvious he had come all this way for romantic reasons.

'Si la dame ne veut pas vois voir, vous serez venu à un excellent endroit pour le ski. Ce sera une consolation. Mais je suis sûr qu'elle le fera. Vous pourrez skier ensemble.' (If the lady doesn't want to see you, you'll have come to an excellent spot for skiing. That will be a consolation. But I'm sure she will. You can ski together.)

'Merci, Monsieur. Elle m'attendra à la gare.' (Thank you, Sir. She will be waiting for me at the station.)

'J'ai un magazin de location de ski. Laissez-moi vous donner ma carte.' (I own a ski-hire shop. Let me give you my card.)

He gave him a business card in the name of *Chambéry Ski Sévices*. His name was written in the bottom corner – Laurent Souchon.

'*Merci, Laurent.' Je viendrai peut-être venir vous voir.*' (Thank you, Laurent. I may come see you.)

'*Il me fera plaisir de vous aider.*' (It will be my pleasure to help you.)

The train slowed down, its destination not far. Inside, the passengers stirred, began collecting their goods, brought down their bags from the overhead rack and stood in the aisle, ready to descend as soon as the train stopped. As if to verify Laurent's comments, Felix noticed a pair of snowshoes (*raquettes à neige*) strapped to a case.

Not sure what he would find, the butterflies fluttered in his stomach as he took his turn to dismount the steps into Chambéry-Challes-les-Eaux.

Chapter 25

Felix Schmidt lagged behind the other passengers hastening along the platform towards the exit. Below the noise of the crowd, he heard two inner voices. One was the voice of hope. Brimming with anticipation, he could not wait to sight Pascaline watching out for her former lover, her slim body silhouetted in the fading light. Another part of him wanted to dawdle and delay the reunion in case it turned out badly. That was the voice of fear. Would he face disappointment? Would she greet him coolly? Or would she warmly throw her arms around him and greet him with exuberance? He had seen her in both moods. People scurried past, dragging their cases behind; a number carried skis across their shoulders. The station looked much the same as on his previous visit, but this time on the walls were advertisements for ski resorts (*Samoëne-Les Saix, Haute-Savoie*) – images of happy people, goggles on their helmets, beaming from the snow. He hoped he would be happy, too, overjoyed, ecstatic, but he was bracing himself, donning an emotional armour against heart-breaking disappointment. The air was chilly, colder than on his previous visits. He remembered a scorching summer sun, but today's overcast skies reminded him he needed a warm jacket.

The sun peeped out as he reached the gate. A positive omen. There she was, as he remembered, tall, slim; her dark hair seemed shorter, tied in a bun. His heart leapt and his loins stirred. She was just as beautiful, a little older around the mouth, but mature and just as desirable. He quickened his pace to join her. She saw him, waved, smiled and stepped forward to greet him. He was wearing his day pack at the front and the larger pack on his back. They got in the way of her embrace so instead he kissed her on both cheeks, and she kissed his in return. They were awkward. He sensed another omen. They had baggage to confront, obstacles to work through.

'Your jacket looks so thin. You must be freezing.' She spoke in English in the same delightful accent.

'Absolument! J'ai besoin d'une veste plus chaud,' (Absolutely! I will have to get a warmer one) he replied in French. He wanted neither language to dominate. He hoped she would believe he was trying to meet her halfway. He felt tense, unable to relax.

'We should have a drink before we drive home. I have parked outside a bar. It will be warm in there.'

'Okay!'

Around them, people were shouting, greeting, kissing, hugging. Their greeting was more restrained, but he felt content she seemed pleased to see him. So far so good. They walked with the crowd to the parking. Most put luggage into boots and themselves into the vehicle, keen to get going as soon as possible, but a small number placed luggage into boots and took themselves to the bar. Inside was warm and they found a booth in a quiet, cosy corner where they did not have to shout above the brouhaha. A young waiter followed them.

'Qu'est-ce que vous voulez, Madam? Monsieur?'

Back in Australia, he would have ordered a beer on a hot summer's night. Here, in wintery Chambéry, he asked for a red wine. Pascaline asked for a white. They received their drinks promptly. They spoke in English. Small talk was safe. He chatted about his conversation with Laurent and showed her his card. She knew of his shop but had never visited because the family had its own ski gear. He felt safe in discarding his armour. She listened and seemed interested. He listened to her words. He listened to her use of words. He looked into her eyes, her subtle facial expressions. He tried to interpret her silences, hear what she was not saying. He tried to gauge her true feelings. He was not having much success. She was restless and wriggled in her seat.

'I need to talk to you before we go home. I have something to tell you.'

Pascaline's manner was subdued and serious. He was apprehensive. What was she going to tell him? That it was all over? That she had another bloke? That she was married? That he could only stay one night because her husband was away tonight and would be back tomorrow? That he might as well go back to Australia? Or was it something about her mother? Was Ghislaine unwell or worse? Or her brother, Anton? Such thoughts flashed through his mind with the speed of light. His imagination was running rampant, getting out of hand, his efforts to contain himself banished. Pascaline could see his consternation. She broke into a smile and laughed.

'Don't worry. I hope you will find it good news.'

He felt calmer. Panic averted, his heart settled down into its normal place. He strained to listen against the inner static and loud laughter from a group in the next booth. Someone was telling a funny story. Pascaline waited until the noise subsided.

'When I left Australia, I was pregnant.'

She paused, staring intently at him.

'*Quoi?*'

'I was expecting a baby. I was not sure until I got back home and had a test.'

A million questions flooded his mind. He reverted to English. He wanted to get everything straight.

'You think it was mine.'

'Yes. Absolutely.'

'Did you have the baby?'

'Yes, of course.'

'Where's the baby now?'

'He's back home.' She smiled, her face softening. 'A beautiful little boy. That is why I needed to tell you now.'

He was stunned and confused but the message was clear. The baby was a boy; he was alive and well; he was about six years old. Another flood, this time, of memories. Their last lovemaking had an air of abandon. Nothing else mattered, their normal precautions neglected. His little sperm found no barriers on its way and did its job. He felt a surge of joy and happiness, the nature of which he hadn't known before. The last thing he was expecting was for Pascaline to tell him they had a son and that he was about to meet him. He had come to France to win over his mother and now he had to win the child as well. He was caught off-guard. He was nervous enough about meeting Pascaline. Now, an extra surge of jitters like an electric current was dancing inside his body, which was doing its best to manage a mixed bag of emotions.

'What's his name?'

'Christophe Felix.'

'Christophe Felix.' He repeated the name. Excellent that she included his name. A beautiful touch. Even after she was back in France, she was not ready to exclude him from her life. Her willingness to stay connected made sense.

'What's he like?'

'He's a beautiful intelligent boy.' She pondered over her reply, a mother's love shining in her eyes and smile. The questions flooded back but the news exhausted him. He was overwhelmed and needed time to absorb this startling and unexpected information. This changed everything. This really was a new chapter. He finished his drink and beckoned the waiter for another. He was a father and, until now, didn't know. He tossed the name around. *Christophe. Christophe. Christophe. Get used to it. You're a dad, Felix Schmidt.*

'Does Christophe know about me?'

'Yes. When he asked about a papa about a year ago, Ghislaine insisted that I tell him the truth. I told him that his papa lived in Australia and could not come because it was such a long way. He wanted to know about Australia, so Ghislaine bought him a book about Australian animals. It is his favourite.'

'Does he know I'm here?'

'Yes. I told him papa was able to get away at last. He's excited but he's nervous and hasn't said much.'

They finished their drinks and left the bar for the short, chilly walk to the car. Night was closing in; the city lights illuminated the way. They drove in silence through the town and emerged in the countryside.

'I've been asking about Christophe; I haven't asked about you. How did you manage? A single mum. If you had told me, I would have sent you money.'

'I have managed well. Maman has been extremely helpful. She loves having a grandson in the house. The government is good at supporting families. I did not need to work. I found a job only recently.'

They continued in silence. He felt comfortable to be sitting beside her without speaking. The surrounding mountains and fields were fading fast into the darkness. Questions had been answered. He would be welcome at *chez* Ghislaine. People were waiting. Other questions remained. Why hadn't she told him? Pascaline had once mentioned that she kicked out Jean-Claude shortly after they returned to France. Did he leave her when he found out that she was pregnant? Another touch of the guilts. He remembered wondering whether Pascaline was sleeping with other men. She would have been busy with her pregnancy, suffering morning sickness and other inconveniences. He wondered if she suffered from postpartum stress. He wondered, briefly, if other men featured in her life. He really didn't want to know. What mattered was that she was with him now in the darkened car, their faces lit by the control panels, both staring ahead. They would be sharing the same house that evening, not necessarily the same bed. She may not be ready. His life, in the form of his son, had gone on without him. He had missed the milestones – his first step, his first word. Did he speak English as well as French? Was he attending school? What about the rest of the family? He was looking forward to meeting his son.

Pascaline turned off the road into the farmhouse. The sight was familiar, the same group of buildings enclosing the courtyard. Last time, leafy vines covered the portico, but this evening the headlights picked out bare vines in their leafless winter dress. Light was coming from every window. The front door half opened and a young boy in a dressing gown and pyjamas peeped out, and, in the background, Ghislaine was gently pulling him back out of the chilly night air. They climbed out of the car, he retrieved his bags from the boot and followed Pascaline into the noisy warmth of the house, the bright light a sharp contrast to the winter gloom. An excited small dog that resembled a Yorkshire terrier was jumping around and barking.

Ghislaine stepped forward and embraced him.

'Felix! How wonderful to see you!' She spoke in English. She looked the same but more wrinkles and grey hairs. Her greeting was warm and enthusiastic, as if she really meant her words. In the meantime, the dog was insisting on being introduced. It continued to bark, wagged its little tail and stood up, placing its paws on his leg. Ghislaine disengaged herself to chastise the dog.

'Arrête! Arrête!'

The young boy jumped forward, leaned down to grab the dog around the neck and cuddled it.

'Arrête! Arrête!' He repeated Ghislaine's command. The dog stopped barking, wagged its tail vigorously, looked up and licked the boy's face. He laughed and looked up at Felix.

'C'est mon chien.' (It's my dog.)

'Quel nom?'

'Coquette. C'est une fille.' (She's a girl.)

'We call her Coquette because she loves everyone,' Pascaline spoke to him in English, then turned to the boy.

'Christophe! C'est Felix. Felix est ton papa.'

Christophe let go of Coquette, stood up, took his hand, and greeted him solemnly. Felix looked down at him intently. In his possessions back home he had a photo of himself taken on his first day at school. Christophe's chin, eyes, cheeks and brow reminded Felix of himself at that age. The likeness finished there. Christophe's hair colouring and complexion were Pascaline's. Felix was glad the boy did not inherit his red hair, which had made him a target for the bullies and caused him so much grief that once he attempted unsuccessfully to dye his hair.

'*Bonjour, Felix. Bienvenue!*'

'*Bonjour, Christophe. Merci beaucoup.*'

Christophe stepped back and clung to Pascaline, seeking shelter from this stranger in the embrace of his mother. He wanted to escape, to bury his face in her skirt.

'*Tu peux dire Felix ou Papa, tout ce que tu veux.*' (You may say Felix or Daddy, whatever you wish.)

Christophe said nothing and looked up at his mother, unsure how he should handle meeting his father for the first time. Felix wasn't sure how he would handle meeting his son either. Although Christophe's greeting was formal and guarded, he welcomed Felix. He had been schooled to be polite. It's not every day that father and son meet for the first time. Up to an hour previously, Felix didn't know Christophe existed. He was happy with this first meeting. Coquette was a nice distraction. Keep it light, Felix, no need for kisses or big embraces yet or heavy emotion. No need to rush in this new ball game.

'I'll show you to your room.' Pascaline led him down the passageway. 'It is better you sleep in a separate room at least for tonight until we have a good talk.'

'Good idea. We have to get to know each other again.' No need to rush in the old ball game either.

'You could have a shower to refreshen up after your travel. You must be cold. I will find something warm for tonight. We will go shopping tomorrow.'

He was wondering about sleeping arrangements. He would have happily jumped into her bed. He was looking forward to it, yearning for it; the seed wanted to leap tumultuous out of his scrotum but, for the moment, it needed to be pent up behind closed doors. Pascaline had marked the bounds he was not to cross and fastened the way with a bolted gate. He accepted the prudence of a short delay.

He remembered the whereabouts of the bathroom. He enjoyed undressing and stepping into the shower, allowing the hot water to stream over him. As he was drying and towelling himself, Pascaline entered with clothes. She did not seem to mind his naked body and he did not mind her gazing at it. His member did not mind either and made its impatience known. She looked him up and down with a smile. Was she tempted to unlock the gates? He would have stepped forward and embraced her, but she put up her hand as if she were a policewoman stopping the traffic and gave him a kiss on the cheek instead. Come thus far and no further.

'You cannot walk around the house naked. Dress yourself and join us for dinner.'

She laughed at her own joke and left him to don the tracksuit. Shortly after, he joined the family in the warm living room. Pascaline was setting the table, Ghislaine was checking the dinner, Christophe was watching the television and Coquette was in his lap. Ghislaine served the meal and Pascaline called Christophe to the table. They sat down and, before they ate, Ghislaine made a speech of welcome, first in English, then in French.

'Je suis heureuse de te voir, Felix, assis á notre table. Bienvenue.' (I am pleased to see you, Felix, sitting at our table. Welcome.)

He replied in French.

'Merci, Ghislaine. Je suis incroyablement heureux d'être ici.' (Thank you, Ghislaine. I am incredibly happy to be here.)

'Je t'en prie.'

He felt he was home, a lost traveller who had been returned to the family. Here was his son, his son's mother and grandmother, sharing a meal, a wonderful way to begin their bonding. In French, he caught up with the news. Both Ghislaine and Pascaline were working at the language school. There were not as many students as in summer, but there were enough, sharing their time between studying French and skiing in one of the resorts. As part of their programme of excursions, the school organised days in the snow. Pascaline and Christophe often went too. Christophe was developing into quite a competent skier. Ghislaine went occasionally. They would all have to go one time, she suggested. Felix mentioned meeting the ski hire shop owner on the train. Ghislaine knew the shop but was sure they had enough equipment for everyone. Her son Anton had been busy with the grape harvest. He still managed the vineyard, and, after a good season, he was processing the year's vintage. He and Mireille decided to marry not long after his last visit. They had two children, a girl and a boy. They led a busy life.

Ghislaine asked for his news. He had resigned from his job. He had wearied of the corporate life and was not planning to return. He had a good payout so the issue of finding another income was not pressing. Ghislaine glanced at Pascaline at the mention of quitting The Champions. She knew the barrier that grew between them was his work, the cancer that ate away at their relationship. Now that it had been removed, his future was open. Pascaline ate her meal and listened to her former lover.

They spoke in French for Christophe. He listened to the conversation but made no comment. It was all adult talk that he didn't understand. He looked often at this new person in his life, observing how he ate, used his knife and fork. Instead of cutting the meat and then using his fork, he cut his meat as he went. This man spoke French well enough but sounded funny, different to Mummy and Grandma. He seemed a good man.

After cleaning up, they joined Christophe who was watching one of his favourite shows, which was about two towns competing for the honour of running a circuit of challenges. The producers had shown amazing ingenuity in creating games in which two teams dressed in their town's colours were pitted against each other. The town with the most surviving members at the end of the course was the winner. Each town had its rowdy chanting crowd of supporters while the compere maintained a frenzied commentary. Christophe shrieked with laughter at the various mishaps – falling into a pool from a tightrope, sliding off slippery slopes, climbing collapsing foam walls. They joined him in his laughter at this comedy of ridiculous frothy nonsense – family entertainment, they called it. Coquette contributed to the fracas, and they laughed at her excitement.

Christophe protested when Pascaline told him it was time for bed. Felix had an impulse to support her, seeing that he was his son, too, but checked himself in time. That would have been a bad, bad mistake. He had to be accepted and to establish trust before he would accept his discipline. He had two people to win over. He did not want to muscle in on the child's routine.

'*Que passe-t-il habituellement au coucher?*' (What usually happens at bedtime?) he asked him.

'*It se couche comme un bon garçon,*' (He goes to bed like a good boy) Pascaline intervened, taking his hand. '*Dis bonne nuit á Felix, er, á Papa.*' (Say goodnight.)

'*Bonne nuit,*' Felix said as he bent down to give Christophe a hug.

To his surprise, Christophe kissed him on the lips, then added, 'Papa.' The look of trust from his lovely brown eyes beneath long lashes moistened his father's eyes.

'*Bonne nuit, Christophe. Peut-être demain soir je te lirai une histoire.*' (Perhaps tomorrow night I'll read you a story.)

Christophe left with his mother. Felix's heart skipped another beat. Christophe had accepted him.

'I think you've been accepted.' Ghislaine echoed his thoughts. She spoke in English. 'I'll go in shortly and give him a cuddle. He likes getting a cuddle from grandmama.'

'Christophe told me you're a nice man,' was Pascaline's comment on returning. 'He wanted to know if you're staying.'

'He wants his story,' he replied.

She laughed at his joke.

'I hope I can stay. What did you say?'

'I said you're staying for a little while.'

'Did I tell you his second name is Felix? Christophe Felix.'

'Yes. I like that. He has my name as well as my genes.'

Ghislaine returned from kissing her grandson goodnight and the three of them settled down with a drink in front of the modern wood heater built into the old farm fireplace. Through its glass door, cosy warmth radiated through the room and kept the winter chill at bay. Time for a talk. They all looked at each other, waiting for someone to start.

'We did not know how your meeting with Christophe might go,' Ghislaine began. 'He hasn't said much but he found a map of Australia and wanted to know which part you lived in. He has books with stories of Australian animals and he has been looking at them.'

'Perhaps he's looking for stuff that he can ask about.'

'He's a curious child and is always asking questions,' added his proud mother.

'I'm pleased that you have come to visit us,' Ghislaine continued. 'I was pleased to see my daughter but I wasn't sure that Pascaline had done the right thing when she left you and came home. She did not want to tell you that she was pregnant. I felt that she should have. I'm pleased that at last you know. I'm surprised that you are not angry with Pascaline that she did not let you know. If you are, you are not showing it.'

'It's wonderful. I'm getting used to the idea of being a father. Pascaline, I am not angry with you, but you should have let me know. Would I have been here sooner? I'm not sure. I was involved with my work, and we were going through tough times. I had to stay to see things through.'

'I'm happy that you have left the company,' Pascaline intervened.

'I wasn't happy when Pascaline came home but I am pleased that I have seen my grandson grow up in my own house. I have been a lucky woman. My three grandchildren have been close to me. I see Anton's family every other day.'

The wine and the warmth were making him drowsy. He drifted in and out of the conversation, waking with a start and snatching the glass just in time.

'You are tired, Felix,' said Ghislaine. 'You have had a long day. You should have a night's sleep and continue tomorrow.'

'Good idea. One thing I wanted to ask you, Pascaline ...' He took both her hands and looked at her closely. 'Are you happy to see me?'

'Yes, of course, you silly boy.' She gave him a gentle kiss. 'I'm tired, too. We have all been tired and tense, waiting for this day.'

'I understand. It's not every day that your old lover turns up.'

'I will leave you and go to bed.' Ghislaine stood up and gave Pascaline and Felix a kiss. She turned the lever to dampen down the heater. 'There might still be coals in the morning to start the fire with. We don't have to get up early. It's Saturday. Good night.'

They sat together looking at the slowly dimming glow. The dying flames and the reduced heat reminded them that, beyond the range of this heater, the night was cold.

'One thing I want to say before we retire, Pascaline.'

'What is that?'

'I want to tell you how sorry I was for allowing the company to come between us.' He spoke quietly, urgently, in a whisper. 'I want to ask your forgiveness for neglecting you. You were on your own. Your family, friends and everything that was familiar was on the other side of the world. You needed me. You had no one you could trust to turn to. Please forgive me.'

'Of course,' she whispered and kissed him. 'I think, Felix,

that you are sorry. I love to hear your words. But they are just words. It's what you do now that proves that you really mean it.'

'I will do my best to ensure nothing comes between us.'

She kissed him again.

'I did feel so lonely. That's why I listened to Jean-Claude when he wanted me to return to France.'

'And he turned out to be a rat.'

'He wanted nothing to do with Christophe, even though he wasn't born. He told me I should have an abortion.'

'Thank God you didn't listen.'

'No, I wanted my baby. Maman wanted me to have my baby. She wanted a grandchild to fuss over.'

'And I'm so happy that he's here, that I have a son, that *we* have a son.'

The fire was dying down in the firebox, but the fire of passion was burning brightly within his body and spirit. The warm glow of love flowed out of him and enveloped Pascaline. He looked at her with the eyes of his heart.

'I've missed you, Pascaline. It was in the quiet times that I missed you the most, away from the busyness when my mind had a chance to wonder and remember.'

She continued to gaze into the fire and made no comment, although he sensed the slightest of movements towards him, just a millimetre or two.

'I should come to your bed tonight. We could make another baby.'

She looked at him as if he were a naughty child asking for something he knew he was not allowed to have. She was wavering; she wanted him, too; their spirits were connecting, but she held back.

'No!' she replied. 'Not yet! Not yet!'

'Tomorrow night?' The naughty child was not giving up easily.

'We shall see.'

They sat in silence gazing into the firebox as if it were a god and they were in silent prayer. A clock ticked somewhere in the room. A sigh from Christophe floated down the passage-way. Outside, a gust of wind whistled around the house as if it were a lost soul seeking shelter.

On the way to their bedrooms, they crept into Christophe's. He was sound asleep, but his blankets were at his feet. Pascaline pulled them up, and the child snuggled into them in a foetal position and sighed. They stood gazing at him, feeling his contentment and sense of security. He was in safe hands. Felix could see love streaming out of her maternal heart. Love poured out of his, too. Silently, he promised his son he would be a good father, be involved in his life and make up for the time they had lost. They crept out, kissed each other good night and turned to their rooms. He was cold in his bed and wished he had Pascaline's warm body, but as sleep overtook him, he prayed in thanks for progress made and hoped that they would continue to know each other. He could have been angry with Pascaline for keeping Christophe a secret, but the joy of seeing them both had smothered any negative feeling. Old ground had been recovered, the healing had begun and in time their relationship would be restored.

It had been a long and tumultuous day.

Chapter 26

That night Felix struggled through a dream of finding himself, except that it wasn't exactly like that. He wasn't a poodle left unattended at a French railway station. Nor was he lost. His genuine self was right there all the time but had been buried under a pile of shit – cultural expectations about ambition and climbing ladders, other people's opinion of his worth and conclusions not always accurately drawn from his studies and rearing as a kid about what was worthwhile in life. In returning to Chambéry, to Ghislaine and her family, he was returning to himself. On the way he had undergone an unlearning, a discarding of irrelevancies and a remembering of who he was before The Champions got their hands on him. Out of this jumbled maze of thoughts, he woke slowly, emerging from the depths into consciousness. He opened his eyes and looked around. A strange room was waiting. Heavy curtains were not doing their best job of blocking the light. At first, he did not recognise his surroundings, but, through fluttering eyelids, he saw the revelations of the previous day.

What really mattered lay in the hands of people such as Pascaline, Christophe and Ghislaine. Anxious to join them, he drew back the curtains and the light revealed a room that served as a study. Crammed bookcases lined the walls looking as if every book that the family had acquired had been read and retained. The overflow was heaped in piles in the corners. His bed was a sofa, set up as a bed for him but comfortable as a couch by day, ideal furnishing for a study. He dressed quickly and emerged. The smell of coffee drifted down the passageway. He found Ghislaine in the kitchen sipping a cup listening to the radio. He heard a news item about the day's itinerary of François Mitterrand, still the president of France, before she turned down the sound.

'Good morning, Felix. Would you like coffee?' She began pouring before he replied, as if it were the custom that every-one began the day with coffee. She refilled her own.

'Yes, thanks.' They spoke in English.

'I am pleased it's the weekend. I do not have to work today. I have been feeling tired of late, thinking about stopping work. It would be nice to retire and do some travelling.'

'You could travel to Australia. There's a lot to see. So many contrasts.'

'Yes, Pascaline has told me about the mountains. They remind her of Savoy.'

'I would love you to visit Australia. I could return your hospitality. What would you do with your house?'

'I could rent the farm, particularly in winter. People come to Chambéry for the ski. They come in summer, too. The British would love the idea of a holiday in a French farmhouse.'

'I'm sure other nationalities would love the idea, Austra-lians included.'

Christophe emerged, rubbing his eyes, then ran to grandma. She hugged and kissed him.

Without prompting, he turned to Felix and said, *'Bonjour, Papa.'*

In that simple greeting, Felix saw acceptance. He was no longer a stranger. He was part of Christophe's life.

A minute later, Pascaline emerged looking just as lovely as ever, tossing her head to allow her hair to flow, just as she always did. They kissed on both cheeks. He was part of her life, too.

'J'espère tu as bien dormi parmi les livres,' (I hope you slept well among the books) was her greeting, continuing the practice of speaking French in Christophe's presence.

'Qui, merci. Je suis plein d'apprendre ce matin. Le lit était très confortable.' (Yes, thanks. I'm full of learning this morning. The bed was very comfortable.) Her bed would have been better.

Ghislaine produced a plate of warm croissants from the oven and the four of them sat around the table to enjoy their breakfast. Christophe drank his orange juice, and the adults sipped their coffee. The smell reminded him of hearth, home and family. After living for so long on his own, he hoped he would become part of this family and the family part of him. Over a simple meal, both his spirit and stomach were nourished.

'Nous devrions aller faire les courses ce matin.' (We should go shopping this morning.)

'Puis-je venir?' (May I come?) Christophe wanted to be in the action.

'Bien sûr.' (Of course) Pascaline beat him to it. *'Nous devrions t'apprendre un peu d'anglais parce que papa parle anglais et maman parle français. Nous parlons les deux langues. Tu devrais aussi.'* (We should teach you a little English because Daddy speaks English and Mummy speaks French. We speak both languages. You should, too.)

'Il apprendra très vite,' (He will learn very quickly) added

the grandmother, proud of her grandson's intelligence. *'Déjà, il connaît beaucoup de mots.'* (He knows many words already.)

As evidence, Christophe counted in English to ten, and, with prompting, made it to twenty.

Joy surged through Felix's heart and hope leapt off the scale. Pascaline was speaking as if she expected him to be around. He hadn't felt so happy for a long time as the three of them set off for their shopping. Ghislaine gave Pascaline a list for the *supermarché* and they dressed for the chilly morning and drove into town. Ghislaine had given him a jacket to wear, a shapeless object with the advice that he should buy something more fashionable. In no time they joined the bustling crowds. They wandered down supermarket aisles, shopped at the market stalls and visited the colonnades for the boutiques where Pascaline selected a smart jacket for him. He was expecting Christophe to be bored and complain, but no, he was happy to be with them. At one time, when the crowd was dense and the little fellow almost disappeared among the thicket of legs and coats, he took his daddy's hand. He had found his papa; he wasn't going to lose him. His father took great joy in hearing the name. However imperfectly, he would be a presence, not an absence, in Christophe's life.

With the shopping done, they found a family friendly bar, which had added a children's playground behind a thick glass wall designed to deaden the noise of screaming children. Christophe was content with an ice-cream. He then peeled off to climb the ladders and slides, leaving them to watch and to chat over coffee. He was getting used to French coffee; it was always so intensely black and strong to his taste, but he knew that Pascaline enjoyed her cup.

'Christophe and you are getting on well,' Pascaline remarked as she took a sip. Christophe stopped his climb and waved as if he had sensed he was the topic of their conversation. Felix didn't wave back immediately. He looked at his son through the glass wall then waved back as Christophe continued his climb.

'I remember once when we discussed marriage you said you would marry if we decided to have children,' he said, then paused to allow her to dig around in her memory banks. 'Well, we have a child. It's time to think about marriage,' he added.

'Are you asking me to marry you?'

'I suppose I am.'

'You're funny, you silly boy. You are putting things back to front. I haven't agreed to let you sleep with me yet.'

'Well, now that you have raised the topic. May I sleep with you tonight?'

She gave a laugh and smiled. She leaned across and took his hand. She didn't exactly say she couldn't think of anything nicer, but he took her gesture as a yes. As for him, he couldn't think of anything nicer than to sleep with her that night. He squeezed her hand. Their little barometer through the glass wall was observing them all the time. Sensing something was going on, he was back by their side glowing with the exertion of climbing. Not wishing to miss the action, he asked for another ice-cream and sat with them while they finished their coffee. Pascaline ordered another, but one French coffee was all Felix could stomach and ordered fruit juice. He felt the glow of family life. He had a vision of being surrounded by children. He didn't know what Pascaline would have thought about caring for a tribe of infants. It was not the time to reveal his inner thoughts. In the meantime, Christophe was suggesting they go home because he had something to show him. They were mates.

Back at the farmhouse, while the ladies were unpacking the shopping and preparing lunch, Christophe led him into his room. They sat on his bed, and he showed Felix a picture book that Ghislaine had bought for him. *Animaux d'Australie* was well illustrated with drawings and photographs – kangaroos, koalas, wallabies, *émeus* (emus), goannas, wombats, and *serpents* (snakes). Attached to each illustration was a description. He paused at the page illustrated with a variety of snakes.

'*L'Australie a beaucoup de serpents venimeux. Ils sont dangereux,*' (Australia has lots of snakes. They are dangerous) Christophe said solemnly. He looked at him as if for assurance that Australia was a safe place.

'*Oui, mais si l'on fait attention, on peut les éviter. Ils ont plus peur des humains et s'enfuient.*' (Yes, but if you are careful, you can avoid them. They are more frightened of humans and run away.)

Christophe seemed happy with his answer and continued to show him the other animals. Felix didn't bother to mention that Australia had plenty of poisonous spiders, too, and enough other dangerous creatures to scare the wits out of the timid European visitor.

'*As-tu un animal préféré?*' (Do you have a favourite?)

'*Oui. Le kangourou.*'

Pourquoi? (Why is that?)

'*Parce qu'ils sautent haut et gardent leurs bébés dans une poche.*' (Because they jump high and keep their babies in a pouch.) He pointed to a drawing of a kangaroo with a joey's head poking out of its stomach then jumped off the bed in kangaroo fashion. Time for lunch.

Ghislaine suggested they walk over to Anton's. After lunch, the four of them rugged themselves for the brisk weather and, Felix in his new jacket, along with Coquette, braved the wintery afternoon and walked through the vineyards. The sun shone weakly through the thin cloud cover. Coquette scampered among the vine rows sniffing and peeing. Christophe threw her sticks, which she chased with speed and when Christophe tired, they took turns to continue the game. Coquette never tired. The more action, the better.

Anton was the same lanky old mate. They took up where they left off years ago. But for the fact that they were speaking French, they could have been good Aussie mates catching up after a lengthy period apart. Felix told him he'd fit in well in Australia. Australian vineyards and wineries would welcome his expertise. He seemed interested, whether from courtesy or from genuine interest, time would tell. Anton knew Australia produced excellent vines, as good as Savoyard wines. Felix mentioned that Australians learned the trade from the French. Christophe enjoyed playing with his cousins. René and Yvette were younger, and they looked up to their cousin to take the lead. Coquette joined in their games, dashing with canine fervour from one to the other. They sat down for afternoon tea and the children demolished little cakes baked by Mireille. For the adults, Anton produced cheese and a bottle of the vineyard's red. The vintage (*cépage*) was *Mondeuse*, which Felix mentioned to Anton was like a heavy Australian red. Before leaving, Anton suggested that they enjoy a day's skiing on one of his days off. Felix thanked him for including him and replied that he would enjoy very much a day in the snow.

On the way home, the cold wind blew them along and, above them, the clouds tumbled through the sky. Christophe walked beside Felix, took his hand and chatted.

'J'aime rendre visite à mon oncle Anton parce que je peux jouer avec mes cousins.' (I like to visit my uncle Anton because I can play with my cousins.)

'C'est très bien.'

'Parfois, ils viennent chez moi.' (Sometimes, they come to my place.)

'Tu as des cousins en Australie. Un de ces jour tu pourrais les rencontrer.' (You have cousins in Australia. One of these days you might meet them.)

As if that was enough new learning for one session, Christophe left him to dash after Coquette and spent the remainder of the walk tossing her sticks.

That evening he was waiting for his story, so the ladies suggested Felix put him to bed.

'Papa, qu'est-ce que tu vais lire?' (Daddy, what are you going to read?)

'J'ai un poème sur L'Homme de Snowy River. Chaque enfant australien apprend le poème. Il est célèbre. La rivière est dans les montagnes avec beaucoup de neige. C'est pourquoi on l'appelle la Rivière Snowy.' (I have a poem about The Man from Snowy River. Every Australian child learns the poem. It is famous. The river is in the mountains with lots of snow. That is why the river is called Snowy River.)

Christophe was fully attentive, eager for more.

'Elle est en anglais. Je traduirai pour toi. Un jour, tu pourrais le lire et l'apprendrai en anglais. Quand tu seras plus vieux.' (It is in English, so I will translate for you. One day you might read and learn it in English. When you are older.)

He nodded. He accepted the potential future challenge. He flipped through the beautifully illustrated pages, a verse to a page accompanied by excellent illustrations of the action.

Felix didn't realise the enormity of translating a nineteenth century Australian bush ballad into French for a nearly seven-year-old boy. He had to take liberties. Words like 'colt', 'crack' or 'fray' had him searching in his vocabulary bank.

There was movement at the station, for the word had
passed around
That the colt from old Regret had got away,
And had joined the wild bush horses
he was worth a thousand pound,
So all the cracks had gathered to the fray.

(Il y avait du mouvement au ranch car le mot était passe que le poulain de old Regret s'était enfui et avait rejoint les chevaux sauvages. Il valait mille livres ainsi tous les cavaliers d'élite etaient rassemblés á la mélée.)

They didn't get far. The first verse stimulated a host of questions. Old Regret was the colt's mother. It was an excellent racehorse, so any foals were worth money. A pound was British money. Australia used to have pounds. Now they have dollars. Countries change their money sometimes. If you're a crack at something, that means you are very good. Felix asked

Christophe if he was a crack at something. He thought about that and replied he was the best reader in his class. There used to be lots of cattle in the Snowy River country so the men looking after them had to be pretty good horse riders because the mountains were so rough. But now, because it is a national park where no cattle are allowed, there are wild bush horses, which are called brumbies. In America they are called mustangs. Christophe knew about mustangs; he had read a comic book (*Bande dessinée*) about cowboys, but he didn't know about brumbies. Christophe knew about the wild west; he had seen films, too. By this time, Felix concluded that his son remembered everything he read. So much new knowledge made him tired, and he yawned. Felix was tired too. He left the book with his son.

'*Pour l'instant ça suffit. Tu peux avoir le livre. Regarde les images pour voir ce qui se passe.*' (That's enough for the time being. You can have the book. Look at the pictures to see what happens next.)

He felt sure that his son, once he put his mind to learning English, would know the poem by heart. He had a vision of him standing in front of an audience somewhere, sometime, reciting *The Man from Snowy River* in English with the same delightful accent as his mother.

J'ai un autre livre que je vais donner á maman. Elle aime les montagnes parce qu'elle est y restée une fois. Tu peux le regarder aussi.' (I have another book which I'll give to mummy. She likes the mountains because she stayed there once. You can look at it too.)

'*Snowy River serait un bel endroit oú vivre.*' (Snowy River would be a nice place to live.)

He felt he was winning as he kissed and hugged his son. He had known him for just over twenty-four hours, but they had come light years in getting to know each other. He had come light years in his understanding of love. Nothing selfish in the love a father has for his son. It's a kindness and compassionate kind of love, a self-forgetting kind of love even to the point of giving up one's own life. No doubt he would settle down to a practical, down-to-earth, matter-of-fact version as he got used to the idea, but right then, as Felix left him to sleep peacefully, his heart was full of the first flush of paternal love. He imagined he felt the same as a father experiences, when he sees his baby child for the first time, except that he was years late. With all his imperfections, he wanted to be the best of fathers. In the years ahead, love would demand the best from him and bring out the best in him. Up to now, Pascaline had borne the responsibility for rearing Christophe. Now, he wanted to share it with her. He hoped he would meet the challenge with energy and courage.

He investigated his room of the night before and found it restored to its former purpose. The sofa had been returned to a couch, the bed clothes were gone and the books were a reminder of the years of learning that this study had witnessed. His backpack was gone, too. Had Ghislaine read the signs and removed it to Pascaline's room? His heart was already full of joy where a yearning for Pascaline surged for space. His love was like a flame that warmed his spirit. He felt a kind of healing, caring, forgiving and a passion bursting out of his chest for connection with his beloved Pascaline. With such a cocktail of emotions, he made his way to her room.

PART FOUR

DAYS OF REALIGNMENT

Chapter 27

The sun had not yet risen, and the mountains were just emerging from the purple darkness. Dawn was the best time of the day to get out and walk. The earth was fresh, and the new day was bursting with promise. He rose from bed and dressed silently to creep out of the house. Everyone was asleep except for Belle. His Jack Russell, alert to his movements, intercepted him as he opened the door, tail wagging briskly, eyes pleading and eager to accompany him. He was hoping to leave her home, but his heart softened.

'Good girl, Belle! Good dog!' he whispered.

With Belle on her lead and day pack on his back, he opened the gate noiselessly and crossed the roadway. The other side of the road gave an uninterrupted view of the lake below, and beyond, the mountains had already donned their caps of snow, reflected in the still stretch of water. Early snow had not long melted and left the town clean and the air pure. These pre-season falls filled the hearts of the residents with hope for a good winter season. They earned their yearly income by providing all manner of services, from cafés to nightclubs, from ski instruction to tour guiding. Soon, thousands of visitors would arrive to enjoy the ski slopes and sample the night life of the town, gateway to the mountains. Already, young people, winter workers, were arriving, looking for work and accommodation.

The autumn morning was brisk, the countryside was quiet. The only sounds were bird calls. He moved along the ridge down a rough pebbly path threading its way through the snow gums, their white trunks silhouetted against the emerging blue sky, the lake on his right, past the sports ovals and descended through a plantation of pine, which, along with their carpet of needles, reminded him of his travels in France. He crossed the main road leading to the ski resorts. This morning there were no vehicles but soon, temporary traffic lights would regulate the flow of skiers aiming for an early start. Once across the road, hopeful that she would not bail up any snakes, he let Belle off her lead and she dashed forward, zigzagging this way and that, sniffing at unseen creatures in the surrounding grass and bushes, snuffing her way through the carpet of autumn leaves, excited to be free, while he lagged behind, confident that she would come at his call. He walked along the lake past seats and playgrounds. By now, the sun had emerged and shimmered through the mist, rising from the waters as if it were a restless ghost from the old town, drowned when the dam was constructed that created the lake. Although man-made, God could have formed it. He felt content, thankful to be surrounded by such beauty. He wanted to live in such a way that he didn't miss the beauty that was all around him.

'I will never take this for granted, I promise,' he whispered in awe.

The mirror image of the mountains was disturbed by a breeze that rippled across the waters. On shore, fallen leaves fluttered across his path and sang a gentle song of nature. Belle had detoured through some bushes and trees, run to the water's edge and had now joined him. They passed the camping ground and its boat ramp. Bursting at the seams both in summer and winter, three caravans, two tents and rows of empty cabins indicated that this was the off season. No one was about. No boats were in the water. Different on the weekend if the weather was fine. He came to the bowling club, a regular watering hole for both residents and visitors. He called Belle and put her back on the lead. He left the serenity of the lake to walk across the empty car park, to the main road into the town to a courtyard bordered by shops. Only one was operating this time of the morning. The baker opened early to catch the tradies for breakfast on their way to work. Later in the morning, and certainly by lunchtime, the place would be bustling with humanity.

'Hi, Felix!' Annette always had a big smile and greeted her customers cheerfully. She knew him as one of her regulars. 'Same as usual?'

'Yes. Coffee for me, Annette, and water for Belle, thanks.'

He sat outside on one of the benches. At his feet lay Belle, happy for the rest and for the bowl of water, which she lapped noisily. Tradies arrived to buy their breakfast, morning tea or lunch. He knew them by name or by face. He found it comforting that he knew people and people knew him. He was part of the community – so different to the large cities where he'd lived such a large chunk of his life. None of the suspicion, or, at best, indifference. Here, he greeted everyone as they passed with no more conversation than a comment on the weather. 'Looks like we're in for a nice day.' 'Not much snow yet.' 'They'll have to get the machines working.' Not the time of day for extended deep discussion with men on their way to work, ready for 7 am starts.

One young tradie, Zac, paused when he saw Felix. He was tall, with long blonde hair tied in a ponytail and an infectious

grin. He often stopped for a chat. He was outrageous, sometimes, but you could never take offence.

'G'day, Felix. Whatcha doing out so early? You're a puzzle.
You're not working. You don't have to get up early. You could
be sleeping in bed still.'

'I like to get up early, Zac, and not waste the day.'

'Mate! Saturday can't come quick enough. I can sleep in to
midday, especially after a few beers Friday night.'

He often saw Zac around the town. On the weekends, he
untied his hair as if he were letting it all hang out. Come Monday morning, his locks were back in place.

He sipped his coffee and thought about Zac's comment
about his not working. He had not bothered with a job since
coming to this town. He was happy to settle into his new life.
Working for someone did not appeal. He was not interested in
returning to the corporate world, in donning a suit and climbing the ladder to nowhere. If he worked again, he would work
for himself in his own business. What that business would be,
he was not clear on yet. He would wait to see which opportunities came along. As it turned out, the local bookshop was
up for sale. The owner, Sharon, told him the bookshop was
doing well. She had a regular group of customers (including
Felix), and visitors were always calling in looking for reading material during their holiday. They returned on their
next holiday. However, her life was a balancing act, trying to
juggle the demands of teenage children with running a business. Although she loved her books, the strain was becoming
too much, and her family's interest won the day. A bookshop
appealed. If he were to enter retail, that would be the field.
His enterprise would become the literary hub of the town, a

centre where book clubs could meet and where local authors could launch their work. He could organise writing competitions for the children and work with the school on schemes to encourage reading. He could sell books as well. He would read every book in the shop. At least, he could always give his customers a personal review.

He returned his cup to the shop. Annette knew he always bought fresh croissants to take home for breakfast and had them ready for him. He retraced his steps out of the shopping centre, back to the tranquil foreshore of the lake where he let Belle off her lead and allowed her to run. By now, people were out walking their dogs. Belle darted here and there, sniffing and weeing, taking no notice of the other dogs, many of which strained at their leashes. He made eye contact and greeted everyone. Most returned his greeting with comments on how beautiful Belle was, but others ignored him. He guessed they were visitors from the big city, absorbed in their own thoughts, focussed on the sounds from earphones that only they could hear, too self-absorbed to return greetings from an over-friendly stranger. Although he had lived most of his life in big, congested cities, he had grown up in the bush and returned to it. He no longer identified himself as a city dweller and hoped he never would again. The camping ground was stirring. A couple was stretching themselves in the sun and walking to the ablution block. No one was swimming. Even in midsummer the water, once melted snow, was cool, more so in autumn.

At the pine grove, he left this peaceful scene, a place you could linger forever. He returned Belle to her lead to cross the road then released her as he climbed the slope. They crunched their way through a carpet of dried needles, towards the sports ground, then walked up the ridge through the snow gums, with the lake on their left, shining brilliantly in the full sun. Islands covered with trees, once the tops of hills, stood out in their detail. On one of their beaches, he could make out a canoe. Someone had taken an early morning row into solitude. On a weekend, sailing boats would be gracing the waters. None today! No noisy motorboats, thundering their way through the water, creating waves that reached the shore. He continued up the hill to home, a simple wooden structure – tin roof, verandah running the full length – his ideal of what a house in the bush should be. This really was home, he reflected, as Belle raced ahead. This was where he belonged. This was his life. He wanted to soak it all up and find joy in the simple things. He wanted to let go of what did not matter and be present in all that he did. Especially, he wanted to be present with those he loved. Hard to believe that the person living his life years previously was the same person living his life now. It had taken him a while, a lifetime, to feel content and settled. This was where his book began. The rest was still to be written.

Belle was waiting at the door. Once inside, she dashed into the laundry to find her food. He found her packet of dried food and poured a handful into her bowl, which she consumed in frenzied time. He was hungry, too. He took the croissants out of his backpack and placed them in the oven to warm. He prepared the coffee and placed the pot on the stovetop. He dipped into the fridge for fruit juice and poured a glass. He checked the rack for eggs laid by his own chooks. He was proud of his three hens, each had a name. His neighbour warned him about foxes, so he built a solid henhouse with wire netting dug well into the ground. From the windowsill he selected two ripened tomatoes grown in his own veggie patch.

The next job was to wake the family with the news that breakfast was almost ready.